Little
Black Dress

Kim Black

ISBN: 1946846044
ISBN-13: 978-1946846044

DEDICATION

For Tammie. Thanks for always being so brave of me.

ACKNOWLEDGMENTS

I'd like to offer a special thank you to James D. Quiggle for your remarkable editing skills, as well as your wealth of knowledge of just about everything. Thank you to Sean Black for the incredible cover art. Thank you to Pamela Fagan Hutchins for your willingness to help me paint my pictures on pages. Thank you to the Story Brewers for your words of encouragement and acceptance. Thanks to Greg and Dianne for all your longsuffering and atta-girls.

Thank you to my sister, Lorna, for helping me flesh out details from the very beginning of LBD. To my dear Lone Star Women of Letters sister-writers, Donna, Suzana, and Brandi, thank you for your honesty, encouragement, and love. Thank you to Kay Stacy for hanging in there and encouraging me to finish this job. Thanks to Ron Cleeton for helping me with fun technology facts.

To my favorite nerds in the whole world, Sam, Whitney, Sean, and Riley, thank you for walking with me on this adventure. The dress never would have come off the rack without you.

CHAPTER ONE

She had never been one for bars or nightclubs, but how else was a good girl like Evan Tyler going to find a bad boy in Paris?

"How many in your party, Mademoiselle?" the host repeated in English when his initial question in French brought no immediate response.

"Jus' mysay-elf," she answered with a diphthong more suited to Paris, Texas than Paris, France.

The thin man looked at his tablet and then shot her a pitying glance over his Poirot mustache. "Without reservations, I can seat you at the bar." He stared as if he had asked a question, and Evan got the distinct impression that he hoped she would reject the offer and leave.

"Merci." She matched the lilt in her voice with a dip in her step as she followed him through the Pub Saint Michel. Her heart pounded as she climbed the neon-treaded staircase, or maybe that was just Daft Punk's "Digital Love" pumping through the sound system. The nightclub smelled like old wood, lemon oil, cigarette smoke, and trouble.

Keep your chin up, the little voice in her head whispered. *Project confidence. You can do this.*

Evan felt conspicuous; a misfit in a dark room crowded with couples sharing designer drinks and easy conversation. The black leather booths on the street level were filled, but the upstairs bar still had a few empty seats. She nodded to Moustache and took the center stool.

Her electric blue strapless dress hugged her curves and usually drew a response, but no one here bothered to notice. She tugged at the purse strap on her bare shoulder and tapped the toes of her three-inch heels on the brass footrest. She resisted the urge to check her lipstick in the mirrored wall behind the bar. *You look fine. Take a breath.*

"American?" the barman asked. He was taller than Evan, with a strong square jaw and shoulders to match.

1

"Yes, sir. How did you guess?" Evan nodded, pushing a loose auburn curl behind her ear.

"May I get you a Cosmo? Or maybe a Mojito?" he said with a broad smile.

"I'd just love a plain dry martini with an extra olive, s'il vous plait."

He nodded and turned away to work.

She considered all the things she'd given up over the last few years. She had traded the glamour and pay of a modeling career for one that required extensive travel and, among other things, the forfeiture of any real relationships. For a split second, she missed home.

She couldn't honestly say that she loved her work, but Evan knew that she made a difference, and for now, that was enough. She had worked hard all day, and tonight she just wanted to find a man.

She used the bar mirror to scan the room. The tables behind her held couples and threesomes, speaking French, Russian, Italian, and English. Saint Michel was popular with both locals and tourists. Most were looking for love, and a few were looking for trouble.

To her left, a large arch-topped window overlooked the bustling street below and the Seine River just beyond. To her right, a man sat alone in a shadowed booth. THE man.

He was perfect, she thought. Mid-forties, slim, but not athletic, gray at the temples, decent looking. He grinned in her direction.

The barman slid the drink in front of her, and before she could thank him, he pointed to the man in the corner. "Compliments of Monsieur."

This is it, Evan. Girl, you can do this. He's your man.

"Merci." She turned her barstool and made eye-contact with him. She raised her drink and smiled.

Don't mess this up.

He looked her up and down with eager eyes. With his gold-ringed pinky, he gestured to the seat across the table from him.

This is it.

She inhaled every particle of audacity from the air and stepped down from the barstool.

"Please join me," he said with a sharp Eastern European accent. "Good evening."

Evan set her drink on the table and took her purse in hand as she slid into the booth seat next to him. "It is a good evening—for me."

His grin broadened, and he looked as if he was about to say something clever, but as soon as he felt the muzzle of Evan's .40 caliber Springfield in his ribs his face turned ashen, and his hands began to tremble.

"I'm unarmed," Shelby Templeton said. His accent was gone.

"I've got him," Evan whispered.

"Good job, Agent Tyler. Bring him out."

CHAPTER TWO

"That's the slimeball," Senator Stanton Grey said. He paced the floor with crossed arms as he watched Shelby Templeton fidget in the interrogation room behind the two-way mirrored glass wall. On any other occasion, the fifty-six-year-old Texas politician looked polished and composed, but at the moment even the creases in his Armani suit looked angry.

Eleanor McKinnon-Grey dipped her chin toward her husband. "Are you sure?"

"That's him, Elle. He had a different accent before, but that's the same man that invited me to the party." He tilted his head and squinted as he looked over Templeton, then turned back to his wife. "Are you going to get him?"

Eleanor nodded. "Oh, yeah. We'll get him, honey. You go on home, and leave this one to me." She stretched up on her tip-toes to kiss her husband goodbye. "Call if you need anything. I should be back in DC next week." Her confident voice and tender touch seemed to smooth the wrinkles from his forehead.

Stan hugged her and gave her his signature wink as he left the room.

Eleanor loved that wink.

Now back to work. She brushed her golden hair back from her face and tugged the hem of her navy-blue jacket into place. Tucking the folder of photographs and notes under her left arm, Eleanor marched to the next room where Templeton waited.

"You can't keep me here. I'm an American citizen," he said when she entered. Eleanor could see in the mirrored wall that he studied her curves as she turned to close the door. His gaze settled on her narrow ankles.

Eleanor took her place on the other side of the steel-topped table from him and sat down. She stared at him for several seconds without saying a word. She considered how quickly Evan had been able to track him down and take him into custody. Good girl. Maybe she envied Evan a little. But looking at Templeton, maybe not. She'd rather be in the field than at a desk, but this—she was good at this. Eleanor would wait a few more seconds, listening to him breathe through his mouth. She allowed time for his imagination to generate a host of nightmarish consequences for all his sins.

Eleanor always appeared cool and collected. She rarely let down her guard. She knew from experience things could go south quickly if she did. She fixed her gaze on Templeton's twitching nostrils and let her long black lashes rise and fall in rhythm with her breath.

"Did you hear me? I'm an Ameri—"

"I heard you, Mr. Templeton. I have your file right here." Her deep alto tone rolled at an even pace.

"Then you know you can't detain me without cause."

"Oh, I have plenty of cause, Mr. Templeton. You're in a great deal of trouble. We know that you sell government secrets, and we intend to stop you." Eleanor's full pink lips formed a Cupid's bow as she spoke.

Templeton looked distracted by Eleanor's perfect mouth. He seemed to strain to keep up with what she said.

"I'm sure you're being manipulated into this treasonous business," she added. "We can help you out of it, but you'll have to cooperate."

"Treason? Secrets?" He looked scared. "What are you talking about? Who are you?"

Eleanor leaned against the back of her chair and blinked serenely. Her blonde curls slipped off her shoulders as if on cue. She noticed Templeton's breath quicken.

"I work for the American government, Mr. Templeton." She opened the file folder and carefully placed half a dozen surveillance photos in front of him. Each shot depicted him shaking hands with a different United States Senator and the same thin blonde woman draped over each senator's arm. The photos appeared to have been taken at parties at various times and locations.

"It's not illegal to have friends," Templeton said. Perspiration beaded at his hairline, and the crease across his forehead deepened.

Eleanor knew she had him. "Of course not, but you seem to only make friends with senators and other government officials." She paused for a second. "And blondes."

She used her Georgia peach accent to charm him. He attempted to smile casually but then appeared to surrender.

"What do you want me to tell you? I just set up parties for friends. I don't sell secrets. I just like to help people have a good time." Dark, damp circles formed under his arms. He twitched and shifted in his seat.

Eleanor waited for more. She could almost hear his heart pounding.

"I don't sell drugs, either," he pleaded. "I've seen them at the parties. At some of the parties. But someone else brings them. I don't mess with that stuff." He straightened his posture for a few seconds and then slumped back in his chair again.

She licked her lips. This was too easy. If it weren't for Templeton's profuse sweating and shattered nerves, she would suspect he was playing her.

"And I don't pimp out the girls. That's someone else, too. All I do is set up the parties and invite the right people." Templeton tapped his fingers on the table and chewed on his lips. After a few seconds of silence, he stopped tapping and shifted his hands to fumble with the buttons on his shirtsleeves.

Eleanor nodded but said nothing. She knew Templeton was on the verge of implosion.

"His name is Hrevic," he said with a quick burst of energy. "Anton Hrevic, the fashion designer. But he's more than that. You've got to protect me. He has people. He'll kill me if he finds out I talked to you."

Eleanor turned to look over her shoulder at the mirrored wall. She raised her eyebrows and smiled. She knew how entertaining this must be for the two agents behind the glass.

Eleanor stood and walked around the table directly behind Templeton. She placed both hands on the back of his chair and stared coldly at his reflection. She could see the panic on his face. She could smell his fear. "I'm going to let you talk to a friend of mine, Mr. Templeton. I want you to tell him everything about these parties that you set up for Mr. Hrevic. Don't leave anything out. Do you understand?"

Templeton sighed and nodded. "Yes. I understand."

Two men from the next room entered, leaving the door ajar for Eleanor to exit.

When Templeton saw the open door, his flight instinct took over, and he jumped up to run. Before he managed to take a full step, Eleanor grabbed his wrist and twisted it sharply behind his back, paralyzing him in his tracks. She pushed her elbow into the center of his spine and pinned him face down against the table. The two men drew their side arms, training them on Templeton's head.

With her free arm, Eleanor signaled them to stand down. She leaned over her suspect and whispered in his ear while she pulled tighter on his wrist.

"Don't do that again, Mr. Templeton, or I'll rip off your arm and feed it to you. I can't protect you if you behave foolishly."

She reached out and took a pair of handcuffs from the man nearest her. She cinched them around Shelby Templeton's wrists as he blubbered, "I'll tell you anything you want to know."

She helped him stand upright and placed him in the custody of her fellow agents.

"Take good care of him, men. This is the one we've been waiting for." She directed her icy gaze back to Templeton and said, "Don't hold anything back. We'll know. And we have our own ways of dealing with traitors."

CHAPTER THREE

Eleanor kept her eyes focused and her breathing steady as she sat across the mahogany desk from the Director of InDIGO, the International Discretionary Intelligence Gathering Organization, for whom she had worked for the last six years.

"Anton Hrevic is a nobody," Max Fischer said. "He's a blip on the radar. Every time we try to put him under a microscope, he comes clean in the wash." He twisted the chunky gold ring on his right index finger and then tapped it heavily on his desk blotter.

Eleanor winced at his mishmash of metaphors. She preferred precision. Liked things neat.

"Wouldn't you like to finally have something concrete on him?" She sat forward in her chair and raised her eyes to study the original Degas that hung on the wall over his century-old credenza.

The old stone storefront looked like an ordinary boucherie on an ordinary street on the poorer side of Paris. No one would suspect it housed the French offices of an international intelligence agency. The smells of raw and curing meat and sausages from the butcher shop below seeped into the office and tickled her nose. She took a second to clear her mind and refocus. She didn't want to be distracted and refused to let Fischer intimidate her.

"Only if it's actionable." He huffed as if he were tired of the subject already. "I don't have the budget or manpower to send agents chasing ghosts and rumors." Fischer tugged at his cufflinks, adjusting his sleeves under his cashmere jacket.

Eleanor raised one eyebrow. She longed to call her boss out whenever he talked about budget restraints. InDIGO's resources seemed infinite when the job was important to Fischer. Not to mention the man didn't own a shirt that cost less than two grand. But she could play nice.

"Sir," she said with a honeyed tone. "I think this is the perfect situation to try out the LBD." Eleanor had been careful not to bring up her pet project until she had to, hoping he'd suggest it first.

"Of course that's what this is all about. You don't care what Hrevic may or may not be doing out here. You just can't wait to get your hands on that dress." Fischer pressed his lips into a thin line. His eyes narrowed to match.

"Sir, with all due respect, this is exactly the kind of assignment for which the dress was designed. It's not as though I'll be the one wearing it." Eleanor wished her words back. Of course, she'd have loved to be wearing the Little Black Dress, but her last field assignment prevented that from ever becoming a reality. She swallowed hard and leveled her tone, knowing that Fischer had to sign off to even get this operation off the ground. She offered him facts. She knew he preferred cold hard facts. "Shelby Templeton provided ample information on how to access Anton Hrevic. We have his addresses. His automobile information. His associates. I've already got a connection with the French police who can help with anything else we might need."

"Humph." Fisher shook his head. He crossed his arms and leaned back in his leather chair. "I suppose. Get your team together. No more than five. You have two weeks. If you want any more than that, I need results. Proof. Real evidence. Not some weasel in rayon crying for protection. Not another Templeton. You can't accuse a world-renowned fashion designer of espionage and then say 'oops' when you find out he's innocent."

"Yes, sir. Thank you, sir." She stood. "Evan Tyler and Rowan Kirk are already here in Paris. They're the ones who brought Templeton in for us."

"Well, what a coincidence." Fischer's voice smacked of sarcasm. "What about Parker?"

"I can have Hedge here with the package in twenty-four hours." Eleanor's heart rate quickened.

"I bet you can." Fischer smirked at Eleanor. He didn't bother to stand.

Her excitement smothered his snide remark. "And don't worry. I'll see who else is nearby to complete the team. I can keep a tight rein on the budget." Eleanor pursed her lips and allowed them to relax into a contented smile. She felt like purring. She smoothed her skirt and picked up her attaché.

"You don't ever turn it off, do you?" Fischer said, turning his chair to face the ballerinas on his wall.

"I wouldn't make a very good agent if I did, would I?"

Eleanor left Fischer's office with a broad smile on her face. "It's finally coming off the hanger," she whispered to herself.

CHAPTER FOUR

Hedge Parker sauntered through de Gaulle Airport with a small black leather carry-on and a hard-side rolling luggage case. While tourists marveled at the snaking tube-designed terminal, he scanned the faces around him for out-of-the-norm expressions and found none. The security guards appeared relaxed. Checkpoints ran smoothly. Public announcements sounded in a clear multi-lingual feminine voice. All was well in this corner of Paris.

Agent Parker's six-foot-four athletic frame drew a little female attention as he strolled across the worn red carpet, but the wobbly wheel on his suitcase had a few others staring, as well.

Women from around the travel hub noticed his broad shoulders, perfectly groomed goatee, and midnight blue eyes. Some went out of their way to step into his line of sight. He nodded politely and smiled as he passed each one.

A few years before he could fly in jeans and tees, carrying nothing more than a backpack or duffle. These days his cover attire was a bespoke charcoal business suit. The suit wasn't bad, but his wingtips were still not quite broken in. They felt tight and squeaked right along with his luggage wheel.

He sighed with relief when he found his exit. He hated traveling alone.

Eleanor met him at the terminal door with a hug. Hedge kissed her cheek. Just a husband returning home after a business trip, as far as anyone else could tell. He passed the leather bag to her and tossed his roller case into the trunk of her sedan.

"How was your flight?" she asked him, placing the bag in the back seat and then sliding behind the wheel.

He closed his door as she peeled away from the curb. *Why did she always have to drive as if she were in a high-speed chase?* "I don't think the plane ever went this fast."

Eleanor snickered. "You're supposed to blend in." She looked at her former partner and grinned. "You look great, Hedge. How've you been?"

He couldn't answer that question. *Not yet. Not with Elle sitting right there. Better to deflect.* "You're really something. I don't know how you did it, but you managed to get the dress activated." He knew she could do anything, but the LBD project had been shelved for months. He never expected it to fly.

Eleanor laughed. "I wouldn't be here without you." She squeezed the wheel and bit her bottom lip. "We're really going to do it."

Hedge watched her drive through the narrow streets. Hedge knew from experience that when she bit her lip like that, she was excited. He gritted his teeth, wishing things could be different. If not for that last night in Mexico City. "You should be the one to wear it. This is your baby. If I hadn't—"

"Don't you dare say that," Eleanor snapped at him. "This is not about me, and it's not about you."

"I know, Elle. You always say it's about the job."

"And it is. We use the best tools we have for the job." She nodded, and her voice seemed to flutter to a higher pitch. "And sometimes we get to develop better tools for the job."

"They said it was your husband that got the ball rolling," Hedge said, almost a question. He pulled at his maroon silk tie to loosen it a bit. He wasn't sure if he was feeling motion-sick or something a little closer to the heart.

Eleanor sat straight in her seat. Hedge could tell she wasn't ready to talk about her husband with him, and he felt a stab of pleasure from making her uncomfortable. He hadn't been comfortable in years; why should she?

"Yes, actually. Stan came to me last month about someone inviting him to a party with girls and celebrities." Eleanor kept her eyes on the road as she spoke. "We've suspected for a while that there was something like this. The French and Greek governments have had similar complaints. Their officials go to a party, and suddenly they change their minds about legislation, policy, and even basic platform issues. In Greece, a judge reversed his decision on a key money laundering case. We think there may also be a connection with the British judge that hung himself last October."

"So, it's blackmail?"

"At least that. It may be a great deal more. We have our suspicions but no proof."

"And the Italian Prime Minister's brother selling the family villa? Was he a victim, too?" Hedge asked.

"I doubt it," Eleanor said. "I've met him. He's just an idiot."

Hedge laughed. "Aren't we all?" The seatbelt cinched Hedge in place as Eleanor maneuvered between lanes and then hit the brakes.

Eleanor parked her sedan at the curb in front of an apartment house and turned to face him. "Are you ready to meet Evan… Agent Tyler?" she asked.

"Who is she?" He scanned the tall cut-stone building at their side.

The purple slate roof sat above the fourth floor like an old woman's hat. The windows were all veiled with scrolled wrought iron. Paris always reminded Hedge of childhood visits to his grandparents' home in New Orleans. Old money, rich food, architecture by day, parties every night. A lace curtain shifted in a window, and he focused again on the job.

"We all read her profile, I know. But who is she? Is she the real deal?" he asked.

A slim redheaded young woman emerged from behind the double-door entrance wearing a tailored gray skirt suit and black leather gloves. She pulled a lipstick-red travel bag behind her. As she approached the car, she lowered her black sunglasses and peered in. When she saw Eleanor, she smiled.

"Get out and help her," Eleanor said, nudging Hedge.

He stepped out of the car and the woman took a step back from her luggage. Hedge took the red case and added it to the contents of the trunk. The woman watched his handling of her bag as she waited next to the rear passenger door. Hedge slammed the trunk closed and then opened the door for Evan with an exaggerated flourish of chivalry. She was from Texas, one of the handful of states where Hedge knew women still appreciated help with luggage and opened doors.

"Thank you kindly, Mr. Parker," she said in a rhythmic drawl. Evan slid into the back seat next to the leather case.

Hedge glanced at her legs—to make sure she was all in—and then closed the car door.

"You can call me Hedge," he said as he closed his door and secured his seat belt.

Evan raised her eyebrows and smiled. "And just how does one get a nickname like 'Hedge'?" she asked.

Eleanor laughed as she charged the car into traffic. "He's had that one for a long time. I always assumed he earned it because he always hedges his bets. This man is never without a backup plan."

"He sounds like a good man to have around during an emergency," Evan replied.

"Oh, if you're in an emergency situation, he's bound to be close," Eleanor said.

"You know I can hear you, right?" he said. He turned to his new team member. "Agent McKinnon and I have known each other for years. Probably since before you were born," he said, jabbing both women about their ages. He knew it was bad manners, but he didn't feel like being careful.

Eleanor seemed to ignore him. "Evan Tyler, this is your new team leader, Hedge Parker. And yes, he's every bit as ornery as you've heard."

"Who else is on the team?" Hedge asked, changing the subject.

"Kirk, of course," Eleanor answered. "He's sweeping the flat as we speak. And Teo Ramos and Jarrett Brawn."

"Will you be staying, Agent McKinnon-Grey?" Evan asked Eleanor.

"Oh dear, no," Eleanor said. "I have a flight back to DC tonight. You all can handle things here."

Hedge nodded. "I worked with Ramos a few years back on a security detail. He's a good man. What do you know about Brawn?"

Eleanor's expression lightened as she pulled up to the flat. She handed Parker a large envelope from behind her seat. "It's all in the file," she said. "Have fun."

Hedge and Evan retrieved their bags from the trunk. When Hedge reached back into the car for the black bag, he shot a sad grimace to Eleanor. "I wish you were staying." The time was too short for the conversation they needed to have.

She nodded. "I know you do. Now get in there. You have your own team now."

Hedge and Evan went inside the small apartment building and crossed the lobby to the tiny elevator. Both of them pulled their luggage behind them, but Hedge kept the black leather bag protected under his arm. Hedge punched the up arrow, and they listened as the carriage descended with a whine.

"Nice," Evan said. "What floor?"

"We're on three." He broadened his shoulders, hoping to make her nervous. Evan was tall, muscular, with the kind of red hair that didn't look fresh from a bottle. She was magazine perfect, and he had no intention of falling for her. "Real estate in Paris is pricey. This place isn't bad at all." He stared straight into her teal blue eyes without blinking. Not falling might be tough.

She just shrugged and met his cool gaze with a warm smile. "No complaints from me. If we plummet to our deaths in this elevator car, well, it was a pleasure meeting you."

Hedge couldn't help but like her. He appreciated that his intimidation tactics merely glanced off her casual defense.

They survived the lift to their floor, and Hedge led her to the first door on the right. He used a key from the file envelope to open the door for Evan and then followed her inside. Eyes up, soldier.

"Hey, Red," Evan said to her partner, Rowan Kirk, who greeted them in the narrow vestibule.

"You finally met Hedge," Kirk answered her with a hug. He turned to shake Agent Parker's hand. "How do you like my girl?"

Hedge raised his brow at their familiarity. He knew they had been partners for a few years now, but he expected their age difference to keep them at a professional arm's length. "Your girl? Hmmm. She's something else, Kirk."

Kirk nodded. "You have no idea. She once turned an asset with little more than a wink and a smile."

"I can imagine," Hedge chuckled. Maybe there was nothing more than admiration.

"You know I can hear you, right?" she said, smirking at both men.

Kirk wrapped his arm around her shoulder and led them both into the small parlor where two other men sat. One jumped up at the sight of Hedge and rushed to shake his hand.

"I don't know if you'll remember me, sir," he began to say. His broad white smile contrasted with his bourbon brown complexion and dark features.

"Teo Ramos. Of course, I remember. Two years ago, in Venezuela. You're the man who can make a three-story parking garage collapse look like an accident." Hedge offered the younger man a firm handshake.

"I thought you said you worked security together," Evan said. She shook Teo's hand, too.

Hedge exchanged a knowing look with Teo. "That's right. Nothing says 'security' like a briefcase of C4."

Ramos laughed. "I'm glad for the opportunity to work with you again, sir."

The other man looked up from his chair at a small table, where he sat sharpening a five-inch knife on a whetstone. He barely acknowledged Hedge, but when he saw Evan, he stood up and stepped into the conversation. "I'm Brawn. Jarrett Brawn." His wispy brown hair gave him a youthful appearance, but the defined creases at the corners of his eyes indicated that he was at least thirty-five.

Hedge sized him up quickly. *Physically strong. Easily manipulated by women. Desperate for the Alpha role.* Hedge tightened his grip on the black bag.

Evan held out her hand to shake his. "Evan Tyler. Pleased to meet you."

Brawn grinned. He circled his left hand on her right arm, just above her elbow, and led her to the small sofa against the wall. "What an elegant accent. You must be from the South."

"Texas."

"I knew it," he said. "Have a seat."

Kirk interrupted. "Actually, we need to get right to work. Eleanor stressed that time was of the essence."

Hedge maneuvered himself between Evan and Brawn and removed a sealed box from the black bag, placing it on the coffee table in the middle of the room. He gestured for Brawn to return to his place at the table. He waited while Evan took a seat in the center of the couch, and then he and Kirk sat on either side of her, almost protectively.

Ramos took the chair next to Kirk.

"What's our assignment, sir?" Ramos asked.

"What's in the box?" Brawn added.

Hedge leaned forward, placing both hands on the package, and said, "This box *is* our assignment."

CHAPTER FIVE

"Anton Hrevic is a fashion designer. I hardly think he has anything to do with international espionage," Ramos said. "My sister loves his boots. She has a jar on her desk labeled 'House of Alexei' for all her extra change."

Evan listened to Hedge Parker's briefing while studying her new teammates. Ramos was chiseled and handsome, in his late twenties, bronzed and brooding. He seemed excited about the assignment and obviously respected Hedge.

Brawn was slightly shorter, maybe five-foot-eight or nine. He had a square jaw set with a grimace that made her wonder if he were chewing gum. His hair was short and light brown, with a wave that seemed uncontrollable. Evan guessed he was in his mid-thirties, but his gaze roamed over her figure like a teenager ogling a girlie magazine. She'd dealt with plenty of men like him and knew how to handle herself. She crossed her legs away from him.

And then her partner of the last three and half years, Rowan Kirk. He was in his early fifties, tall, with a narrow frame and silver-white hair. Like her daddy, Kirk kept her safe. Reliable, funny, he was her anchor in the field, and she trusted him with her life.

Evan focused on Hedge. *He was going to be a challenge.* Everything she'd heard about him—all business, aggressive, intimidating—all seemed to ring true. But she detected a softer side when he spoke to her and to Agent McKinnon-Grey. There had certainly been something between them at one time. Maybe there still was. He had a military air about him, like her dad. He stood eye to eye with her, literally and figuratively. She enjoyed being pushed to match his strength. *Just like Daddy taught me.*

Hedge looked good in his tailored suit, and she wondered what a tee shirt might do for his arms. And his shoulders. And his chest. *Okay, girl. He's your superior officer. Really not appropriate.*

Brawn nodded. "Why does Agent McKinnon—or Grey—or whatever, think he's a criminal?" He flipped his assignment file opened and closed, as if bored.

Hedge gestured to Evan and Kirk. "Thanks to these two, we have a man in custody who says that Hrevic pays him to find and invite government officials from all over the world to his parties. Hrevic provides women, drink, and drugs."

"So, it's like every party I've ever been to, but the girls are hotter," Brawn said.

Kirk raked his fingers through his prematurely gray hair and shook his head. "Once they've attended the parties, the statesmen—or whoever they are—start receiving extortion threats? Is that it?"

Hedge nodded. "We think that's what's happening. The problem is that if these women can get them into these compromising positions," he said, referencing photographs in their file, "then they could also be stealing government secrets. The fact there are signs of this from multiple countries indicates that Hrevic is a free-lance power broker. He could be making deals or selling information to the highest bidder." Hedge crossed his arms and shot Brawn a narrow gaze.

Evan watched Brawn drop his chin and look down to his knife. *Hedge: 1, Brawn: 0,* as her scoreboard read. She noticed Hedge turned his attention back to the sealed box. He lifted the package from the table and handed it to Kirk like it was a gift.

Kirk just smiled. "The dress is perfect for this assignment." He patted the box and then passed it back to Hedge.

Ramos propped his elbows on his knees and held out his hands, palms up. "What dress?"

Evan watched as the box moved from Hedge to Kirk, from Kirk to Hedge, and back again while the men discussed which one should open it.

"You're the team leader." Kirk handed the box to Hedge.

"Yes, but you're the brain-child behind it," Hedge said.

"For Pete's sake, let me open it," she said, grabbing the box and ripping through the taped edges like a kid with a birthday present.

Hedge and Kirk both leaned away from Evan's elbows.

Once she'd unsealed the thick cardboard box, Evan lifted the lid to reveal a shimmering black cocktail dress bathed in white tissue.

She slid her fingers around the silken fabric and carefully grasped the bodice. The buttery soft material shone like a black pearl in the light of the ancient chandelier hanging above. Evan's heart pounded. *Love at first sight.* She held the dress gently and stood up, letting the wrapping, the box, and all the other items under the dress spill onto the floor. She hugged the dress against herself. Her imagination soared.

Nearly a year ago, she'd been ordered to InDIGO for a suit fitting, as it was called. Eleanor told her about the plans for a weaponized field suit with surveillance and defensive technology. Evan had no idea it would be so beautiful.

Kirk scrambled to pick up the accessories from the floor. He grabbed the black tulle scarf, the handbag, and the left shoe. Hedge retrieved a roll of black fabric and the right shoe.

"You'll need these, too," Kirk said, handing his items to Evan. "It's all part of the suit."

"Well, this has been a lot of fun," Brawn said. "Where is the cake and ice cream?" He wiped the edge of his knife blade on his cleaning cloth and folded it closed. He propped his right ankle on his left knee and slid the weapon into his boot. Once it was out of sight, Brawn rocked his chair back on two legs and balanced with his fingers laced behind his head.

Ramos laughed, still looking confused.

"Here," Hedge said, holding out the right shoe and the roll of black fabric to Evan.

Evan took the pieces from Kirk and Hedge, tucking the shoes under her arm. She was careful not to snag the dress on the heels. When she reached for the roll of fabric in Hedge's hand, it unfurled to reveal a lace-covered corset.

Brawn rocked forward, letting his chair crash down on all four legs. He immediately responded. "Dibs on stake-out with Tyler."

Hedge and Kirk both shot him their deadliest laser stares. Ramos watched with wide eyes, and Evan blushed. She tucked her field suit back into the box quickly.

Hedge stood and marched two steps to face Brawn. "There are a few things we need to get straight before we go any further. We are a team, and we will treat each other with respect. Tyler is an agent, just like you. She is not property or dessert. She is not a toy or a reward for good behavior."

"Yes, sir," Brawn said quickly, sitting up straight in his chair.

Hedge continued. "Just as you are not a punching bag for my frustrations and bad temper."

"I apologize, Agent Tyler," Brawn added.

"Apology accepted," she replied, sitting back down.

"Another thing I need to say," Hedge said, stepping to the opposite side of the room, where he had space to move freely. "I will not tolerate any screwing around on this mission," he said, looking pointedly at Brawn. "We are here to do a job. I don't want anyone thinking they can get grabby just because we have a beautiful woman on the team. I've seen operatives get into a lot of trouble when they start playing house on assignments. You do that, and feelings get involved, judgments lapse, and then people get hurt or killed."

Hedge's team nodded in agreement. Evan heard the emotion in his voice. She again wondered about his relationship with Eleanor.

Ramos lightened the team's tone. "Right, no make-out stake-outs. Yes, sir."

Everyone smiled at Teo's levity before Hedge continued.

"This dress, worn by Agent Tyler, will be tested for the first time on this assignment. It is a tool, developed by Agents Kirk, McKinnon, and myself, to aid operatives in the field. It listens, it sees, it analyzes, and protects. The details are top secret. Need to know only." Hedge gestured to the dress. "Its success is vital to the success of our mission. Tyler has the most difficult job of anyone on the team. Not only must she carry out a regular field operation, but also, she must do it as she's learning to use this new equipment. On top of that, she must protect the equipment at all times and at all costs."

Evan carefully arranged the dress and all the accessories within the box. She smoothed the fabric with her fingers and folded the tissue wrapping back into place. The dress might be as light as air, but wearing it would be a heavy burden.

"When she wears that dress, I want you all ready to act. Is that clear?" Hedge asked.

"Yes, sir," the other three men said simultaneously.

Hedge drew a long slow breath and nodded as he faced the others. "Good. You all have your assignment files to study. If you have any questions, you can see me privately. Tyler and I need to unpack our gear. Dismissed."

Evan picked up her bag and the dress box and looked around the small apartment. Kirk motioned to the door beyond the kitchenette. "You're both in with me."

Hedge furrowed his brow. "Can't she have her own bedroom?"

"This is the only bedroom, Hedge," Kirk explained. "Two twin beds and a settee. Teo has the recliner, and Brawny claimed the sofa."

Hedge frowned. "This is ridiculous."

Evan shook her head. "Don't worry about me. I've been camping before."

Kirk laughed. "She's tough, Hedge. She can handle it." Kirk showed them into the tiny bedroom.

Evan looked from one bed to the other and then to the settee. "I'll take the settee since I'm smaller than either of you."

"No. I'll sleep on the floor," Hedge stated. "I have to have a firm surface anyway."

Kirk went back to the parlor as Evan dropped her bag onto the bed nearer the window, and Hedge opened his duffle on the settee. Evan unzipped the red case and began hanging her clothes in the small wardrobe. When her luggage was empty, she reopened the box and sat down on the bed to fondle the gown again. Hedge walked to her side as she admired the dress.

Evan's eyes lit up as she examined each stitch.

She noticed that Hedge appeared nearly as excited.

"It looks just like I imagined it," he said, stroking his goatee. "Elle and Kirk and I worked on this for months. And now you get to wear it."

Evan looked up at him and smiled. "It's gorgeous. I'm nervous just touching it. When I think of all the clothes I've ruined with spaghetti sauce."

He laughed. "No Italian for you, then. Elle would cry if you spilled marinara on her seven-million-dollar cocktail dress."

Evan's hands trembled at the words. "Seven million dollars?"

"Give or take," Hedge said. "Kirk put in a lot of really sweet features."

Evan shook her head in shock. She remembered trying on her best friend's prom dress and immediately spilling Dr. Pepper right down the front. She thought about getting screamed at by an Italian designer for dripping coffee on a tank top before a runway show. "I can't wear this," she said.

"Oh yes you can, and you will. You were chosen for this dress, not because of your size and your looks, though they are certainly a plus, but for your brains and your physical stamina and abilities." Hedge crossed his arms. "There aren't ten women in the world that could wear this dress. You better not even think about letting me down."

Evan sat up straight. The full weight of the assignment began to sink into her brain. This wasn't a fashion show. This wasn't a dress-up party. This wasn't even a typical "wiggle your hips, wink at the man, and convince him to tell you his secrets" assignment. She blinked, put the dress down, and faced Hedge. "Thank you, sir," she said with a fountain of emotion bubbling in her voice.

"It's still Hedge," he said. "And you're welcome."

Evan smiled and relaxed her shoulders. "I also want to thank you for what you said in there in front of everybody. How you defended me. I appreciate that a whole bunch."

Hedge inhaled and raised his chin. "I expect that from now on you can take care of yourself."

"Sir?"

"I was just laying down a few ground rules for our team. But I'm not your body-guard, and I'm not your father. Next time Brawn makes a crack like that, I expect you to knock him down. Do you understand me?"

"Yessir," she said. *Yep, he was going to be a challenge* .

CHAPTER SIX

Once Hedge returned to the parlor, Evan locked the bedroom door and slipped into the high-tech corset and the black strapless dress.

Strange. She'd modeled haute couture from all over the globe, but nothing had ever made her feel the way this little black dress did. Never mind that she was standing in the middle of a drab, thread-bare bedroom of a low-rent Parisian flat. She was a pearl resting on the slimy oyster in a dirty half shell. Energy flowed from every pore of her skin, physically connecting her to the fabric of the dress, sending her to another time and place. She was Botticelli's Venus, born again.

Evan stood in front of the mirrored armoire door and admired the glove-like fit. The creamy texture caused her to wonder at the fabric's bulletproof capabilities. She played for several minutes with the adjustable ruching down each side seam, making the dress longer and shorter at whim. She decided she liked the hem best sitting just above her knees. That length allowed her to wear her sub-compact pistol strapped most comfortably to her right thigh without showing. That was the key to her fashion sense these days.

Growing up she'd been conservative in her style. She had pored over fashion magazines like most girls, but that was before she was the one in the full-page glossy ad; before she knew what went on behind the runway. *No longer a girl. No longer a model. Well, still both, but something more.* Now she played dress-up with knives and pistols. But she wasn't playing.

She heard a quiet knock at the door. Hedge probably wanted to inspect the equipment.

"Just a sec," she said. She took another glance in the mirror, then two more steps to slide back the bolt on the door.

Rowan Kirk stepped into the room to admire the dress. "I feel like the father of the bride," he said, raising Evan's hand over her head and turning her like a ballerina.

"Am *I* the bride or is it the dress?" she asked him. She realized she'd been holding her breath and relaxed as she let it out. She was glad it was Kirk and not Hedge. Mostly.

He hesitated for a split second and released her hand. "Maybe both." Kirk shrugged and scratched the back of his neck.

Evan knew that he tended to get nervous around other women, but this was the first time since they'd worked together that he seemed tense with her. She tried to diffuse his anxiety by focusing on the dress. "It's just lovely," she said. "No one would ever guess what this little number is capable of."

"How does it feel?" Kirk asked.

"Like a cloud. Are you sure this is bulletproof?" She stepped back toward the mirror and turned a few more times for him.

"It's not technically bullet-proof. Like Kevlar, it's bullet-resistant. The laminated fabric minimizes the impact and penetration. But when the dress is activated, it has another feature that I really like." Kirk turned her to the side slightly and drew her attention to two silk-covered buttons on the right side of the waistband. "Look here."

"I was afraid to touch those," she said. "I noticed that they didn't actually fasten anything together."

"Good girl," Kirk said. "You'll activate the top one if you want the dress fully-armed. It sets you up for all the bells and whistles, so to speak. Once it's on, if someone fires upon you, the sensors will detect it instantly. The fabric will emit a sonic electro-magnetic pulse that will create an invisible ripple in the air around you, using ultra-high frequency sound instead of microwaves. It should feel like a hiccup to you, but it will cause enough disruption to alter a bullet's trajectory, increasing the protection against penetration from the projectile. Even if the bullet hits you, it shouldn't have enough force to pierce the dress—or you."

"And it won't hurt any more than a hiccup?"

Kirk raised his eyebrows and shot her a sideways glance. "The SEM pulse won't hurt. We calculated the strength based on your frame, bone density, muscle mass, and heart rate. But if the bullet does strike you, *that* will sting like crazy. The energy burst will slow it down a bit, but getting hit will still knock the wind out of you."

"Okay, an important safety tip: don't get shot." She looked down at the buttons again. "What's the bottom one do?"

He smiled. "This turns it all off. It's the system blackout button. You hit that one if you're going into a bug sweep, and it will cut all the signals emitting from you. If you even think someone is checking you for wires, punch it."

"And it turns into an ordinary dress?"

"Better than that." Kirk stood a little taller, looking proud. "It also masks any auxiliary devices you may have on your person. It works like a kind of white noise so anything you need to conceal can be cloaked. The only down-side is that our little two-way com set will go dark, too. Only because it's routed through the dress when you're wearing it. But don't worry, once everything is clear, you just punch the top one again, and I'll be right there in your ear again."

Evan smiled again. "I love that you're the voice in my head, Red."

"Me too."

"So, the top one turns everything on, and the bottom one turns it all off?" Evan looked in the mirror again. "Tell me about all these other features you stitched in."

"Let's start with the basic defenses," Kirk said. "You have the SEM pulse, which is automatic if someone shoots at you. You can also manually activate the pulse to jam or disrupt other signals, but use that sparingly—it messes with other stuff in a really bad way."

"Ok, only if I really need it. But how do I do that?"

Kirk reached up to her neckline but stopped before making contact. He realized that he'd never worked with the dress while it was on a real person. "Look straight down. See the little notch in the corset, between your ... well, if you need an SEM pulse, you just pinch that gap closed. It's not something you can do by accident. Once you set it off like that, you'll feel the hiccup, and the dress will shut down. You'll have five minutes that you will be offline completely. After that, the dress can be manually restarted with the top button."

"Can I restart it manually within those five minutes?" she asked. Five minutes didn't seem long, but she knew from experience that even just a few seconds could make the difference between life and death.

"No. The whole system has to reboot, and it just takes that long. I won't even have a read on your vitals. I'm working on that, but right now, this is all we have." Kirk grimaced. "I've been working on a few ideas while the LBD file was shelved, but without the dress in hand, I couldn't run any tests."

Evan nodded. "Okay, so I'll just be your guinea pig. We'll both learn along the way. What about water or fire?"

"The dress is water-proof and flame-retardant, but don't play around," he said.

Evan grinned. "Who? Me?" It wasn't that Evan was careless, but she knew that she wasn't always the most graceful swan in the pond.

"You also have a bug-sweeper of your own that will let you know if you are under surveillance. Let me tell you about your reconnaissance capabilities. The outside of this dress is covered with thousands of micro cameras, and just as many monitors. It's like tiny little TV screens. Basically, the same technology that they use in cloaking suits, but of course, if I turned on the cloak feature on the dress, everyone could still see your arms, legs, head, and shoulders. You'd just look like a goofy weather-girl." Kirk laughed at his own imagination.

Evan waited patiently for Kirk to return from his comical daydream.

Kirk started again. "Yeah, these cameras all work together to form a single image. It's kind of like they have a brain. They detect and focus on movements." He held her arms out slightly. "If you want me to do any detailed analysis in a busy area, you just aim yourself straight ahead, and the cameras will do most of the work. Well, you don't have to aim. The ones in the back and on either side do the same, so you don't have to be standing directly in front of your subject. Just figure out a way to let me know where you want me to focus. In some cases, if you can't get a clear line of sight, it can even extrapolate unknowns."

Evan raised her eyebrows and nodded. "That would mean what to me?"

"It can basically see around corners. It can fill in the blanks if your target is standing behind a pole." Kirk looked like a child with a new toy. "It's a big deal."

"And what about sound? Where are the microphones?" she asked.

"This is what separates this dress from all the other wired devices out there. You have, running all over this garment, dozens of micro-thin fiber-optic threads. At the end of each one is a microphone that transmits directly to me. I gather it all up and decipher, disseminate and analyze everything you're hearing."

"Everything?"

"I can bump up the volume in your canal receiver on anything you want. I can even change the frequency on the transmission so that you can hear it clearly, but someone holding another mic to your ear cannot." Kirk crossed his arms, proudly.

"What about other languages? Can the dress translate for me?" Evan tilted her head with a coy smile. Even the latest and greatest translation gear struggled with accuracy in real time.

"Yes, but I can do that without the computer. I'm fluent in hundreds of languages."

Evan blinked in wonder. "Hundreds? I've heard you speak Portuguese, French, and Italian. Eleanor told me you spoke seven languages now and that you were learning two more. How do you get hundreds?"

Kirk took her hands in his and smiled until dimples formed high over his cheekbones. "Eleanor doesn't count all of the encryption ciphers and computer scripts I know. I can crack passwords and security codes as fast as my notebook. I can translate for you, all right."

Evan laughed at his excitement. He was like a kid during show-and-tell.

She knew he wanted to have his hands all over the dress, and not for the usual reasons.

She twisted and stretched and tugged at the bodice. "Okay, tell me the rest so that I can get out of this corset. It feels like body armor."

"I know it's not super-comfortable for you, but that corset is half of the dress. It is body armor. You must be wearing it for everything to work. Even the bullet-resistance is diminished without it." Kirk stared into her eyes without a hint of nerves.

He put his hands on her shoulders and gently pushed them back so that she stood squared. She watched as he swallowed hard and let the tips of his index fingers slip just inside the straight neckline. "Right here, on either side, there are contact points. There are ten on the inside of the dress, and ten on the outside of the corset."

"The little lines of ribbon?" she asked, feeling with her own fingertips after his.

Kirk retracted his hands and shoved them into his pants pockets. "That's right. Uhmm, they must connect, or you could have trouble. When they touch, the dress and the corset work together. The corset will shield you, not just from bullets, but from electric shocks, x-rays, and other things." He drew his hands from his pockets for a moment but put them back as soon as he started talking again. *Yep, he wanted to touch.*

A second later, he started again. His hands came back out of the pockets, and he gestured as he spoke. "The umm … underwires … in the … top of the … corset have sensors for me," he said with difficulty. He pointed, shifted, and glanced in the most uncomfortable-looking way.

Evan smiled, trying to put him at ease. "For you?" She looked down at her chest and then back up to meet his gaze.

His cropped white hair seemed to lighten in comparison to the deep red hue that flushed over his cheeks. He nodded, his gaze settling on the bodice of the dress. He seemed to realize his faux pas and turned his attention to his computer.

"For me to monitor you. Your heart rate. Your pulse. Your perspiration and your stress level. I can even defibrillate you if I need to. Actually, the corset will do it automatically, but I can do it manually if it becomes necessary." Kirk sighed. "Also, if anyone else starts chest compressions it will defibrillate."

"Okay, good to know. I'll be careful about tight hugs. I don't want to end up fried," she said with a giggle.

"That's a good point," Kirk agreed.

"I'm kidding, Red." She raised her eyebrows. "Is it really that sensitive?"

Kirk took a deep breath and then laughed. "No. You can let people hug you."

Evan laughed as Kirk appeared to relax a little more. "I have a question.

If it's got all this stuff in it, how do I clean it? I'll try not to muss it too much, but you and I both know that this job can be messy."

He nodded. "The dress and the corset are both lined with antimicrobial silver and copper. Not only will it help to keep the dress germ-free, but it also boosts your immune system when you wear it. It's actually healthy." He retrieved a black zipper bag in the bottom of the dress box. "When you're done for the night, put the dress in its garment bag and plug it in for recharging and sonic cleaning."

"All right," she said. "What else do I need to know?"

"There's a ton, but let's take a minute and see if the monitors work. Once we get that test out of the way, you can take everything off and relax while we go through some more specs." Kirk shook his head. "You can put on your regular clothes. Obviously, you won't be naked."

Evan laughed again. "Relax, Red. Take a breath. The dress is perfect. The technology is amazing. Everything will be fine. You just tell me what to do."

Kirk took a few minutes to set up his notebook computer in the parlor, and Evan left the flat and walked to the end of the dingy hallway. Brawn and Ramos stood behind Kirk and watched the monitors on his screen. Hedge stood in the doorway of the apartment where he could keep an eye on everyone.

Evan took a position at the window facing the street, at the far end of the corridor. The glass was rippled with age, and the paint on the frame was peeling back from decades of wear. The sunlight blasting through the window caused Evan to blink several times until her eyesight adjusted from the contrast of the dark hallway.

"I feel a little weird all decked out in a cocktail dress at three o'clock in the afternoon," Evan said quietly. She imagined what others might think if they saw her now. Over-dressed, talking to herself. "Like I'm taking a walk of shame.

"I hear you fine," Kirk answered.

His even-paced voice sounded comfortable in Evan's ear. The micro-receiver, implanted in Evan's ear canal last year, adjusted slightly with pitch and volume so that no transmission ever carried above 45 decibels. Despite Kirk's occasional nerves, the voice in her ear was always relaxed. For reasons Evan couldn't explain, Kirk's voice reminded her of a favorite flannel shirt. Kind, soft, but strong and warm.

"What should we test first?" she asked him, pausing to look out of the window and down to the street at the front of the apartment building. No view of the Eiffel Tower from this window. She could be anywhere in Europe, as far as she could tell from here. Cars darted from curb to corner, and shadows began to stretch up the sides of the building across the street. Even through the glass, Evan could feel the heat of the afternoon. She glanced at the sky and noticed a dark weather front heading in from the west.

"I'm going to run a full camera check. Tell me what you see." Kirk's voice dropped almost to a whisper.

"Clouds in the distance. It looks like it might rain later," she said, as though she were talking to herself. "Warm. Even for late spring. Traffic is bustlin' this afternoon."

"I've got three men at the corner near the bicycle rack. There's a woman in a green dress picking out a bunch of flowers from the shop behind them," Kirk said.

"Very good," she confirmed. The storefronts across the street looked old but busy. The apartments upstairs all had drawn curtains. No one from the street looked up. *Keep your heads down. Mind your business.*

"The men are arguing about a football game," Kirk said. "The tall one likes *Les Bleus*, and the short one doesn't."

"Can you hear them? I can't hear them." Evan turned and looked over her shoulder to Hedge. He shrugged and leaned back against the doorframe.

Kirk hummed softly in her ear. "Among all my other talents, I can read lips, too. I think that's a successful camera test. Turn back to the window for a minute, though."

"Yes," she said. He had known she turned. *Wearing this dress was going to take some gettin' used to.*

"Now turn your head so that your receiver ear is aimed directly toward our flat."

She did as instructed.

"And tell me what you hear," Kirk said.

Kirk's voice murmured something, and a second later Evan could hear the clicking of computer keys. This was a new experience for her. Their com system had never been so sensitive before.

She smiled and was about to respond when she heard Brawn's voice. "Look at the shadow she's throwing on the wall, Teo. Now that's a figure I could—."

"I hear the voice of someone who's about to get a jolt," she said, marching back to the doorway.

Hedge held out his hands to stop her. "Kirk told him to say something. He just wanted to get a rise out of you."

"Evan, hold up. Your heart rate climbed for a second, and now the feed is flat. I need you to come back in, so I can see what happened," Kirk said.

Evan returned to the room to find Ramos and Brawn sitting back at the table reading file notes. She glared in their direction.

"Let Kirk fix the problem," Hedge ordered her.

"Yessir," she said, reporting to Kirk.

"Stand up straight and breathe normally for a minute," Kirk said.

Hedge stood between the other men and Evan. Turning to face Brawn and Ramos, he said, "You don't need to watch her breathe."

Kirk typed away on his keyboard, but couldn't seem to shake the confusion from his face. "I'm going to have to check the contacts."

He carried his computer into the bedroom and motioned for Evan to follow. He closed the door and sat for a few seconds watching the feeds on the monitor. "I don't get it. Everything worked just fine a minute ago."

Evan shrugged. "I don't know what I did. The sound was great. The cameras all seemed to work. You could see and hear everything I could."

"When you heard Brawn's voice, your heart rate elevated. Did you cross your arms or twist or anything? Tell me everything you did." Kirk set his notebook on the bed and circled Evan, studying her for answers.

"I might have held my breath for a second. I don't think I crossed my arms." She held her arms out away from her sides to allow Kirk's inspection.

He wrinkled his brow and rubbed his chin, looking frustrated. "Okay, I have an idea. I need you to take off the dress for a minute."

Evan reached under her arm and pulled down on the zipper at the side seam. She let the dress drop and stepped out carefully, handing the silky black sheath to Kirk. He immediately pulled out a pair of reading glasses and began studying the contact ribbons inside the seam at the neckline.

After a few seconds, without finding any obvious problems, his presence of mind seemed to return, and Kirk said, "Okay, three things."

Evan watched his face carefully. "What is it?"

"First, thank you. That was by far the fastest that any woman has ever undressed for me."

Evan blushed and grabbed the coverlet from the foot of the bed to wrap around her. "I cannot believe you just said that. You should be ashamed."

"Second," he added quickly. "Don't you ever do that again. I don't care if it is me, don't you take that dress off for anybody without Hedge's authorization unless it is specifically described in a mission."

Evan lost her blush and straightened her spine. "Yessir." She knew the rules of this dress and of the mission. Kirk's lapse didn't excuse hers. As a model, she was used to stripping out of her clothing on demand. As a covert operative, that didn't happen as often, thank goodness. This dress brought with it a whole new mindset. She would adjust.

"Lastly, and I know this is awkward, but I need to check the contacts on the corset."

Evan allowed the coverlet to drop just far enough to reveal the exterior contacts embedded in the lace overlay.

Kirk adjusted his glasses and examined each one, comparing them to the contacts on the dress. Evan saw that he was satisfied that they were not the problem, either. He put the dress on the bed and stared at the corset. Evan had been examined before, though usually not in her underwear. Never by her partner.

Evan waited as the wheels in Kirk's mind turned. She'd seen him analyze problems, and knew it was just a matter of time for him to find a solution. "What do you think is causing the glitch?" she asked.

Kirk raised his eyebrows suddenly, and Evan knew inspiration had struck. "Let me see how the corset fits in back," he said.

Evan turned her back to him and loosened the blanket to fall to her waist. Kirk noticed a pucker in the hook and eye placket in the center of her back.

"Have you lost weight since you were fitted?" Kirk asked.

"I don't know. A couple of pounds, maybe five."

"Enough to drop a cup size?"

Evan blinked, startled that he would ask that kind of question. "Maybe, but that's a little personal, don't you think?"

Kirk shook his head. "Nothing about this is personal. You just can't do that, Evan, not even five pounds. We built this outfit to conform precisely to your body. For the time being, I may have to adjust the hooks a half inch tighter around the bust." He gently pulled her to stand in front of the full-length mirror. "See, the underwires aren't getting good skin contact because the bodice isn't tight enough." Kirk pinched at the hooks until the pucker disappeared, and the heart monitor on his computer screen blipped back on.

Evan's eyes widened. "Are you kidding me?" she said with a sigh. No one had ever told her to put on five pounds.

Just then, Hedge entered the bedroom. At the sight of Evan out of the dress, and Kirk holding the back hooks on the corset, Hedge slammed the door closed.

"What's going on in here?" he asked. He raised his hands and shook his head. "I don't think I want to know, but you better tell me anyway."

Evan cinched the blanket up to cover herself completely. "Red— Agent Kirk is just trying to fix a little problem."

Hedge inhaled a deep breath and appeared ready to growl when Kirk interrupted.

"She lost weight. We have to make an adjustment," Kirk explained. He shrugged and released the hooks so that Hedge could see the gap in the contact. As soon as the pucker returned, the signal vanished from the computer monitor. "I'll fix it. I just have to move some hooks and recalibrate the program."

Hedge almost looked disappointed.

Evan rolled her eyes and sighed. She hated that she was letting down her team already. "What do you want me to do?" she asked.

Hedge threw up his hands. "You're in Paris. Eat a pastry."

CHAPTER SEVEN

"Are there any questions?" Hedge asked as he slid his comb into his jacket pocket.

In the two hours since he arrived and met his team, Hedge felt as though the third-floor apartment was shrinking. It would have been more than enough space for Elle and himself, but with a team of five, the walls seemed to close in on him tighter than his necktie. He was anxious to get out of the flat and get this operation underway. *Contact Anton Hrevic. Size him up. Take him down.* The other men shook their heads. *No questions. No worries.*

Kirk, wearing khakis and a golf shirt, sat at his notebook and typed away. Ramos and Brawn, both dressed in black jeans and tees, packed a gray duffle bag with weapons.

"It's just a basic face to face to see if Hrevic will let us into his organization," Hedge muttered, mostly to himself. "We go in, shake hands, let him look us over, and get out. Easy."

Kirk smiled as Hedge paced the tattered rug in the middle of the room. "Yeah, Hedge. We got it. It's going to be fine."

Hedge stared at the bedroom door, waiting for Evan. It had been a while since he'd been in the field with a woman. Elle had often taken hours to get ready to go out, but it had always been worth it. They didn't have hours. He checked his watch. He twisted and tugged at the cuffs of his pale lavender dress shirt, trying to straighten them beneath the charcoal gray suit coat. The creases in his slacks were as straight as the expression on his face.

Evan emerged from the room wearing the little black dress with the mesh scarf swathed around her shoulders like a cloud. She had secured the billows with a pink jeweled brooch pinned below her left breast. No one at the runway show today would suspect the pink accessory had Taser capabilities.

She crossed the room and reached up to straighten Hedge's silver silk tie.

"Not too tight," he complained.

"I'm not tightening it. The knot is crooked." She adjusted the half-Windsor and took a step back to appraise her team leader. She nodded in approval, took a moment to work with his purple striped pocket square, and then dusted his shoulders.

"I swear, if you lick your thumb and touch my face," Hedge warned.

"I'm not your momma," Evan said.

"You can be my …" Brawn started to say, but Ramos hit him in the center of his chest with a box of ammunition and shook his head in a warning.

"She's gonna kill you, Brawn," Teo muttered.

Evan marched the four steps across the rug to face Brawn. "I have orders to knock you on your butt for remarks like that. But I don't want to muss my outfit." She took a half step back. "Look, you don't know me, and I don't know you. Maybe we'll have time later to become friends. I don't know. But right now, we have a job to do, and making rude comments does not help get that job done. Understand?"

Brawn raised his hands in surrender but didn't apologize. Evan turned back toward Hedge and nodded again.

Hedge snarled at everyone.

Kirk laughed. "That's why I won't wear ties. It seems wrong to provide people with such an easy weapon to use against you."

Evan turned to Kirk. "What are we waiting for?"

The men all glanced at each other and then looked at her.

Brawn zipped the duffle closed. Kirk shut the notebook. Ramos moved from room to room, turning off lights and grabbing a camera bag and tripod.

Hedge studied Evan's ensemble carefully. "Your turn." He waggled his finger, and she turned in a circle in front of him. He adjusted the scarf in the back and smoothed the pleats in the back of her waistband. He lifted her glossy red hair and let it drape over the scarf on her shoulders.

"Do the alterations show?" she asked.

"Negative. You look good for this first test." Hedge smiled at her. He felt a rush of pride in his project. The dress looked beautiful. Evan was perfect.

"Do you have any advice before our first date?" She raised her eyebrows.

"Keep your eyes and ears open. Protect yourself. Protect your weapons. Keep your skirt down and your knees together," Hedge said with a laugh.

"You sound just like my daddy." Evan batted her lashes and coyly tipped her chin.

Hedge laughed again and gave Evan her handbag. He stuck out his left elbow for her to take. "Let's get 'em."

The team left the flat together, but Ramos, Brawn, and Kirk jumped into their small black SUV and disappeared into traffic. Hedge and Evan hailed a taxi and headed to the fashion district in downtown Paris.

Photographers and paparazzi crowded the awnings erected around the designated entrances of the mall, and Hedge instructed the driver to stop the cab half a block before the Carrousel du Louvre. Tourists everywhere. In the distance, he could see the top of the Eiffel Tower peeking over the trees surrounding the nearby gardens. The closer they got to the mall, the more organized the lines became. Hedge assessed the security. Cameras, guards, metal detectors, and a few plain-clothes officers. Typical for an event of this size.

They walked the short distance to the entrance and flashed their invitations to the guards at the doors. Finding the right hall for the House of Alexei show proved easy. Banners directed designers, reporters, and buyers to their appropriate destinations.

Hedge and Evan watched for Hrevic in the crowds but didn't find a single face they recognized. Once through the security sweeps at the inner doors, Evan switched the dress into active mode. Almost immediately Evan gave the signal that Kirk was in her ear.

"We're all here," she said with a smile.

"Good," Hedge answered. He pointed to the chairs that lined the runway. "We should find our seats. This place is filling up fast."

The skirted catwalk ran nearly the full length of the room, with a velvet backdrop at one end. Folding chairs flanked each side, allowing fans and photographers a close-up and personal view of the newest fashions to debut from the House of Alexei.

The couple scanned the room as they maneuvered through the crowd to their seats. Lights at the back of the room began to dim, and they quickly located the chairs designated on their tickets. A few seconds later, Hedge felt a firm grip on his shoulder.

"Excusez-moi," said the man behind Hedge.

"Yes?" he replied, making sure to sound extra-American. He stood to face Hrevic squarely to ensure that his six-inch height advantage was evident right from the beginning of their relationship.

"I don't mean to be rude," Hrevic said with an accent that sounded like a blend of Russian and French. "But could you verify that you are in the right seats, please?"

Hedge smiled and offered his hand. "You must be Anton Hrevic. I'm Hedger. Brandon Hedger. It's a pleasure to meet you."

"Yes, the pleasure is all mine," Hrevic said in a polite but automatic tone. "But you see, I think you may be in the wrong seats."

"I'm sorry. I suppose you haven't heard the news," Hedge said.

"What news?" Hrevic said quietly. He appeared to want to hurry the conversation.

"I'm Shelby Templeton's assistant. His right-hand-man. Or at least I was. You see, I inherited these seats. He wanted me to keep his business meeting with you." Hedge nodded and grabbed Hrevic's right hand. He began pumping it, and Hrevic began nodding, too. It was a test to see how easily Hedge could manipulate Hrevic. It worked.

"Where is he? What happened to Monsieur Templeton? He messaged me just two days ago. Everything was fine then." Hrevic appeared concerned.

"That was the day it happened. His car hit a pole and exploded. It was such a tragedy." Hedge swallowed hard as if he really felt the loss. "But don't worry at all. I'll be your new contact. You can call me Hedge."

Hrevic narrowed his pale blue eyes and raked his fingers through his intentionally messy mass of reddish blonde hair. He chewed on his lower lip as the hall went dark and sub-woofers from all over the room began to thump.

He motioned for Hedge to sit, and he joined him in the next chair. "Do you mind if we talk about this after the show? It's quite a lot to take in at once."

Hedge nodded. "Of course. I can't wait to see your designs. Shelby said you are a genius."

Hrevic looked around the room as the music started. He appeared nervous as if his plans for the day had been spoiled, and he was searching for elucidation. His focus landed on Evan's smile.

Hedge noticed the connection and was pleased. "I apologize, Mr. Hrevic, this is Eve. She's the woman that Shelby wanted you to meet. The model he thought you might be interested in signing."

"Yes, he mentioned you in his last message." Hrevic took her hand, leaned in, and kissed her cheek. "Enchanté."

She grinned, blinked demurely, and poured out her sweetest Texas drawl. "I'm anxious to see your handiwork, Mr. Hrevic. Shelby told me that you were simply amazing."

"Call me Anton, please," he said.

"Anton it is," she replied with an intentional blush, just as they had planned. Hedge had only known one other woman who could blush on cue. Elle would be proud.

The three turned to watch the runway light up in a bath of yellow and pink fog. A tall, pencil-thin blonde stepped from behind the black velvet drape. Hedge recognized her as the woman in the photographs from Eleanor's files.

She wore a creamy white pantsuit with a mint green floral scarf looped at her neck. A canary yellow satin bra showed from beneath the jacket. She turned to face Anton for a split-second and then began her strut to the end of the catwalk.

At the foot of the platform, she pushed her angular hips to her right and then back to her left. Her shoulders seemed to automatically adjust for counter-balance. As she walked past them again, Hedge noticed her black-lined eyes glance down to Hrevic and then back up to oblivion.

When she disappeared to the right of the black velvet curtain, another model appeared at the left. A series of blonde stick-figures paraded up and back on the stage for half an hour, each wearing one of Hrevic's designs. Several of the pieces consisted of sheer fabrics with strategically placed stripes or dots in citrus shades of yellows, greens, and oranges.

Hedge and Evan both raised their eyebrows at the ensembles, though Hedge guessed for different reasons.

Anton beamed with pride as the show continued. Cameras flashed, and the audience gasped and sighed as though they were watching a professional fireworks display. At the finale to the presentation, the first model returned to the head of the runway, this time dressed in a dark tangerine-colored gown edged in ivory ostrich feathers at the hem. The neckline plunged to just above the model's navel.

As the volume of the music lowered, and the lights came up, Anton leaped from his seat to join his models on stage. The room exploded with applause. Camera flashes blinded from all sides.

Hedge and Evan waited patiently as Anton received praises and air kisses from his adoring fans. They watched the stream of celebrities circle Hrevic. Most of his models retreated to the dressing room, but the woman in the tangerine gown remained at his side.

Hedge squeezed Evan's elbow as he scanned the room again. "Two o'clock. That's Congressman Forsythe in the blue Armani," he whispered.

"Mrs. Forsythe isn't with him," Evan said. "Kirk tells me Mrs. Forsythe is attending Reading Hour at the West Branch public library in Tucson."

"How does he know that?"

"Twitter." Evan smiled.

Hedge's gaze focused on a young brunette starlet on the other side of the room. He recognized her from a recent action movie in which she performed her own stunts. He had been impressed before, but even more so after seeing her in person.

"Isn't that Tammra Suzette?" Evan asked. "I think she's the one from that movie with the race cars."

"I think it is," Hedge answered. He knew he was staring.

"You should go talk to her," Evan said. "She's been watching you through the whole show."

Hedge turned to face Evan. His eyes narrowed. "No, she hasn't." He didn't need surveillance cameras to know that Suzette hadn't even glanced his direction. She was just a distraction. "We're not here to play," he said more to himself than to Evan. "We need to focus on the job."

They went back to studying the room. Everyone appeared busy and preoccupied with their own conversations. Hedge tightened his jaw and motioned to his right.

She turned to see two men in black pinstriped suits standing on the opposite side of the runway from them. They both stared at Evan and her dress.

Evan made eye contact, and they quickly turned away. She raised her eyebrow and shrugged at Hedge. He shook it off and turned his attention back to Hrevic.

Anton kissed his model and sent her backstage. He motioned for Evan and Hedge to join him at the steps at the head of the catwalk.

"Listen, I have a press thing in a few minutes, and that will tie me up for the rest of the night. I'm having a big party at my mansion tomorrow evening, though. I'd like for you to be there." Anton took Evan's hands in his again. "Both of you."

Hedge nodded. His plan was proceeding perfectly. A little too perfectly. Either Hrevic was on to them, or he was blinded by his blatant lust for Evan. Hedge looked at Evan and then looked at the way Anton looked at Evan. Lust. "We can be there," he said. "Is there anything, or anyone, that you'd like us to bring? I have access to everyone in Mr. Templeton's little black book." Hedge patted his jacket pocket containing his comb and started to reach for the non-existent black book.

Anton shook his head, barely acknowledging Hedge. "For now, just the two of you. We'll see about the next time."

"Sounds good," Hedge said, shaking Anton's hand firmly.

"I can't wait to see you again," Evan said with a flirtatious nod. "I'd love to wear one of your gorgeous designs."

Anton took her elbows in his hands and pulled her close for a kiss on each cheek. Hedge knew that Evan was familiar with these events and the fake affection that accompanied them. He watched her draw a deep breath before pressing her cheek against Anton's.

"I would like that very much," he whispered into her ear.

Evan fixed a smile to her lips, but Hedge thought she looked as though she might run. Steady, Evan. He wondered what Kirk might be telling her.

They both watched as Anton vanished into a flood of his admirers. Evan looped her wrist into the crook of Hedge's arm, and they left the building the same way they entered.

"Well, wasn't he charming?" Evan said when Hedge shot her a look of utter disgust.

"Yeah, adorable," Hedge said as he inhaled the cool evening air.

The meet went smoothly, but he couldn't help but feel suspicious. Evan was mesmerizing. He didn't doubt her ability to influence. But if Hrevic was so easily swayed by a beautiful woman, could he really be the mastermind behind an international extortion ring? And if so, what would his end game look like?

They walked several blocks until they had passed the Louvre. "You want something to eat?" Hedge asked, nodding in the direction of a sidewalk café across the street.

"That would be great."

They maneuvered through the traffic to the opposite curb. "We should take something back to those models, too. They all looked hungry," Hedge said, and Evan laughed.

As they found a small table at the corner of the sidewalk, a server snapped to their side.

"Je voudrais saisir votre commande?" he asked, looking everywhere but at them.

Hedge nodded. "Nous voudrions deux cafes et une patisserie pour mon ami."

The waiter tipped his chin and went inside.

"Very nice," Evan said, obviously admiring his linguistic skills. "Have you spent a lot of time in France?"

Hedge shrugged. "Not much lately, but speaking French is like riding a bike. How is your command of the language?"

Evan looked up at the stars. "Je parle couramment le français, but I've found that my native tongue gets better results from the men over here."

The sun had set, but a haze of blue-green still held the horizon against the dark night sky overhead. Evan's eyes mirrored the color precisely, including the flicker of the just-appearing stars.

"I'll bet. Speaking of results, tell me about Anton. What insights does Kirk have for us?"

Evan sat up straight in her chair and cleared her throat before beginning her report. Before she could start, Hedge noticed two figures standing in the shadows across the street. He furrowed his brow and raised his right index finger to stop her.

He tilted his head and propped his elbow on the edge of the table, leaning closer to Evan. "I want to know every detail, so speak slowly and quietly." He sent her a knowing look wrapped in a quiet laugh. "On a night like this, you can never know for sure who is listening."

"Where?" she asked.

He took her hand in his and stared into her eyes.

"Two men at your seven. About eight meters back. The same guys who were watching you after the runway show. They followed us from the mall, and now they're stopped across the boulevard. It could be a coincidence, but I want to be sure."

"Red's got them," Evan paused for a moment before relaying Kirk's report. "Facial recognition software says that they are designers for Dior. He'll try to catch what they're saying."

Evan tilted her head and dipped her chin as Kirk tuned in her receiver to focus on the men in question.

The server brought out their coffee and pastry. Hedge paid him and nodded. "Merci." He was anxious to know if they were a threat.

Evan listened to the men conversing in French then translated. "The short one says that Hrevic's girls all look as though they are constipated. Ray Milland thinks that's funny and wants to … never mind." Evan coughed. "I'll flag them in the file, but I'm not sure they're anything to worry about."

"Ray Milland?" Hedge asked quietly.

"Kirk called him that."

Hedge laughed, nearly choking on his coffee. "The taller one does look like Ray Milland."

Evan smiled, leaning closer. "Kirk says they're probably harmless, but he'll keep an eye open, just in case."

"Now to Anton," Evan said, sipping her steaming coffee. "What can you tell me, Red?"

She waited until Kirk finished. "Hrevic wasn't wearing any wires. Kirk didn't detect any feeds or signals at all in the room, other than me. There were lots of cameras, but we knew that going in, and nothing trained in on either of us for any length of time. Anton was clean at the show."

"Did Kirk get everything he needed tonight?" Hedge asked, inching closer to her face. To any observer, they were just lovers in a Paris café. Not partners doing a job. Not operatives gathering intelligence. Not saving the world.

"He gleaned all of the SIM card information from his phone. Once Anton gets back home we shouldn't have any trouble tapping all the other lines on his property," Evan explained. "I didn't like the way he kissed me, but it sure made it easy to swipe his information."

Hedge slid his finger up under her chin and bore deeper into her eyes. Her lashes fluttered at his touch. This was fun. He knew she was a pro at seducing others. She might even have a little pull on him. But he could feel her pulse quicken. He could feel the heat from her velvet skin. "You know what I just realized?" he asked. His gaze dropped to her full, pink mouth.

She licked her lips. "No, what?"

He spoke in soft, deep tones. He knew Evan liked him.

"Shorty and Milland are gone. Finish your éclair so we can go home."

CHAPTER EIGHT

Evan rolled her head from side to side, exhausted from the day, and anxious to get out of the dress and into bed. She waited patiently in the tiny bedroom as Kirk pecked away at his computer.

"Can you hear the ticking?" Kirk asked with an expectant look on his face.

She listened for a second until a faint tick-tick-tick filled her ear. "It sounds like an old pocket watch," Evan said. "Is this the polygraph feature?"

"Yes. Don't stop breathing just to listen." Kirk made a few more adjustments in the program, and the ticking grew louder and then softer. "You need to play with it, so you can get used to it. Walk around. Make sure you recognize the sound when there is other noise around you."

Evan stood up and twirled in a circle between the narrow beds. "Every girl needs a pretty dress with a built-in lie detector," she said. "I wish I'd known about this feature earlier tonight. It might have come in handy."

Kirk shrugged. "You didn't need it for this evening's trip. You were fine without it."

"Why can I hear the ticking, though? Nobody's lying to me right now."

Kirk adjusted again. "I just wanted you to know what to listen for. You shouldn't hear anything now."

Evan closed her eyes to focus on what she could and couldn't hear. Silence. "I want to try it out on the team." She smoothed the skirt of the dress into place and headed for the door. She wanted to ask Hedge a few questions.

Kirk grimaced. "I already have all of our voice data dialed out. We do too much lying when we're undercover. It would just cause a constant ticking, and you wouldn't hear when others lie."

"You said you want me to get used to it. How can I practice if I can't try it on you guys?" She felt like a kid with a new toy that she wasn't allowed to play with. "Can't you put your voice data back in, so I can test it?"

Kirk shook his head. "I don't think that's a good idea. I'll go and talk to the others and see who is game for an interrogation. Give me a second, and I'll be right back." Evan remained in the bedroom while Kirk went to talk to the rest of the team. He returned shortly and started typing away at his keyboard. He looked up and nodded. "Okay, go get 'em."

Evan felt butterflies in her stomach. "Which man do I get to question?" she asked, rubbing her palms together. This would be fun.

"I can't tell you that. If we're going to really practice, you must use your own senses as well. This program just monitors vocal patterns and intonations. It's not one hundred percent accurate, just like regular lie detectors. Some people can beat them when they're lying, and some people fail them, even when they are telling the truth." Kirk patted her shoulder. "You've got to learn how to use that little tick to make them tell you the truth."

"Are you gonna coach me any?" She pulled her hair over her right shoulder and took a deep breath.

"Not unless you need it." Kirk walked to the door and held it open for her. He went back to the settee to monitor.

Evan walked into the living room, pulling the door closed behind her. All the men turned to face her. She felt like a teenager at a party playing Spin the Bottle, and she was the bottle. Her gaze shifted from Ramos to Brawn to Hedge. She took a step toward Ramos, and he sat straight in his chair and smiled.

"Good, I get to be first," he said. He wiggled his eyebrows at her and motioned for her to sit on the sofa at his side. "What would you like to know? I'll tell you anything."

Evan tried to recall the details in Ramos' personnel file. She remembered that he had served as a mechanic in the Air Force before joining the agency. He had worked on just about every type of vehicle under the sun and loved all things with wings or wheels. What secrets would he have? She looked him over from head to hoof and smiled. There was something about him, but she wasn't sure what it was. His muscular build would look equally suited for a cover of a romance novel or a recruiter's flyer. But his smile had a glimmer of mischief that she wanted to know more about.

Evan took a deep breath and constructed a question that might put him at ease. "Well, tell me about your first car, Teo."

Ramos' eyes lit up as he leaned toward her. "She was a slick red '69 Dodge Charger 440 two-door hard-top with four-on-the-floor. She was a tiger. The black vinyl interior was near perfect, but it would fry your butt in the summer. I called her Lux. She flew like a streak of light."

Evan grinned. He was telling the truth. "How many miles did you put on it?"

He leaned back into the couch and twisted his lips to one side. "She had sixty-eight K when I got it and almost one-ninety when I ... when I sold it."

Suddenly the ticking started. She watched his face. He looked at his left shoe for a split second. He added, "She was a great car."

Evan leaned closer and nodded. Ramos looked tired and a little sad. Why would he lie, though? "I bet she was, Teo. But what really happened to her? You didn't just sell her, did you?"

He furrowed his brows and blinked with a twitch. "I sold her." His voice sounded strained and defensive.

"What kind of condition was she in when you sold her?" she asked. She tilted her head in a gesture of compassion. She let her lashes flutter to draw his attention. It worked like a charm. He made eye contact.

"She was hurt," he confessed. "I rolled her when I was racing for pinks. The winner didn't want her 'cause she was so messed up. My best friend bought her from me, so I could pay off my race." He scratched his chin as though he wanted to take off his end-of-day whiskers. "I still miss that car."

"Sorry about that." Evan patted his knee and nodded. Not a big lie, not really even a lie. The dress could pick up on intention to deceive. Good to know.

Teo sat back in the chair, giving Evan a clear sign that he was through with this game.

Evan looked over her left shoulder to where Brawn sat at the table. She crossed the room to the empty chair opposite him and sat down. She didn't speak for a few seconds. She just studied his face for a second. She sat as though she were interviewing to become a nun, so as not to encourage any of his suggestive comments.

"My turn. Ask me anything you want; I'll tell you the absolute truth," Brawn lowered his tone. "And I do mean anything." The ticking began immediately.

"Seriously, Brawn? You're already lying to me." She started to get up, but Brawn held up his hands in surrender.

"Give me a chance," he said.

She stayed. "Why should I?" She figured that was about as good a place to start as any. Everything he said would probably be a lie, but as members of the same team, she should at least get to know him a little.

"Look, I know we got off on the wrong foot," he said.

Evan watched his body language. He was relaxed and breathing normally. He rested his hands on the table, toward her, palms up. She listened. The ticking stopped. "Yes, we did."

Brawn pulled his hands back and turned to face everyone in the room.

"I know I get on people's nerves. I'm sorry about that. I never had many friends growing up, so I try to act big to impress people, and it always backfires."

Evan paused to listen to the silence ringing in her ear. She sighed, unsure of what the quiet really meant. The dress said he was telling the truth, but her gut warned her to be careful.

Brawn turned back to Evan and crossed his arms in front of himself on the table. He let his shoulders slump. "I'm not good at talking to women. I never have been." He seemed to stumble over his words. "I mean, women that actually, I don't know, mean something to me. I can think of all kinds of pick-up lines, and they usually work well enough for a good time here and there. But a meaningful conversation with an intelligent woman is something I've never experienced."

Evan smiled sympathetically and stared into his eyes. And just like that, the wicked gleam returned. "Wow," she said. "I don't even need the lie detector for that one." She raised her brows. "Nice try, though."

"What gave me away?" Brawn asked, rocking onto the back two legs of his chair.

"Now you know I can't betray a whole sisterhood," she said. "But you are good."

"At so many things," Brawn said with a sly wink.

Hedge stood up quickly. "Okay, I think we're done here. We should go over our plans and get some sleep before tomorrow. That's when the party starts."

"Oh, hun-uhh," Ramos said. "We went through it. It's your turn."

Evan frowned. She wanted Hedge to answer a question or two.

"I'm the senior agent." Hedge crossed his arms. "No more games." He rapped on the bedroom door with his knuckles. "Kirk?"

"You didn't really think Hedge was going to let you interview him in front of the others, did you?" Kirk whispered in Evan's ear. She could hear him gathering his gear.

Kirk joined them, and Hedge dismissed the levity. Evan exchanged a glance with Kirk and gestured with a quick nod for him to join her on the couch. Hedge commanded everyone's attention from the center of the room.

"Let's go over all the details for tomorrow's operation," Hedge said. "Kirk, you and Ramos will be positioned in the SUV just beyond Hrevic's gates. Kirk, I want you to keep Evan hot at all times. We will only go dark if there is security at the front door. We'll do our own sweeps as we go through the house. Is there anything else we should know?"

Kirk nodded. "This test tonight was successful. Evan will be a human polygraph by tomorrow evening. Also, unless Anton has invested in better gear than I have, I should be able to piggy-back on his signals and monitor any security or surveillance feeds he's using. If that's the case, I can get video and audio pretty easily."

Ramos raised his index finger for an opportunity to speak. "What are the chances Hrevic has better equipment than InDIGO?"

Kirk scoffed. "I didn't say 'better than InDIGO,' I said better than anything I have. He doesn't."

Ramos nodded in obvious admiration.

Hedge turned to Teo. "I want you behind the wheel and ready for anything. Playing in someone else's sandbox can get tricky. Hrevic is probably running background checks on Evan and me as we speak."

"He is," Kirk affirmed. "I hacked all of his social media accounts, too. Don't worry. He's only finding what you want him to find."

Hedge wore an expression of satisfaction. "That being said, we still may need a quick exit or even an outside diversion."

Ramos saluted. "Roger that."

Evan guessed he was ready to blow something up if the occasion called for it. She smiled at the thought.

"Brawn, you're coming in with us." Hedge stared at him. "We may need an inside diversion as well."

"It's a tough job, but somebody's got to do it," he said. "Are all those blondes from Kirk's videos going to be at this party?"

"Yes, and I want you to have one on your arm all night," Hedge ordered.

"Does it have to be the same woman the whole night?" Brawn whined like a spoiled teenager.

"Let me put it to you this way," Hedge explained. "If you keep a girl busy, she won't be entertaining any senators, judges or other government officials. The fate of the free world could be in your hands tomorrow night."

Brawn stared down at his palms. "I love the feel of fate."

Evan rolled her eyes. She suddenly understood what it was like to have brothers. She watched Hedge as he turned to face her. He looked as though a smile was forming at the corners of his eyes. She felt a warm flutter of excitement.

"Your job is simply to get into Hrevic's stable of models."

"I'll get in," she said confidently. "I'm not blonde, but I'm everything else."

Hedge's smile spread across his whole face. "That's why we're here."

Evan took a deep breath. She thought about her college days, modeling to pay her tuition. She loathed the hours and superficial atmosphere of the industry. She despised the drugs, the dysfunction, and the perverts. She was grateful that by God's grace she'd avoided most of that ugliness. But, bless her heart, she loved the fashion. Jumping back into that world would mean wearing the latest couture designs in all the right places, but this time her motivation was much more important than a paycheck. Entire governments, world politics, human lives hung in the balance.

Hedge's expression turned serious. "Our main objective is to find a real connection between Anton Hrevic and the officials he seems to be influencing. We are looking for proof. We are looking for a money trail or an asset that can lead to one." He raised his eyebrows. "Any questions?"

Everyone shook their heads.

"All right, then. Get some sleep tonight."

Brawn and Ramos sat where they were while Evan and Kirk crossed to the bedroom. Evan hoped to have a private word with Red about the dress, but Hedge followed them in.

"How are you wearing the dress tomorrow?" Hedge asked.

"I hadn't really thought about it," Evan said. "Do you have any suggestions?"

"You wore it long to the runway show," Kirk said.

Evan nodded. "I let the skirt out straight. Shows are kinda formal, so I kept the hem just above my ankles." She really wished she could take it off and let the men play with the dress. She was ready to call it a night.

Hedge studied the dress on Evan. "How short can you make the skirt and still, you know, conceal?"

Evan tightened the skirt ruching until the bottom edge sat about four inches above her knees. She hadn't had her appearance critiqued like this in a few years, but it was part of the assignment. "This is as short as I can wear it and still carry my Springfield normally. I'm assuming that's what you mean?"

Hedge looked at Kirk and shrugged. Kirk picked up the black pumps from the floor where Evan had dropped them and handed them to her.

"Slip these on for a second," Kirk said.

She stepped into the shoes. Her feet were tired. Even with state-of-the-art design, four-inch heels on Paris pavement did not feel like sneakers. She looked up in time to see the men exchange a glance that she couldn't quite decipher.

"I know," Hedge said. He appeared to speak to Kirk without words. He stroked his goatee with his right thumb and index finger and shook his head. "Can we lose the side arm?"

Kirk shook his head. "That dress is our way of keeping you both armed. Even in black-out mode, the dress can shield any weapons worn beneath it. She has to carry your Glock in, too," he explained.

"I think it's still too long," Hedge insisted. Evan couldn't imagine what this dress was 'too long' for.

"Raise the hem another inch," Kirk said. "I think we can fix the holsters to sit higher, and you'll have plenty of leg to spare."

Evan raised her eyebrows at their casual regard for her legs. They ignored her response, so she swallowed hard and obeyed. She adjusted the side gathers again. "Any more and I'll have my own website," she joked.

Both men scowled. Evan could plainly see that they wanted the skirt shorter.

"You're as bad as them." She pointed to the door and reluctantly pulled the skirt up another inch. "I practically had Hrevic nibbling my fingers when I was completely covered this morning. I don't even want to think about his reaction to this."

"And no scarf this time, either. You're going bare-shouldered strapless," Hedge instructed. "We don't know what he likes. We want to show off all of your assets."

"Oh, goody," Evan said. She unpinned the brooch and unwrapped her shoulders from the tulle scarf. At this point, the dress barely covered more than the corset. "Can I at least wear a chunky necklace or something?"

"You're not supposed to wear a necklace with a strapless gown," Hedge said, almost defensively.

Evan frowned. "It scares me that you know that," she said. "But that rule is dated, anyway. If I don't have a necklace or a scarf, I'll feel naked."

Kirk shrugged. "I do have a nice red jasper piece with a digital magnification device."

"Great," Hedge said. He regarded Evan with a nod. "Now take off the dress and try to get some sleep."

Evan waited for the men to at least turn their backs, but they just remained in place, studying the dress. She cleared her throat and glanced at Kirk and back to Hedge, who looked almost hypnotized by the dress. She cleared her throat again. "May I have a little privacy, please?"

Hedge seemed to startle, and for a split second, Evan thought he might have been embarrassed. "You have two minutes," he said, returning to his stony façade and the men left her to undress in private.

Twenty minutes later the flat was dark, and the dress hung in its garment bag on the wall hook beside Evan's narrow bed. Kirk took his turn in the flat's only bathroom, and Evan sat cross-legged in her nightshirt thinking about the day and how to prepare for tomorrow. Meeting Hedge, seeing Hedge and Eleanor interact, meeting Teo and Brawn. She had never worked with a big team like this. The dynamics would take a little getting-used-to. As an only child, she wondered what it would be like to have brothers. Now she had four.

Red was the oldest and the protector. The brains. Teo was the athlete. The gearhead. Trustworthy and loyal, she knew he gave one hundred percent of himself, one hundred percent of the time. And then Brawn. The ladies' man, at least in his own mind. She could have him eating from the palm of her hand, if only she wanted to.

Hedge was different, though. He was a mix of everything. Smart, strong, protective, serious, faithful. Pretty sure he knows his way around a dress shop, too. He knew his job, and there was a lot to learn from him. But she was right about one thing. He was a challenge. Easy to tangle with, and maybe she wanted to do just that.

The meeting with Anton Hrevic went just as she had expected. He had all the fake niceties down to an art. Polite conversation about his self-importance, cheek kisses, air kisses. He had all the slick moves of a spoiled rich boy. Eyes that could never see enough. Hands that reached for more than what was offered. She had dealt with men like him before, and she knew how to handle him. But she'd be glad when she didn't have to.

Her nightly ritual of self-debriefing usually helped to clear her mind, so her body could reap the benefits of a full night's sleep. Tonight, she wasn't sure. She hoped her sheer exhaustion would do the trick.

Hedge came in and rolled out his pallet in the floor space between the twin beds. "How long have you known Kirk?" he asked her.

"A few years now," she said. "He recruited me and ran surveillance on my first official assignment. We spent a lot of time together on that one. Red's the one who got me into the LBD project."

"I know. Eleanor and I were the leads on the whole idea. We brought in Kirk early on, even before we got the green light for production." He laced his fingers together and slid his hands behind his head as he lay back on his pillow. "Why do you call him Red?"

Evan stretched out her legs and rocked onto her side to face him. "Did you ever watch the old Star Trek television series? The original ones?" She thought about the first time she met Rowan Kirk after a runway show in Milan.

"Yeah, I like science fiction well enough," he said.

"Kirk and I are both Trekkies. We discovered this about each other on that first mission. I used to tease him about his name, Captain Kirk, you know?" She paused for a second. Hedge didn't respond. "Well, he told me that he wasn't anything like Captain Kirk because he didn't 'boldly go' anywhere he didn't have to. He said that he was unlucky out in the field, like the guys on the show that wore the red shirts. You know, the ones with names like Jones or Smith, how they always get killed off in the first ten minutes of the episode? He thought he was like that. A redshirt. He preferred to stay out of sight, working from behind his computer."

"So, you call him Red to remind him of his bad luck?" Hedge asked as if he disapproved.

"Oh no. It's not like that," she insisted. "That would be mean. A few assignments later we got into a bad situation. We got made by a drug lord off the coast of Italy, and we were forced to jump from a yacht and swim to shore. I helped him when he thought that he wouldn't make it back. Later that night, he told me that if I ever needed a redshirt in the field, he'd go with me. We've been partners ever since."

"That's the stupidest thing I've ever heard," Hedge said.

A faint ticking began in Evan's ear. It took a second for her to realize what it was. Once she knew, she was intrigued. "What do you mean?" she asked.

"A job is no place for the warm fuzzies and kumbaya moments. Here he is, offering to go with you anytime you need a sacrificial pawn, and you just keep rubbing it in," Hedge muttered. "Heartless."

His words sounded sincere, but the ticking betrayed him.

"What about you and Eleanor?" she said, risking his anger. "You two seem pretty close."

"We're colleagues. Our relationship is purely professional. Always has been. She's married to one of your Texas senators now, and she's happy. I'm happy for her."

The ticking grew more intense.

The door opened, and Kirk entered. He placed his watch on the nightstand and got straight into his bed.

"G'night, Red," Evan whispered. She smiled as mischief danced through her thoughts.

"Goodnight, Evan. Sleep well," he replied.

"I will." She propped herself up on her elbow. "Only … can you double-check that you have everything powered down on the LBD program on your computer?"

"Sure thing," Kirk said, sitting up and opening his notebook. "Sorry, looks like I tried to shut down the master program without confirming the settings to close the individual monitors." He tapped on a few keys, and the ticking went away.

Evan stretched her arms over her head and yawned. "Thanks, Red."

"How did you know it was still running?" The light from Kirk's computer projected a pale blue fog around the room.

"It's so weird. I guess because the dress is so close to my bed and to my ear receiver, but I've been talking to Hedge for a few minutes, and the ticking in my ear is just drivin' me crazy." Evan leaned over the edge of her bed to face her superior. Even in the dark, she could see his eyes narrow. She smiled playfully, and Hedge exhaled and rolled to his side, away from her.

Kirk closed the program and powered down the notebook completely. The room turned black.

"G'night, Hedge," she whispered.

"Shut up."

CHAPTER NINE

Hedge, Evan, and Brawn got out of the taxi and took their place in the short line at the entrance to Anton Hrevic's mansion. The large white estate sat center stage on a small lot backing up to the gardens west of the Eiffel Tower. The whole property was lit from every angle, and a thumping bass beat pumped through the open double front doors. Evan hadn't been to a party like this for a while now. She didn't miss it.

Hedge looked professional in a midnight blue suit. Brawn sported a chocolate brown suit without a tie, and he had the top three buttons of his silk shirt undone. Evan shivered as the cool evening breeze raised goose bumps on her very exposed shoulders, arms, and legs.

"I can't believe that's the same dress," Brawn said as they waited in line. "It looks like half the dress. It actually looks like a really nice belt."

"Zip it," Hedge muttered. His eyes scanned the door frame as they approached. He gestured to a wire leading from the bottom right side of the casing to a covered console table in the foyer.

He held out his hand to Evan. "You look nice. Black suits you."

That was her cue to go dark. She put her hand on her waistband and depressed the bottom button. "You're awfully sweet," she chimed loudly with an over-emphasized drawl.

"Invitation only," said the man-and-a-half that guarded the entry.

"Brandon Hedger," Hedge said. "We should be on the list."

The guard paused for a moment and put his hand to his right ear and nodded. He stepped aside to let them enter. "Enjoy the party."

Everywhere Evan looked was white, silver, or gold. The polished white marble floors reflected a thousand points of light from the crystal chandelier overhead. The curved stairway to the right was lined with silver and gold-plated ironwork that looked like scrolling ivy vines. The only color in the room was a hot pink, life-sized crocodile sculpture on the floor in the corner. *Who thought that was a good idea?* Evan decided not to ask Anton for his decorator's number.

Within seconds Anton appeared in the foyer. He wore a dark gray pin-stripe over a pink shirt. His hair was shaped into a blond fin held in place with pomade and wishful thinking.

"Brandon, I'm glad you made it tonight," he said, pumping Hedge's right arm. "I forgot. You like to be called Hedge. I like that. It sounds like shrubbery."

"You've met Eve already," Hedge said, gesturing to Evan. He then motioned to Brawn. "But I don't want to make the same mistake my predecessor did by not introducing his right-hand-man. Anton Hrevic, I want you to meet my chief of staff. This is Jason Brown."

Anton shook Brawn's hand quickly and then focused his attention on Evan. He planted real kisses on both her cheeks and immediately looped his arm around her narrow waist.

"You look fantastique," he said as his gaze roamed over her. He glanced over his shoulder at the other men. "Follow."

Evan carefully inched her left hand across her waist to turn the dress back on, but as soon as she accomplished her task, Anton's fingers crept around her and took her hand in his.

"Eve, let me get you a drink," he said, leading her to the bar. "All of my muses drink mineral water. It helps keep them trim."

Evan bit her lip. "That would be lovely," she said.

He handed her a champagne flute filled with sparkling water. "From Texas?" he asked.

"I am. How could you tell?" she said, sprinkling in a few extra syllables.

"My dear, I have traveled all over this great world of ours and have come to a singular conclusion." He handed Hedge and Brawn each a cocktail and took one for himself. "The creator gifted the earth with beautiful creatures we men rightly call the fairer sex. Three locations on this planet received more than their share of beauty: France, Russia, and Texas."

Anton lifted his glass in a toast, and the other men followed. "To beautiful women," he said. "De belle femmes."

"Vive la France," Brawn added.

"Za zhén-shsheen," Hedge toasted in a burst of Russian.

Evan smiled and raised her glass. "Remember the Alamo."

The men laughed, and they all sipped at their drinks.

"Hedge, come with me to my office, and we can take care of our business. Mr. Brown, please take advantage of my hospitality. Your boss will join you shortly." Anton directed him to the closest blonde.

"What about me?" Evan was anxious to roam the house. She had already noticed a couple or two leaving the dance floor for more privacy. She wanted to see who was here and what they were doing.

"My dear beauty, you are not leaving my side." Anton cinched her closer.

Brawn nodded and stepped through another pair of doors into a room filled with flashing lights and people dancing. He finished the rest of his drink and jumped into the circus.

Hedge followed Anton and Evan down a hallway to a room furnished in dark wood and purple velvet drapery. A wide mirror in a gilded frame consumed most of the wall to the right. A built-in credenza anchored the wall on the left, and French doors lined the opposite wall.

"What a pretty room," Evan exclaimed, as Anton started to close the door behind them. She hoped Kirk saw everything. He had been quiet so far.

"Anton, here you are," said a woman pushing through the door before it clicked shut.

Evan recognized her as the head model from the runway, but tonight her hair was pulled back in a tight bun at the nape of her neck. She wore a short, metallic gold sheath and black platform sandals with gold studs around the heels. Her face was precisely symmetrical, with cold gray eyes and a straight nose aligned over expressionless frosted lips. Her chin could direct traffic.

"Hi," Evan said, enthusiastically. She held out her hand to the woman, who looked at it but didn't take it.

The blonde raised her eyebrows. "Has the party been moved back here?" she asked. Her voice carried a sharp Russian accent.

Anton shook his head and jutted out his lower lip. He moved quickly to the woman's side and away from Evan.

"Xandra, darling, I want you to meet someone. This is my new associate, Brandon Hedger, from America. And this is his friend, Eve." Anton circled his arm around Xandra's waist and kissed her cheek.

Evan watched as Anton's attention shifted solely to Xandra. No doubt as to who was in charge in their relationship.

Hedge offered his hand to Xandra. "It's a pleasure to meet you," he said.

Xandra's eyes widened as she seemed to compare Anton's average build to Hedge's muscular frame. "How nice," she said with a bite in her voice.

She faced Evan. "Eve? Are you a model?"

Evan smiled and exercised her lashes, intentionally creating contrast from Xandra's stone expression. "Why, yes ma'am, I've been in shows all over the world."

Xandra looked her up and down. "Hmmph. You are fat for Paris couture."

"Xandra, be kind," Anton admonished. "Not everyone can be as naturally slim as you are."

Evan blinked the comment away. *Yep, she really didn't miss the fashion world.*

Hedge put his arm around Evan's shoulders defensively. "Eve's working on her figure." He looked at Evan and grinned.

Evan forced her lips to smile, but her eyes warned Hedge not to push his luck.

Anton patted Xandra on the backside. "Why don't you go back to the party, and I will be right out. I just have a bit of business to work out with Mr. Hedger."

Xandra led him to the door. When he opened it for her, she took his face in her hands and kissed him full on the mouth. As she pulled away, she drew his bottom lip into her mouth and released it slowly from between her teeth.

She glowered at Evan as if she were claiming her territory before she left.

Evan thought she might throw up a little in her mouth. "Shake it off," she heard Kirk whispering. "I need you to walk around the room. I'm picking up blips, and I need to isolate them."

She tilted her head at the men. "Y'all don't mind me. Go ahead with your business, and I'll just look at all the pretty things."

Hedge and Anton sat in the leather chairs on either side of the desk.

"What exactly do you know about Templeton's function in my organization?" Anton asked.

Hedge leaned back and appeared utterly relaxed. "Templeton told me all about everything he did for you. He said that you needed big names for your parties. He said that important politicians needed to meet you and your models so that you could become famous and your girls could become super-models. Shelby said that you liked to do favors for powerful men."

"That's very true," Anton said. "Tell me about the powerful people you know."

Hedge began reciting a list of names carefully designed to elevate Anton's interest. Some were American businessmen, others were elected officials. He threw in a few celebrities and authors for good measure.

Evan walked around the room, picking up knick-knacks and objets d'art, careful not to show too much interest in any particular thing. Kirk advised her as to where cameras and listening devices might be located. A bronze monkey with black crystal eyes, a cigarette lighter shaped like a racecar, a sculpture of a nude woman picking a flower. As she identified them, Kirk remotely hacked into their signals. Within a matter of minutes, Evan and Kirk had every feed secured.

"How can I be sure you don't have ambitions to take over my whole operation?" Evan heard Anton ask.

Hedge laughed. "Oh, no sir, I don't know anything about clothes and such things. I know about having important friends, though. Templeton taught me all about that. He often told me that if anything ever happened, he wanted me to take over for him. He said you were his most important client."

"It's a shame that Shelby met such an untimely end," Anton said. "How did you say he died? A car accident?"

Hedge knew that Anton expected more information than what the newspapers included. Luckily, the newspapers only printed the article that Hedge had given them.

"Yes, it seems he ran his Peugeot into a telephone pole just outside of Paris four days ago. The police tell me that he was probably under the influence of alcohol and perhaps a number of other chemicals." Hedge sighed. "I knew he drank, but I never suspected that he did drugs, too. Too bad."

"He was clever, that one," Anton said, apparently satisfied with Hedge's answer. "He never let me down. I shall miss him."

Hedge nodded. "I feel the same way. Shelby was a decent man. I just want the chance to live up to his reputation."

Evan finished her tour of the room while the men discussed their business. She listened to both remarking about her figure and her face but pretended not to hear anything as her temper started to warm. She leaned over the back of Hedge's chair, intentionally giving Anton an eyeful. Anton smiled as she joined the conversation.

"I'd like you to take Templeton's place, Hedge," Anton announced grandly. A button on his desk phone flashed. "Excuse me for just one minute," he said, rushing to the office door. "I'll be right back."

As soon as the door closed behind him, Hedge grabbed Evan's wrist and pulled her around the chair to his lap. Before she could react, he fixed a firm kiss on her full pink lips.

"I think he's going to let you model for him, baby," Hedge said, as soon as their lips parted.

"You think so?" she asked. She tried to play the part of a young, excited model whose star was about to rise to a new level. Earlier they had discussed how to handle their cover relationship. They decided that an equal mix of sex and money would be their prime motivators, and would allow for emotional reactions when necessary. Good diversions. Easier to surprise targets. But Evan didn't expect Hedge to kiss her at the first opportunity, and she was a little shaken by it. Had he even been listening to his own 'Evan's not a toy' speech?

Hedge nodded and stood, lifting Evan and then planting her backside onto Anton's desk. He placed his hands just above the bends of her knees and pulled her tight against his legs.

Evan felt his fingers under her skirt retrieving his pistol from the holster on her thigh. Once he discreetly dropped it into his jacket pocket, he reached back under the dress for the micro-dot trackers from the back of her holster. He slid the one-inch card of trackers into her hand. She grinned and then slipped them into the top of her corset. Where they should have been in the first place, but Hedge had been afraid that they might be too visible. As if anyone looking down her dress would notice something the size of a postage stamp. She huffed excitedly and threw her arms around his neck. She was tempted to squeeze him tighter than necessary.

"I'm gonna walk the runway in Paris, Hedge. People are gonna hear my name and see my face all over," she said, alerting him to the cameras and microphones all over the room. She could stay focused on the job.

"I know, Evie. Anton likes you. I can tell. One day you'll look in the mirror, and the whole world will be toasting you." Hedge kissed her again, lifting her off the desk and letting her legs down slowly until she was standing between him and the desk.

Evan remained in Hedge's embrace until Anton returned to the room. She smiled and blushed as Anton resumed his seat at the desk.

"Sorry 'bout that. We're just so excited to be here," she said.

Anton nodded, eyeing the edge of his desk where she had sat only seconds before.

"As I said before, Mr. Hedger, I want to give you the chance to impress me. I would like for you to enjoy my party tonight. See what I do here and have fun." Anton stood at his desk and made a sweeping gesture toward the door. "I'm planning another party for next Saturday evening, and I want you to attend that one as well. But that night I want you to bring a few friends with you. I want them famous, or powerful, or both."

"You won't be disappointed, Mr. Hrevic." Hedge shook his hand again. "What about Evie? Can you find a place for her in your next show?"

Anton reached out for her arm. "Eve, do you know what I call my girls?"

"No sir, what?" she asked.

"I call them my muses. You see, all of my women inspire me." Anton's regard for Evan had cooled slightly. Evan guessed he'd been watching them from behind the huge mirror. "I think you will be of great inspiration to my designs. I want you to come and meet some of my friends."

He led them back down the hall to the crowds of carousers. He tried to cinch her body to his, but Xandra reappeared and foiled his maneuver.

He looked over Evan from head to toe. "I want you to impress me tonight, cherie."

Evan pushed her shoulders back and raised her eyebrows. "How do I do that?" She kept her tone flirtatious.

He smiled and waggled his finger at her, exaggerating as Xandra watched him. "I want to see you dancing with as many men as you can collect."

Evan beamed. "Y'all don't two-step here, but I'll do my best."

Evan and Hedge folded themselves into the mass of revelers, finding Brawn dancing with two models at the same time.

"Hedge, you want one?" he offered loudly. He raised his right hand, which held the hand of one of the women. "This is Olga." Raising his other hand, he called, "and this one is Tatiana."

Tatiana quickly switched to Hedge's arm. "Hello."

"Nice to meet you," Hedge said, stepping side to side to keep the beat. His tall, muscular frame looked slightly awkward at first, but soon the music caught him up in the tide of rhythm and flesh.

"Hello," she said again. Tatiana's long, sinewy arms waved over her head and toward Hedge, luring him like a siren.

Evan nodded to the men and continued dancing to the other side of the room. She danced with one man and then another, staying with each just long enough to move a micro-dot from her décolleté to the back of his neck. She made sure to allow time for Hedge and Anton to see her with each partner. When all eight of the trackers were distributed, she stayed longer with her companions, trying to glean information that Kirk could use.

When she could no longer dance, she took a narrow path back to the bar and asked for another glass of mineral water. She was approached by a handsome dark-skinned man with a sage green two-button suit and a polished British accent.

"Wouldn't you prefer something a little stronger?" he asked.

"I surely would," she admitted, "but for tonight I'm sticking to water." She watched as his piercing brown eyes studied her face and neck.

"Maybe I'm not talking about your drink," he said.

She let her head rock back and laughed. "I like that one," she said, raising her glass. "I like your accent, too." She steadied herself against the bar as she felt the cool bubbles from the mineral water rush down her throat. This man was pretty. And she could listen to his smooth-as-silk voice all night.

He reached out and cupped her elbow in his hand when he saw her shiver. "I like yours. Are you one of Anton's friends?"

She nodded and sipped again at her water. "Are you?"

He took a step closer. "I dare say we all are."

Evan took a deep breath and enjoyed the scent of sandalwood and patchouli. "My name is Eve." She let her hand brush against his. "What's yours?"

He laughed. His index finger made a gentle trail up her arm to her shoulder. "You'll think I'm making this up, but my name is Adam."

Tick, tick, tick. Evan had been concerned that she wouldn't be able to hear the ticking over the music, but it sounded loud and clear. *Liar.*

"You're kidding." She giggled and leaned closer to the man.

"I'm not." He gazed into her eyes without blinking.

Ticking. *Pants on fire.*

"Evan, he's lighting up. He's wired," Kirk whispered. "Be careful. He could be one of Anton's men."

Evan winked at him and pushed herself away from the bar. She finished her water and took his hands in hers. "Let's dance, Adam."

She pulled him onto the dance floor where she saw Brawn dancing with Xandra and Hedge dancing with Olga. She positioned herself between her team members and took her turn with Adam.

Both men watched her as she swayed and moved in rhythm with the Brit. Before the song ended, Anton cut in. Evan couldn't decide if she was relieved or disappointed.

"You're doing quite well," Anton told her. He let his hands settle on her hips.

Evan moved closer to him, circling her arms around his neck. She raised and lowered her lashes as slowly as she could, hoping to keep his attention on her eyes. "I am getting a little tired."

Anton nodded and took her to a pair of chairs in the corner of the room. "I want you to spend tomorrow with my muses. I want you to get to know them."

Evan slid her hands down her sides to hold her skirt securely as she sat down. She saw that Anton's gaze focused on her legs and she didn't want him to catch a glimpse of her sidearm, or anything else. She crossed her legs demurely.

"I'd love to," she said, once he was seated at her side. "What will we be doing?"

"You're going shopping. Xandra will show you how we do things here. I promise you'll have a good time." Anton squeezed her knee. "They'll help you get ready for Saturday's party."

Evan leaned close to Anton's face and placed her hand over his. "I don't think Xandra likes me," she whispered. She hoped that Xandra noticed how intimate they were getting. People make mistakes when they let their emotions run wild.

Anton nodded and squeezed again, moving his hand up her leg a fraction of an inch. "Don't worry about Xandra. She knows that I like you, and she is a very jealous woman." He took her hand, and placed it on his thigh, above his knee. "I'll make sure she's nice to you. And I will talk to Nastya." He gestured over his shoulder to the dance floor. "She is the one dancing with Hedge now. Nastya is more … generous."

Evan watched Hedge's new partner winding herself around his shoulders like a python.

"I can tell that about her." Evan raised her eyebrows. "She's sure taking good care of Hedge."

Anton laughed. "Maybe you are jealous, too." He waved to Hedge and to Brawn, motioning for the men to join them. Anton stood and helped Evan to her feet.

Evan smiled and discreetly nodded to her partners.

"I think it is time for you to take Eve home for the night. She will tell you about the plans for tomorrow." Anton placed Evan's hand on Hedge's arm. "She needs rest tonight. And you need time to invite your friends to my house." He looked at Brawn with an arrogant sneer and then smiled warmly at Evan. "Eve amazes me. I hope you do as well."

He led them all back to the foyer, where Xandra appeared behind him again.

Evan noticed the security guards were all gone for the night. Olga was leaving with another party-goer. She waved at Brawn and blew him a kiss over her shoulder.

Anton kissed Evan's cheeks carefully, making sure not to overstep his bounds in front of Xandra. Hedge and Brawn both kissed Xandra on the cheek and then shook Anton's hand.

"I expect great things from you," Anton said to Hedge.

Adam strode into the foyer and reached out for Evan's hand. "You're leaving so soon?" he asked. "I was hoping for another turn on the dance floor."

Anton raised his hand. "She has a big day tomorrow, but don't worry, my friend," he said. "Eve will be back for you on Saturday."

Adam fixed a hurt expression on his face and placed his manicured hand over his heart as if he suffered her loss. "That gives me something wonderful to anticipate for Saturday, then."

Hedge tipped his chin to his host and turned Evan to face the door. Brawn followed close behind as they left the mansion.

When they cleared the gates of the house, Evan turned to Hedge and pushed her index finger into the center of his chest. "I thought you said that there would be no make-out stake-outs." She dropped her other hand from his arm and walked ahead of the men down the block to where Teo waited in the SUV.

Brawn gasped. "Oh, boy! What did I miss?"

CHAPTER TEN

"We need to move quickly," Hedge barked into the Bluetooth speaker connected to Evan's ear canal receiver. "These poor saps are all going to be compromised within the hour if they aren't already."

Hedge, Brawn, and Evan sat around the speaker on the coffee table in the apartment while Ramos and Kirk took point in the SUV, searching for everything they could find on Hrevic's party guests, and chasing down their current whereabouts in Paris.

"Who do we go after first?" Ramos asked.

Evan raised her left eyebrow. "Congressman Forsythe is a priority. He's easy prey for any one of those girls."

"I took care of him myself," Brawn said with a sinister laugh as he pulled his shirttails loose from his pants.

"What did you do?" she asked.

"I might have slipped a little something into his drink that will make his evening considerably less romantic." Brawn made a mock-cramping gesture. "Trust me. It won't be pretty, but he'll be alone for the night."

Evan cringed. Hedge nodded in appreciation.

"Okay, I'll ask again." Hedge could hear the frustration in Teo's voice, even over the speaker. "Who's first?"

Hedge regarded Evan with an open palm. "Your call, then."

Evan took a moment. "The first man I pinned was a big-time banker from Chicago. His name is George Hogaboom."

"Hogaboom?" Ramos asked.

"He's single, forty, an advisor on two national banking committees," Kirk said, tapping away at his notebook. "He has a rented Beemer on the street in front of Hrevic's. It's still here. Pretty blue, too."

"I've got it. Give me a second," Ramos said.

"What is he doing?" Hedge asked. He could hear the vehicle door open and close.

Kirk typed away. "Not sure what Teo's doing. At the moment, I can't see him."

After a minute of air, followed by the door opening and closing again, Ramos' voice chirped, "I'm afraid that Mr. Hogaboom is going to have a blow-out tonight."

"I hope that's enough to keep him out of trouble," Hedge said.

"Next?" Ramos and Kirk sounded anxious.

"I danced with a couple of men who had wedding bands missing, and one who forgot to take his off," Evan said, kicking her shoes off and pushing them to the side of the couch. "Perry Adyta, Les Bernard and Reginald Lampert."

Kirk laughed. "Ah yes, hold on." Kirk typed for a minute. "All three of them will be getting phone calls from their wives and children very shortly. All arranged."

They could hear Ramos snickering. Hedge smiled. He pulled off his tie and rolled his shoulders forward and back to ease the muscles.

"This is too easy. Give us one that will at least get me out of the car." Kirk's voice sounded tired.

"I thought you didn't like being out in the field," Brawn said.

"But being in this SUV is worse," Kirk said. "Ramos is giving me a weird look. I'm afraid he's going to pull a make-out stake-out."

The speaker crackled with laughter. "You know it," Ramos said.

Evan exhaled loudly. "You want a challenge? There was a tall Viking. Jensen. I don't know whether that was his first or last name. Take care of him."

"Suggestions, anyone?" Ramos asked.

"He won't be at a dance club after the party, that's for sure. I think tonight might have been the first time he'd ever heard music." Evan rubbed her forehead. "Talk about stoic."

"Go wash your makeup off," Hedge told her. "We've got this."

Evan nodded and retreated to the bedroom.

Hedge's lip curled with an idea. "Let's post a BOLO with the locals and give them an anonymous tip for his approximate location."

Ramos asked, "What is he suspected of, sir?"

"Prostitution," Hedge said without a second thought. He remembered Jensen. He was polished. No facial hair. A little too shiny for his own good.

"Done," Kirk said. "I even uploaded a picture of him." More clicking on the computer keys. "Of course, the charges will be thrown out as a big misunderstanding as soon as he's put into the system."

"But he won't be anyone's date tonight," Ramos assured them.

"Evan, who was the German man? A member of Parliament?" Kirk asked. "What do you recommend for him?"

"Evan's in the other room," Brawn answered.

"No, she's not," Evan said, rejoining the men in the living room. "I think he was a banker, too. Krieger." She now wore sweatpants and a tee shirt.

"Hans Krieger?" Kirk asked. Hedge noticed his voice sounded somewhat surprised.

"That's him," she said. "Something special for him. He kept trying to look down my dress."

"Special? Yes. Blue plate special, coming up," Kirk said.

Hedge crossed his arms over his chest and grinned. "Love the blue-plate special."

"What's the blue-plate special?" Brawn and Evan asked at the same time.

Evan plopped down on the sofa and tucked her foot underneath her. She pulled a fabric-covered band off her wrist and used it to twist her hair into a ponytail. Hedge noticed that even without makeup, Evan looked like a cover model.

Hedge grinned and took a deep breath. "Ramos, are you up for a little pick-pocketing?"

Teo snorted. "You know, when I was a kid, my mom worked two jobs and put me in every kind of sport under the sun just so that I wouldn't end up a thief."

"What is he going to steal?" Evan asked. She pulled her other foot up and began massaging her soles.

"Everything. Kirk will check him out of his hotel before he gets back there. He won't have his ID, money, or phone with him. They'll put him out in the street. He'll be lucky to get a blue-plate special before lunch tomorrow."

"What if he goes back to Anton's with his girl du jour?" Brawn asked.

"I doubt any of the models will find him attractive without cash or a room," Kirk said. "I listened to several of their conversations. They're just not that benevolent."

"You guys are mean." Evan shifted her position to work on her other foot.

"Keeping him out of the embrace of Mata Hari," Hedge rationalized. He watched Evan's expressions change as she hit the different pressure points on her foot. He resisted the urge to take over the massage.

"So, you're puttin' one in jail, three in the doghouse, one in the bathroom, and one in the gutter. That leaves two others that I marked and then my sweet Adam."

"I think he likes you." Brawn unbuttoned his shirt and leaned back in his chair, letting the shirt fall to either side of his bare chest.

Hedge noticed that Evan pretended not to notice.

"Every man likes a redhead," Hedge said, wanting to ignore the whole exchange.

Kirk's voice interrupted. "I'm sending one, a Stephan Englewood, an urgent text from his boss. He must come home right away if he wants to keep his job. The second one, Gabriel Doss, will have a gas leak at his hotel. This is pretty easy stuff, really."

"Then finish the special and get back here," Hedge ordered.

"Yes, sir," Ramos said.

CHAPTER ELEVEN

After a late night keeping tabs on the men from the party, and an even later night waiting for Kirk and Teo to return, Evan finally managed to decompress and get a few hours of sleep. Her alarm woke her before the sun did, and the team spent a couple of hours working out the plan for the day. Evan would be at the mercy of women who didn't like her to please a man she could barely tolerate. At the very least, she could gather intel while shopping in the heart of the Paris fashion district.

The sun was just high enough to cast a little color onto the gray stone buildings lining the narrow street. Brawn and Evan waited on the Rue du Faubourg Saint-Honore for the muses to arrive. The exclusive designer shops were just beginning to open around them.

"You look nice," Brawn said. He reached out to brush back a wisp of Evan's red hair from her face.

She smiled, surprised at his gentle touch. "I feel strange without the dress now."

Brawn rocked his head to one side. "You'd look strange wearing a cocktail dress on the streets of Paris at ten-thirty in the morning."

She nodded and tugged on her cardigan, feeling the chill of the morning air. "I know. At least I have Kirk with me."

"Yes, you do," Kirk whispered in her ear. "I'll be here all day."

"How does that work without the dress? You're not wearing a wire or an earbud," Brawn asked, looking in her ear.

"I have a receiver implanted in my ear canal. I took the leap last year."

Brawn shook his head and pushed his hands into his slacks' pockets. "I wouldn't like that," he said. "I enjoy my privacy."

Evan laughed and nudged him with her elbow. "So do I." She lowered her voice. "I have special earrings I have to wear to activate the signal."

"Oh." Brawn watched the traffic on the street for a moment and then turned back to Evan. "I could deal with a nice diamond stud. Chicks like that, right?"

Evan rolled her eyes and laughed. "I don't know. The surgery was a piece of cake, but the recovery and training were pretty painful."

"But so worth it," Kirk whispered. Evan smiled.

She noticed a black limousine approaching and straightened her stance. "They're here."

Brawn waited for the car to come to a complete stop and then opened the car door for Xandra. She stepped out and examined Evan with a critical expression.

Her eyes scanned from Evan's chocolate brown kitten heels up her cream-colored lace stockings to the navy-blue leather skirt. She scrutinized the gold-linked belt at her waist and then reached out to feel the composition of the salmon-pink sweater twinset.

"Cashmere?" Xandra asked.

"It's a silk-cashmere blend," Evan answered.

Xandra motioned for the other girls to join her on the sidewalk. "At least she knows how to dress for shopping." Her Russian accent seemed heavier in the daylight.

Brawn offered his hand to each woman as she stepped out of the limo. "Nastya, Olga, Tatiana and … I don't think I've had the pleasure," he said, still holding the last woman's hand. "I'm Jason Brown."

"I am Maria," she said with a glitter-glossed smile.

Evan guessed that she was the youngest of the muses, probably no older than eighteen. She found herself feeling sorry for the girl. "I'm Eve." She held out her hand.

"Are you sure that you don't need me to escort you all?" Brawn asked. "I love watching women shop."

"We'll be fine on our own," both Evan and Xandra said simultaneously. They looked at each other and smiled.

"I'll call if I need you." Evan squeezed his hand. "Thanks."

Brawn nodded. "Then I'll be on my way." He turned to walk back to the SUV.

Xandra leaned down to instruct the limo driver. "We will need you back here at four o'clock." She closed the door and watched the car drive away.

Nastya looped her arm around Evan's. "Let's go to Hermes to find you a scarf."

Evan took a deep breath and nodded. The women giggled and entered through the keystone arched opening into the department store directly behind them. They spent an hour inside, following the basket-weave tiled floors at ground level, delving into the basement lined with ornate wrought-iron rails, and touching and trying out every scarf they saw.

Evan picked one with hints of each color in her current ensemble and knotted it at her neck. The silk twill felt like angel kisses. As she removed it to examine the design more closely, she felt around the edges for a price tag. She allowed the sunlight from the window to filter through the leaf and branch pattern, and she found herself falling more in love.

Nastya nudged her arm. "That one is a bargain. Only three-hundred-eighty-five American," she said. "Very pretty."

Evan coughed. She remembered modeling haute couture, but she had forgotten the prices. "It is beautiful."

Xandra snatched it from her hand. "Anton would want you to have it." She placed it in a small pile of items at the counter. "Let's find you a decent handbag."

The women moved to the next department filled with leather bags and accessories, all displayed in sparkling glass cases. While the others admired the colors and stitching, Evan examined the purses for weapons compartments and places to hide surveillance equipment.

She picked up one purse with tailored straps and silver buckles. The ruby red leather seemed to glow from within. "Get that one," she heard in her ear.

She laughed at Kirk's blind recommendation. "Mmm," she hummed to herself, wondering how Kirk could know.

"Your heart rate just amped up to the point that even I could hear it. You like it," Kirk said.

"What do you think about this one?" Evan asked.

Xandra shrugged and nodded in a non-committal way. Nastya grinned.

"I wonder," Evan started to say.

Nastya murmured close to her ear. "It's about twelve hundred dollars."

Xandra scowled. "Why do Americans always have such cheap taste? In Russia we had nothing. We made dinner with last week's broth and stale bread. Now that you can afford nice things, you should get nice things."

Again, Xandra added Evan's choices to the pieces at the counter.

Maria and Tatiana bounced up to Xandra. "We are going to look at shoes," they said.

Xandra shook her head. "No. We will go to Versace for shoes. You are too young for these. Tell the clerk we are ready to go."

Xandra waited for them to leave her sight. "I feel like their mother sometimes. Are you having a good time?"

Evan nodded. "I am. I've never seen so much, well, so much everything."

Xandra motioned for Nastya to find Olga. "You will get used to this. Anton wants us to look a certain way whenever we go out."

Evan smiled. "I suppose I don't understand. Why does he want us to be seen wearing other designers' clothing?"

Nastya joined their conversation. "He wants us to be seen everywhere in

Paris. In every boutique. Our last stop will be his shop, and we can pick out things there. When the photographers snap our pictures, and we are carrying bags with everyone's names, the world sees the label, House of Alexei, on the same level as Versace, Chanel, and Dior. You see?"

Xandra smiled. "Also, we like to buy beautiful things, and Paris is filled with beautiful things."

Evan raised her eyebrows as a shiver of excitement climbed up her spine. "But will Anton be angry if I spend so much money? I don't even know if he's gonna let me model with y'all."

Nastya shook her head. Xandra grabbed the shopping bags and distributed them to Olga, Maria, and Tatiana. Nastya held the door open for the others as they left for the next shop.

"Don't worry about Anton," Nastya assured Evan. "He saw how you handled the men at his party last night. To him, that is more important than walking in any fashion show."

Evan laughed as they entered the next store. It smelled like jasmine and vanilla. "I guess I'm just a simpleton," she said.

Nastya appeared confused. "What is 'simpleton'?"

Evan explained. "I just don't understand the party thing. All I did was dance with some handsome men. What else is expected of us?"

Xandra directed the group to a display of blouses.

"You won't have to do anything you do not want to," Xandra said. "But with the selection of men who come to Anton's house, you can have just about anything you like. I saw you with Adam. He likes you very much."

Nastya sighed. "Adam is delicious." She had a buzz in her voice. "He's very rich."

Xandra agreed. "He has a Ferrari."

Evan blinked at their conversation, trying to decide if it was real. Risking the chance of offense, she gasped. "Oh my gracious! Are you," she lowered her voice to a whisper, "prostitutes?"

Kirk guffawed in her ear. She bit the inside of her cheek to keep from laughing.

Xandra hardly seemed fazed. "No, we're not prostitutes," she replied loudly enough for the store attendants to hear. They didn't seem fazed either.

Nastya laughed. "You are funny, Eve. We are celebrities. You would be surprised how many rich men want to be seen with us. We let them, and they give us things."

"But you don't sleep with them," Evan said with an exaggerated sigh of relief. She fanned herself with her hand in the same way her Aunt Talley did whenever she was embarrassed.

"Yes, we do," Olga chirped. "Only if they aren't ugly. They give you more things if you sleep with them. You should know this at your age," she added.

Evan stopped her fanning and just froze in disbelief. She couldn't decide whether to be offended, shocked, or entertained. She thought that nothing would surprise her anymore. She was wrong.

Xandra held up a sheer blouse against Evan's shoulders. "You don't have to sleep with anybody. I saw how you look at Mr Hedger. I saw how he looks at you."

She snapped her fingers for Nastya to bring her the skirt that she was holding.

Xandra moved the skirt to sit under the blouse. She wrinkled her nose. "No, you need something with more color. How long have you known Mr. Hedger?"

Evan smiled. "For about a year," she said. "He's trying to help me pick up my modeling career. I was doing a lot of shows for a while, but things have slowed down lately."

"Face it," Nastya said. "A model's career is short. We get old or fat or both. When that happens, who wants us to wear their clothes?"

Evan listened to every word Nastya said. She had heard this all before. Those were the rules of high fashion. Don't get old. Don't get fat.

"We are beautiful women, so we have to take what we can for now. We put it away for the rainy days. The days when we are not so beautiful," Nastya said, and Xandra nodded.

"Anton helps us the way that Mr. Hedger helps you. If they work together perhaps we all do better," Xandra explained.

They shopped up and down the blocks of Paris' most exclusive district, taking only a short luncheon at the Hotel Costes' lounge. As planned, they ended their tour at the House of Alexei where they selected a dozen more pieces for their wardrobes.

Evan kept reminding herself that she was undercover. She lost count of the money that Anton spent on her somewhere after $8000.00. Her mother would scold her if she were present. Her father would likely shake his head in complete disbelief. That's what Evan wanted to do.

She couldn't fathom that these beautiful women would sell themselves for stuff on hangers and rides in fast cars. They were smart, capable women. Why?

As they left Anton's shop, Evan took the bags containing her spoils just as the limousine pulled up to the curb.

"Four o'clock. Time to go home," Xandra announced.

"I had a wonderful day," Evan said, somewhat sincerely.

"You cannot leave yet. No, you're coming with us," Nastya said. "Get in!"

"What?" Evan asked. This wasn't the plan she had worked out with her team.

"Hang on," Kirk whispered. "Brawn is forty-five seconds away."

Xandra tossed her bags into the car after the other girls got inside. "Anton will be angry if you don't come," she said. "We all go shopping, and we buy whatever we like, but when we are done, we have our own little fashion show for him in private."

Evan swallowed hard. "Well, then I suppose I *must* go with you," she said, joining the other women in the limousine.

"We've got you covered," hummed Kirk in her ear. "Just keep me posted as to what you want."

As she settled into the buttery leather car seats, Evan decided to go fishing. "I'm awfully glad that Anton sent me home early last night. I'd have loved to stay and dance, but I'm starting to get tired now, and the day is only half done." She sighed. "Did he have y'all go to bed right after I left?"

Nastya gasped. "Oh! My first date was terrible! He was Swiss or something. We were just about to leave, and his wife called him. He left me standing at the front door." She made a face like a sad puppy. "And then I went out with the tall blonde man, Mr. Jensen."

"How did it go with him?" Evan asked.

"Worse!" Nastya said. She waved her hands wildly to make sure the other girls listened. "We left Anton's to go to his hotel. As we were about to go inside, the gendarmes—the police—they took him."

"For what?" Olga asked before Evan had the chance.

"For being a gigolo, I think." Nastya rolled her eyes. "They asked me if I was paying him! Can you imagine?" She shrugged and allowed a long slow breath to escape her lips.

Kirk laughed in Evan's ear. "It was priceless."

Evan managed to keep a straight face as the next woman told her story.

Olga put her hands on her cheeks. "At least you got to ride back home in a taxi. I was out with the big American man from Chicago. Everything he talks about is money or Chicago. We drive to see the Arc de Triumph and the Eiffel Tower, and BOOM! His tire is flat."

The other girls gasped.

"That was his name, too. Hoga-BOOM!" Olga laughed at her joke. "He said he could fix it, but he didn't have a spare. I had to walk back home. I ruined the heel of my shoe in the first block, and I had to throw away my stockings. There was nothing left of them."

Maria poked at her. "That is no different than your other dates. You always have to throw away your stockings." They all laughed.

Evan thought she heard another snicker from Kirk.

Maria took her turn complaining. She was to spend the evening with Congressman Forsythe. "He caught a virus or something. It was awful," she said. "We never even left the front step. I just stayed in my room and watched TV."

65

Tatiana's plans ended abruptly when both of her dates got calls from home and work. "It's bad enough when another woman calls. But a child or a boss, and the night is over."

"Did any of you have a good night?" Evan was almost sympathetic.

"I had a little trouble with my first gentleman, but I ended the night with your friend, Adam." Xandra purred like a cat. "We went to his hotel and enjoyed some champagne."

"Don't tell Anton about the champagne," Maria said. "He won't like that."

Xandra nodded. "Adam had a phone meeting that interrupted us for a few minutes, but after that, well, I can tell you that he is very romantic."

"What business is he in?" Evan asked.

Xandra raised her eyebrow suspiciously as she regarded Evan.

"You said he has a Ferrari. His business must be doing well," Evan added.

"Good save," Kirk whispered.

"He has a petrol company, I think." Xandra shrugged. "I don't pay attention to things like that. I just like to dance and have fun, you know. We all like to have fun."

The rest of the drive back to Anton's house was filled with laughter. Olga and Maria started a tune in Russian that sounded like a nursery rhyme. Tatiana and Nastya joined in the chorus, and Evan decided that it was more likely a drinking song. Her feet ached, and she wished that she could trade everything in her shopping bags for a Margarita. Except for the red purse.

Anton greeted them at the door with hugs and kisses and smiles all around.

"Hurry upstairs and get everything ready," he ordered. "I can't wait to see what you found today." He took Evan's hand and led her to the stairway. "Go with Xandra and let her help you. This is the fun part!"

"Yeah, for him," Kirk muttered. "What a creep."

CHAPTER TWELVE

Evan looked around the dressing room in wonder. "I wish my friends back home could see this," she said. The room had high ceilings, with a crystal chandelier that hung much lower. The walls and ceiling were painted eggplant purple, almost black.

"You're forgetting," whispered Kirk. "I hacked his security cams. I can see a pretty good portion of the house, just not everything. Talk to me. Without the dress, I can't tell exactly where bugs and cameras might be, but I can guess with fair accuracy. I can't see you right now, though. Tell me everything you see."

She looked at the mirror-lined walls with lighted vanities and purple plush-covered chairs. "This dressing room is beautiful. The mirrors all have lights and dressing tables," she said.

"Watch out for the mirrors. You know as well as I do that they probably have cameras behind them. Just because he doesn't have them in his security loop, doesn't mean he isn't keeping them in a private feed," Kirk advised.

The thought irked Evan. She immediately refocused. "I love the chandelier in the center," she said with a sigh. The six-tiered crystal fixture refracted its light into tiny diffused rainbows that danced across the ceiling.

"Good chance there are concealed cameras there, too," he added.

She walked to the doors at the end of the room. "And we'll model for Mr. Hrevic in this other room?" she asked.

"Yes. That's where he will be waiting for us," Olga replied.

"You should put together a few outfits from our shopping trip this morning. If you need anything more to finish a look, just grab something from the center rack," Nastya said, gesturing to a full wardrobe of tops, skirts, scarves, and shoes in the center of the room.

"You can have this seat next to me," Tatiana said, clearing space at the make-up mirror adjacent to hers. Each dressing table was fully equipped with a stack of drawers on either side and a shallow drawer just above the knee space. The tops were covered in white marble, polished to a reflective glow. The mirrors above the tables rose nearly to the ceiling, making it easy for the models to study their reflection whether they were sitting or standing. The clear glass light bulbs in the vertical fixtures between each station put off a blindingly bright glow.

"Any more places for bugs or cameras?" Kirk asked.

"My goodness!" Evan exclaimed. "I can't believe how many nooks and crannies there are all over this place."

"Sorry, kid, without the dress I can't jam any signals, either." Evan could tell that Kirk was trying to cheer her up. "But once we take Hrevic down, we'll confiscate all the pictures. At least the ones he hasn't already uploaded to the internet."

"Isn't this just *fun?*" she said, cloaking her sarcasm with a smile.

Evan pulled together three outfits from her shopping bags. Using items from the garment rack in the center of the room, she made one more.

Evan watched as Tatiana made her face up with false eyelashes and pearlescent powder. She opened the shallow vanity drawer in front of her and picked out five or six pieces of glittering jewelry. Evan's jaw dropped at the sight of all those facets.

"You have some in your drawer, too," Tatiana said, pointing.

Evan inched back in her seat and pulled open her jewelry tray. The embellishments inside reflected the vanity lights and stunned her. "Wow," she said aloud.

"These are nice," Nastya said from the seat on Evan's right. "But if you are good, Anton will let you see the others."

"The others?"

"Only if you're good," Tatiana said.

"What makes me good?" Evan asked.

The girls all laughed. Nastya leaned close to her ear and whispered, "Just do whatever Anton says to do."

"Don't you dare," Kirk whispered.

Evan stared into the mesmerizing gemstones. "These are just gorgeous. Are you sure I'm allowed to wear these?"

"Of course," Nastya said.

"Don't be stupid," Tatiana added. Evan liked that her Russian accent made the word sound like *stew-pit.*

"We wear these to the parties, too." Nastya picked out a diamond necklace that looked like drops of rain. "This would be nice with your new blouse," she said. She picked up the matching earrings and held one to Evan's earlobe. "See how pretty?"

As soon as the earring touched Evan's skin, a high-pitched squeal of feedback pierced her eardrum. She pulled it away and blinked in pain.

"Are you alright?" Nastya asked. "Your eyes are watering."

Evan snatched a tissue and wiped away the tears. "Oh yes. Just a little bit overwhelmed," she said.

"What was that?" Kirk asked, obviously sharing her pain.

"These earrings are just dazzling. The moment they touched my ears, I couldn't help but cry," Evan said.

Kirk scrambled for a minute. "Earrings caused that? They must have an audio transmitter in them. That's not great."

Evan took a deep breath and stared confidently into the mirror, grasping at a sense of calm.

"Anton made them special for us," Nastya said, playing with a pair of earrings from her drawer.

Kirk whispered. "I want you to look at the backs of them. If they are real gemstones, the setting will be open behind the stone."

Evan examined the drop design closely. "I see how the gems are sealed into their settings. That must keep them very secure."

Tatiana nodded. "I've never had one even come loose. That is very good because when I dance, I just go wild." She waved her hands over her head for emphasis.

Evan smiled and listened. She put the earrings back into the drawer without letting them touch her ears again.

"Check the other pieces, too. There's no telling what he's putting in these things," Kirk said.

Evan looked at the necklace in front of her. She turned the design over to see the settings and studied the unusual closure. "I like the way the gems and beads on the necklace lay flat against the skin. And the diamonds must be very high quality—look at how the centers look almost black." She nodded to Nastya and the other girls. "Ooh, and the clasp is nice and thick. I'll bet that this doesn't come unhooked while we're dancing."

The other girls ignored her chatter and dressed for the fashion show.

"If the stones look black in the centers, they probably have cameras on board," he said. "It would be an easy way to accumulate black-mail material. The clasp could have a storage chip as well."

"I suppose I should be getting myself all dressed up now, too," Evan said as she powdered her face and put on her pink lipstick.

The other women helped her dress, and soon the music started in the adjacent room. The models formed a line at the door. Maria and Olga waited to enter first. Tatiana was next. Nastya pushed Evan in front of her, and Xandra stood last in line.

Nastya tapped Evan's shoulder. "Eve, remember one thing. Keep your eyes focused straight ahead until you get to the end of the walk. Then look down and smile at Anton. He likes that."

Evan waited, unsure of what to expect. She found herself humming low. She hadn't modeled in a while now. She was dressed to the teeth, and her nerves started to flutter with energy.

Don't worry," Kirk whispered. "You can do this. You catch bad guys for breakfast. You carry a .40 caliber in your purse. This is a piece of cake."

"I'm ready," Evan said to Kirk—and to herself.

The music pulsed, and Maria began her strut. Olga waited a full ten seconds before starting her rhythmic walk. Tatiana stepped aside to let Maria reenter before she crossed the threshold. Evan was next.

Wearing a chestnut brown satin mini-skirt and a gold chiffon blouse with coppery threads woven through, Evan let her arms fall straight at her sides and began the stylized step.

She expected to see an elite crowd of admirers or critics around the dark room—typical for a designer of haute couture. Instead, she saw only Anton sitting in a leather chair at the end of the long, raised stage. The rest of the room was dark and empty. He held a highball in one hand and a smoldering cigar in the other. His shirt gaped open, just like his eyes, and he wore a pair of silk lounge pants that revealed too much. A greedy grin covered his face.

Her skin crawled as her gaze met his hungry stare. She paused and turned, just as she'd been taught, with her hips leading the way.

As she re-entered the dressing room, she quickly stripped off her first outfit and pulled on her next. She jumped back into her place in line as Maria walked through the door. Her turn again. This time she wore a long teal blue charmeuse gown that hugged every curve. It seemed like a good idea when she bought it, but the idea of wearing it for Anton unnerved her.

Ten minutes later the show was over. The muses chatted as they put away their jewelry and accessories. Evan sat at her mirror trying to control the tremors in her fingers. She never expected to feel as used and degraded as she did at this moment. The look in Anton's eyes as he watched her last trip down the runway turned her stomach.

Nastya handed Evan her shopping bags. "I'll help you gather your things."

"Thank you," she said.

"Eve, you don't look well," Xandra said with a sharp tone.

"She's just overwhelmed," Nastya explained. "Today was a big day for her. She is probably tired."

Evan and Nastya put all of Evan's shopping finds into her bags and placed the other accessories onto the center rack. Evan headed to the door, wanting desperately to leave, but Nastya held up her hand to stop her.

"Wait, your necklace has to go back into the drawer at your station," she said.

"Oops." She raised a hand to her throat and stepped back to her dressing area.

70

Evan was glad to take the jewelry off. She knew Kirk would want to examine it, but she couldn't wait to get it off of her. She unhooked the clasp and spread the ornament flat on the tray. Evan looked around the room. Six dressing tables. Five models, plus her. She turned to Nastya.

"Was there another muse?" she asked. "My vanity station already had jewels in it."

Nastya nodded. "Sophie used to sit here, but this is your place now. She got married a few months ago to one of the rich young men she met here."

"Where is she now?" Evan asked. She heard Kirk's typing in her ear.

"I'll see what I can find," he said. "A model for Hrevic named Sophie. Got it."

Nastya shrugged. The other girls filed out of the room with their bags, and Evan followed. They each took their finds to rooms off the hall on the opposite side of the stairway. Evan waited on the balcony for them to return. As they all reached the foot of the stairs, Anton stood clapping his hands. He greeted his girls with another round of air kisses. For Evan, he added a full-bodied hug. She was never so grateful that her hands were full of shopping bags.

"What do you think of our little rituals?" he asked her. "You found some marvelous things on your shopping excursion, yes?"

Evan swallowed hard against the rising acid in her throat. She smiled and tilted her head. "It's difficult for me to take it all in." She chewed on her lip, trying to sound excited and impressed. "I'm sure I'll spend the rest of the night reliving today. I may not get a moment's sleep."

Xandra squeezed her arm, and Evan was surprised at the thin woman's grip. "You must be exhausted." Turning to Anton, Xandra added, "You should call Mr. Hedger to come for her."

Anton frowned, obviously disappointed. "Only if Eve wants me to call him." He thrust his bottom lip out in a childish pout, pleading with Evan to stay.

Evan nodded. "Maybe I should go. I need my rest for the next party."

Anton shoved his hands into his pockets and walked to his office. "I'll be back in a moment. We can all enjoy an aperitif before dinner. I'm sure Mr. Hedger will be an hour or more."

"Give us one minute," Kirk assured her.

Xandra took her aside as the other women found a place at the bar. "Soon you'll be living here with us," she said. "You'll have to learn how we do everything. Girls who don't learn don't get to stay."

Evan blinked, again astonished by Xandra's candid statement. "What about Sophie?" Evan asked, trying to sound as innocent as possible.

"Who said anything about Sophie?" Xandra snapped.

"Nastya told me that she married a man she met here. That sounds like a wonderful fairy tale."

Xandra nodded, and her tone softened. "Some are luckier than others."

"Where does she live now?" Evan asked. "I bet she's very happy."

Xandra raised her eyebrow. "I wouldn't know anything about that. I haven't heard from her since the day she left the mansion."

A knock caught the women's attention. Xandra opened the door to find Hedge on the stoop. Anton shuffled back down the hallway with a look of frustration on his face.

Hedge grinned at Xandra and pumped Anton's arm for a second. He took the shopping bags from Evan.

"Did you have some fun today, Evie?" He nodded a greeting to all of the other women. "I'm sure you all had a nice time."

"I'll talk your ear off about the whole thing," she said. She turned to Anton and offered her cheeks for kisses. "Thank you for just a beautiful day, Mr. Hrevic. I simply can't wait for the next party."

His hands gripped tightly at her waist and hips. "I'll count the hours," he whispered into her ear.

He patted Hedge on the shoulder as they left. "Take care of my new muse, Mr. Hedger. And don't let me down. I expect great things from you."

The door closed, and Hedge walked her to the car. "Did you get us anything we can use?" he asked.

Evan clinched her fists as she walked through the gates and slid into the car. "Can I have half a minute to think?" she protested. "I've had people pulling me one way or another all day, and I'm kinda sick of it!"

Hedge circled the front of the SUV and slid in next to her. He slammed his door in response to her eruption.

"Evan," Kirk hummed in her ear.

"My priority is the job." Hedge started the engine and then turned to face her straight on. "What's yours?"

"It's important," Kirk said. Evan could barely hear him over her frustration.

Evan glared as Hedge poked at the shopping bags. "Do you think I spent the day having fun? I was on the job, just like you!" she said, her volume rising.

"Yeah, except that I don't have a four-hundred-dollar scarf to show for it!" Hedge shouted.

"You can have mine!" she yelled back.

"Evan!" Kirk barked, this time commanding her attention.

"What is it, Kirk?" She held up a hand to preclude Hedge's next outburst. She pulled Hedge's earbud from his shirt pocket and pushed the plastic form into his ear.

"We have a problem. I found Sophie Ivanov, one of Anton's last models," Kirk said.

"Yes?" Evan said. She held her breath to listen.

"French police found her body three weeks ago in a landfill. She was strangled and stabbed a dozen times."

CHAPTER THIRTEEN

Evan sat in the darkening room on her narrow bed. She could hear the four men in the living room playing poker and talking about Anton and his set-up at the mansion. She had spent an hour rereading the files. She knew her assignment. She knew her objective. She knew her role in the mission.

The moonlight sifted through the ironwork outside the apartment and poured through the slender bedroom window, casting a golden-white beam through the deep blue and black shadows. The room looked like a picture from one of Evan's childhood storybooks. She wondered how she got from once-upon-a-time to the here and now.

In school, she had wanted to be a model and actress. Now she did both. She had longed to travel the world. Now she did. Back then she imagined that life to be romantic. Tonight, she sat alone in an apartment in Paris. Dark in the City of Lights.

The door opened, and Hedge peered in. Light spilled into the dark bedroom, and they both had to adjust their eyes to the relative change. He came inside and closed the door behind him.

"You okay?" he asked.

"I'm fine." It was a lie, but it was also the expected answer.

"Did something happen out there that I need to know about?" Hedge took a seat on the small couch at the foot of the bed. He didn't turn on the light, and for that, Evan was thankful.

"Just what I told you earlier." She kept her answers short and professional.

"I don't have a special lie-detector in my ear, but I know when someone's not fine." Hedge took a short breath. "You've been on other jobs that were more dangerous than this one. You've taken lives and saved lives before."

"Yes, I have."

"I've been talking to Kirk. He's worried about you." Hedge seemed to study her silhouette in the blue glow.

"I'm glad I can be a conversation starter for you both."

Evan watched as Hedge tightened every muscle in his face, and then let the tension release as he exhaled. "I'm the team leader. I need to know my people are okay. He'd worked with you before, and I asked him if this was your MO. Would you prefer me to ask you point-blank why you're acting like a stuck-up diva?"

Evan dropped her chin and stared at her hands. She shook her head. "No, sir. I apologize." She shifted back into professional mode.

"Evan, I swear," he said, and then took another breath. His mouth twisted and then calmed. "Talk to me. You're upset about something. You may think it's just nerves or left-field emotions, but in my years with the company I've found a weird common thread among us. Our guts tend to tell us more than we realize."

She looked up at his face. He stared into her eyes. She blinked, but he kept his gaze steady.

"We live with so much subterfuge, both on and off the job, that we forget our feelings and instincts are there to help us." He slowed his voice, and his tone had a softer edge. "We stuff them, thinking they're distractions. But they can be our greatest assets." Hedge nodded as she listened. "It took me a long time to learn that."

Evan pressed her lips together into a tight, thin line. She knew he was right, but she felt more comfortable talking to Red. She shot a glance toward the door.

"It's just us for now. I need to know what's going on in your head."

She sighed. "I'm not sure that I know," she heard her voice say. Her words sounded detached as if someone else spoke them.

"Okay, that's a start," Hedge said. "Let's just go through your day. Don't tell me about the specific things that happened, but about how you felt."

"Are you a shrink, now?" She turned her body slightly to face him. She pulled her foot up from the floor and tucked it beneath her. This job required absolute confidence, and the only thing she was sure about now was that she was failing.

"Give me a chance, alright?" He leaned forward and propped his elbows on his knees. He appeared eager to listen.

Evan crossed her arms at her waist and then noticed that Hedge was appraising her physical attitude as well. She let her hands drop to her lap. "Starting out this morning I was pretty excited. You know, going out with the girls for a day of shopping."

"No nerves?"

"Not until they started telling me what everything cost." Evan punctuated her sentence with a nervous laugh.

"Paris is expensive," he said without smiling.

"Yeah," she said. "I know it is, but when I saw it in a running total, I flipped out a little."

"It bothers you to spend money." Hedge said it more like a statement than a question. "You were concerned about the cost of the dress, too."

Evan nodded. "My family was never rich. Dad was career army. We always had enough. It was just my parents and myself. No brothers or sisters. But we didn't spend lots of money on anything. I started modeling because my drama teacher in high school sent me to a friend of hers who was a talent agent." She smiled at the memory of Mrs. Tomkins and her Theatre 101 class. "I started out doing local fashion shows and commercials. It paid for college."

Hedge leaned forward and laced his fingers together. "So the shopping stressed you out a little?"

"Yes. It was fun, I suppose, but …"

"Even good stress is stress." Hedge's voice sounded supportive. "I understand."

Evan recounted the conversation in the limo. "I felt a surge of, I don't know, self-assurance maybe when they started talking about how bad last night went for all of them."

"Good. And then what?"

"Nerves again once I was with the others for Anton's private show." Evan tried not to think about the actual walk down the narrow runway.

"You were uncomfortable? Because you were modeling or because of Hrevic?"

How could he know? "I just don't like Anton. He gives me the creeps," she explained.

"What about him exactly?" Hedge's voice sounded eager.

"He looks like he's hungry. More than hungry. He's gluttonous. When I modeled before, most of the designers I worked with were grateful for their success. They were demanding, but most of them seemed happy just being able to make money at something they loved." She found herself relaxing as she talked about the past.

"Not Hrevic?"

"No. Anton's like a spoiled child who has been given everything and still wants more." Evan shivered. She hoped that Hedge didn't notice.

"Are you cold? Wrap this around your shoulders if you need it." Hedge picked up the coverlet and offered it to her.

She took it and held it in her lap. She chewed on her lip. "I'm okay."

"What about him makes you uncomfortable? Is it the way he talks to you? The way he touches you?"

Evan held her breath, wanting to scream. "All of it," burst from her lips.

She wasn't sure how loud it came out but judging by the look on Hedge's face it was loud enough.

"If you could have done whatever you wanted to him this afternoon, what would have happened?" he asked.

"I'd have had his house stormed and had him taken into custody."

Hedge looked up at the ceiling and back to Evan. "I don't want the 'right' answer. I want the truth."

Tears burned in Evan's eyes. She knew that they glistened in the moonlight and that Hedge could probably see them. She refused to let them loose. She blinked until they retreated. "I wanted to run away. Is that what you want me to say?"

"If it's the truth, then yes." Hedge scooted to the edge of the couch. "What's wrong with running sometimes? It's instinct. It can save your life on occasion."

She hated talking like this. "So, we're good now?" she asked, hoping Hedge was satisfied.

He laughed. "Not hardly. Why don't you want to talk to me? Every female I've ever known wanted to talk all the time about everything."

"Why do you *want* to? Every man *I've* ever known wants to say as few words as possible. Most of their vocabulary revolves around beer and sandwiches." She switched into defensive mode.

"I grew up with ten sisters. My repertoire is a little broader than beer and sandwiches."

She stared at him in the moonlight, in complete dismay. The personnel files contained almost zero personal information, and this was the last thing she expected from Hedge Parker. "You have ten sisters? You poor guy."

"This is why I know so much about clothes," he said. "My mom taught me to sew when I was nine so that I could help her make dresses for my sisters."

"You were the oldest?"

"No, I have two older sisters. I knew more about girls by the time I was a teenager than most men ever know. And I know enough to realize that still isn't very much."

"Like how you acted like a jackass in the car."

"Yeah, I apologize for that. I was a little stressed, too."

"I know you're the boss, but maybe give me a minute to breathe before jumping on me next time." Evan hoped she wasn't overstepping. Hedge nodded.

She smiled. She finally felt safe again. "I wanted to run because I was afraid of being trapped in that house. I was afraid of becoming like those women."

"Being a slave to Hrevic?"

Evan shook her head. "I'm already like those girls, you know. I use my looks and my voice and everything else to collect secrets and manipulate people."

"For different reasons." He rubbed his palms on his knees.

"Yes, of course. But it's not that different. When I was in school, I hated modeling. I felt like I was making people spend money that they didn't have. I was lying to them with my body." She sighed. "I'm still doing that."

"You don't like your job?" Hedge seemed surprised. "You're incredibly good at it."

"I like that I'm doing it for my country. I like that I get to help catch the bad guys. But honestly, I'm not your typical intelligence agent. Men are chosen for their minds, their skills, their strength. If it weren't for the way I look, I never would have been recruited." She shrugged. "It was never as clear to me as when I saw the look in Anton's eyes as I walked toward him on the runway. I became his own personal doll. A living, breathing doll. He was just playing dress-up with me."

"You felt sick to your stomach?"

"I did. I could barely breathe." She swallowed, trying to move away mentally from that moment. "I've been threatened before. I've been assaulted and attacked in just about every way possible. Not like this. I suppose I'm not as tough as I think I am." Evan closed her eyes tight, waiting for Hedge to say how disappointed he was with her. Or maybe he'd just pull her from the assignment and send her home. He did neither. She opened her eyes and saw him just sitting and nodding. He almost looked like he was smiling.

"What do you think we should do next on this mission?" Hedge asked.

Evan laughed quietly and took a long deep breath. "It's not my place to say what happens next."

Hedge shrugged and leaned in once again. "Maybe not, but you're the one in the middle of this whole situation. You've had the up-close and personal experience. I just wonder what you would do if you *were* in charge."

"Well, I think we should get all the evidence we need on Hrevic and take him in," she said without a moment's thought. "Burn him to the ground. I don't want him as an asset. I want him gone."

Hedge kept his expression steady. "Is that the 'right' answer, or is that the truth?" he asked.

"That's the way I truly feel." She nodded and finally allowed a smile to spread across her lips.

Hedge's face relaxed into a confident grin.

Evan continued. "I want to get him and anybody else involved in his organization. He's hurting people and destroying lives. For all we know, he may be killing people with his bare hands. I want him to rot in prison for the rest of his miserable life." Evan let out a long breath. She almost felt better. As if her doubt was transforming into determination. *This job was probably going to cost her soul, but if she were going to pay the price, Anton Hrevic would, too.*

"Well then," Hedge said, standing up and moving toward the door. "I'd say you're a lot tougher than you think you are." He stopped and turned to face her again. "And Evan, you weren't recruited just for your looks, or your body, or even your brains. You were recruited because you had all of that and more. You were not only in the right place at the right time, but you were willing to do what needed to be done. I think you still are."

Evan felt her heart pounding in her chest. She strained her eyes to make out Hedge's expression in the moonlight. She thought he was studying her. Maybe smiling. She hoped so.

"Yessir, I am." She watched him walk back into the other room and close the door.

He was good.

CHAPTER FOURTEEN

Evan climbed the gilded stairs of Hrevic's mansion linked arm in arm with her new best friend, Nastya Alenko. She felt as fully-charged and prepared for the night as the little black dress she wore. She joined the other women in the dressing room and spent half an hour playing with lipstick, jewelry, and hairspray.

"That's a nice perfume. What is it called?" Nastya asked, leaning her face close to Evan's neck.

"Orchid, by Cara Samir," Evan said, holding up her wrist to her own nose. "I wasn't sure if I liked it. What do you think?"

Nastya inhaled with closed eyes and smiled. "It smells just like my aunt's greenhouse in the Caribbean. It's wonderful."

Evan pulled out an emerald necklace from her drawer and secured it behind her neck. She leaned toward Nastya and whispered. "I just love these jewels. I wish I could take them home."

"Don't be silly," she replied. "This will be your home soon."

"Will Anton get angry if I don't wear his earrings? My piercings are very sensitive, and I haven't had the chance to talk to him about it yet. I just think it would be terrible to break out with weeping sores on my earlobes while I'm trying to entertain a guest." Evan kept her voice low. "Don't you?"

Nastya cringed at the suggestion. "It will probably be alright tonight, but you should talk to him soon. And you know that if a guest takes you back to his hotel room, you are supposed to take the necklace off and leave it flat on the nightstand, right?"

"What?" Evan asked, nearly choking at her friend's casual instruction.

"That is the proper way," Nastya said. "You may leave on your other jewels unless you are going to get wet—in the shower or pool or something. Mostly Anton doesn't want the necklace broken. You must take it off."

"My goodness gracious," was all that Evan could think to say. "And I'm supposed to place the necklace on the nightstand?"

Nastya rolled her eyes. "Yes; flat on the nightstand beside the bed. You should keep it in sight so that nobody steals it. And lay it flat, so that it will not get tangled or fall to the floor." She stared at Evan as if she was speaking to a child. "It is not a difficult thing to remember, Eve."

"I see," Evan said. Her head was swimming in images of hotel rooms and strange men.

Xandra stood at the door and cleared her throat.

The muses all turned to face her.

"It's time."

Evan raised her brows and smiled, but the other women behaved as though this was simply their weekly routine. They nodded and followed Xandra to the door.

"When you walk down those stairs, you must become a muse like us, Eve. You must be every man's dream come true," Xandra said. "Do not spend the party dancing with Mr. Hedger or Mr. Brown. You need to find a rich guest and keep him happy."

"I understand," Evan answered. She smiled and tilted her head as she slipped past Xandra and bounced to the stairway like a debutant going to a ball.

The song from the sound system drew all six women downstairs and into the mix of laughter and dance. Alcohol sparkled everywhere, though Evan knew she mustn't drink anything but mineral water.

She saw Hedge and Anton speaking in the corner, wearing serious looks and making discreet gestures to guests around the room. Evan identified Senator Stanton Grey at the bar, and former Press Secretary Denny MacDonnell leaning on the white grand piano in the niche beside the foyer. MacDonnell made himself available as a means to pay off a favor that he owed to Hedge. Senator Grey agreed to play his part to score points with his wife, Eleanor.

Brawn quickly took Olga's hand and led her to the center of the room to dance.

As per the plan, Evan made her way to the bar to catch Grey's eye. She employed her most sultry stare but found Stanton looking like a panicked teenager at his first prom. She smiled warmly, trying to ease his mind. He looked like he might hyperventilate.

Evan moved her fingers to her upper lip, appearing to cover a bashful grin. "Kirk, tell Hedge we may have a situation. Grey looks like he's gonna yark."

"I'll tell him, but you're going to have to handle it for now. Hedge has problems of his own. Anton doesn't appear to like Mr. Brown," Kirk said.

Evan approached Grey and offered her hand. Grey took it and squeezed. His palms felt cold and damp. Evan took another step closer, hoping to calm his nerves.

"I'm Eve."

"I'm Senator Stanton Grey, from Texas," he said.

"Why, Senator! You're from my home state. Imagine flying halfway around the world just to meet your next-door neighbor!" Her voice fluttered with charm. "You need to relax," she said, pressing his hand for emphasis. "Let me get you something to drink."

Grey exhaled a short breath and scrubbed his palms down the front of his jacket. "Maybe we should dance."

Evan nodded and followed him onto the floor. A slow-tempo song faded in, and Evan draped her arms around his neck. He settled his hands in a stiff hold at her waist.

She rested her cheekbone lightly at his jaw and let the music lull him for a minute. When his shoulders relaxed, she moved back to look into his eyes again.

"Are you okay?" she asked, truly concerned.

He nodded and swallowed. She watched his Adam's apple jump a few extra times. She let her right arm slide down to his chest, and she played with his necktie, loosening it and unbuttoning his top shirt button.

"That should help," she whispered. "You look scared."

"I am," he confessed. "I know what I'm supposed to do tonight," he said. He moved his angular lips close to her ear. "But whether I do it exactly right or screw the whole thing up, I still must face the single fact that my wife carries a gun, and she will be briefed thoroughly on every aspect of my evening."

Evan laughed. She moved her hand up to his face and let her fingertips settle on the cleft in his chin. "Just let me take care of you, Senator."

The music switched to a faster song, and Grey put his arm around her waist. "I think I'll have that drink, now."

They walked side by side to the bar, and Evan handed him a whiskey sour. "You look like a man who enjoys a cherry with his cocktail."

His eyes widened. "You're going to get me into trouble, I expect," he said.

"That she will," a deep British voice boomed from behind her.

Evan felt a strong arm around her waist, pulling her back against a muscular frame. She rocked backward, nearly losing her footing.

"Adam," she exclaimed.

"Eve!"

Senator Grey watched with fascination. Evan turned her head just in time for Adam to kiss her full on the lips.

She pushed herself back from him, controlling her ire, trying to fix a fresh face on the complication. "Adam, this is Senator Stanton Grey. Senator, this is Adam. I'm afraid I never caught your last name."

"Dooley. Fantastic to meet you, Senator. Do you mind if I steal Eve away for one dance?" Adam asked, without removing his arm from her waist.

"I suppose I can live without her for one dance," Grey said, watching them walk away.

"Brilliant," Adam said. Once in the room's center, he turned Evan to face him. "I missed you."

Evan blinked at his lack of inhibition. "That's sweet," she said, dancing in his arms. She felt the steel mass of his muscles under his jacket. She smelled the mix of her orchid perfume with his sandalwood aftershave. Her focus drifted for a split-second.

He lowered his chin and held her tighter, leveling his dark eyes with hers. "There are very few things about me that are sweet," he said. "I don't waste time with candy or flowers. When I see what I want, I take it."

Evan didn't bother to listen for ticking. His voice carried no doubt or hesitation. She smiled as they danced, but something nagged at her mind. She wanted to run back to Grey.

Adam, or whoever he was, pulled her against him. "Let's get out of here," he said.

Evan peered up at him. "What?" she asked, hoping to sound innocent.

"You don't have to pretend, Eve. I heard the way you talked to that senator back there," he said, not mincing words. "I want you to go back with me to my hotel. I need to make a business call in half an hour. When I'm done with that, we can have some fun. I'll bring you back here tomorrow morning, or afternoon, perhaps."

The ticking was loud and clear. Evan's heart contracted. She turned and looked around the room for Hedge or Brawn. "I can't leave just yet. I promised the senator another dance."

Adam took her arm before she could walk away. "Anton said you were mine for the night, Eve. And I don't take 'no' for an answer."

Kirk assured her. "I'll alert Hedge. Stall as long as you can."

"Where is your hotel?" Evan asked. "Is it very close?"

Adam laughed. "Don't worry. If we leave right away, I won't miss my call."

The ticking grew stronger, and Evan tried to walk as slowly as possible. "What do you really have planned for us? You can tell me. I'm adventurous." She tried to keep her body relaxed and her voice light.

Adam ignored everything she said. He held a firm grasp of her arm and walked her to the front door, where Anton waited.

"I see that you're leaving already, Mr. Dooley," Hrevic said. "I trust that you'll take good care of my new muse. She really is something special."

"She'll be safe with me," Adam said, shaking Anton's hand.

"Anton," Evan said. "Will you tell Mr. Hedger where I am? I would hate for him to worry about me."

"Excuse me," Anton said to Adam. "May I speak to her for just a moment?" he added, taking Evan aside.

Adam nodded and took a step back to offer the appearance of privacy.

"Mr. Hedger left about a minute ago. I assured him that you were in capable hands with Mr. Dooley. Your dear senator became ill and had to leave. I must say that I'm a bit disappointed in Mr. Hedger. I hope that you won't let me down, too." Anton squeezed her shoulders. "Nastya told you what's expected?"

Evan smiled and shrugged. "What exactly do you mean?"

"The jewelry. She was supposed to tell you about…"

"Oh yes, Nastya told me all about that. Don't fret, Anton. I'm a big girl," she said with a smile.

Kirk whispered, "You're doing great. Hedge will tail you."

As they left the party, Evan caught a glimpse of Brawn dancing with Xandra. *Good. Keep an eye on Anton. If he's on to us, this could be a diversion tactic.*

Walking to Adam's car, Evan clung to his arm with a tight grip. "When we get to your hotel room, do you suppose I could get a real drink? Anton doesn't let us have the good stuff in the house."

Adam opened the car door for her and helped her down into his shiny black Ferrari. As she waited for him to round the front of the car and join her, she debated which side of the coin she should play, worldly or naive. This was not her first Ferrari.

He slid into the car and took a moment to look her over as if he was creating a story in his head from a photograph.

Evan turned her knees toward him and got comfortable in the seat. She fixed a smoky expression on her eyes and bit her bottom lip. She wanted to make the most out of this hurdle, and get back to Anton's as quickly as possible.

Adam raised one eyebrow with a determined expression as he started the engine. "I'll get you some champagne after my business call," he said, starting the ticking in her head once again. "Maybe you should have a glass before the call, to help you relax. You seem a slight bit on edge."

Evan wasn't as worried about the fact that he lied, but what he was lying about. Her priority was to maintain control of the situation. "What is your call regarding?" she asked. She wondered why he kept bringing attention to it.

"Just business," he said, watching her reaction as he drove.

Tick. Tick. Tick.

From the corner of her eye, Evan saw a flash of light in the side mirror. It looked like the senator's rented Jaguar. She was glad they were leaving plenty of distance.

"What business are you in?" she asked, smiling. "I mean, this is a beautiful car. I would suppose that it's probably expensive, so I guess you're very successful at whatever business you do." She caressed the leather seat on either side of her.

"You suppose it's expensive? You like my car?" he asked with a chuckle.

"Yes, I like the little horses, especially." She pointed to the yellow and black Ferrari emblem in the center of the steering wheel. Kirk laughed in her ear.

Adam swatted her hand away. "Don't touch the wheel while I'm driving," he said with a razor-sharp edge in his voice.

Evan feigned pouting and crossed her arms. "Sorry."

"Let's not be cross with each other," he said. "After all, we're going to have a lot of fun tonight." He brushed the back of his hand on her cheek. His skin felt smooth on her face. His fingers inched down her neck and over her shoulders.

The image of a dead model, strangled and stabbed, flashed into her mind. She never knew Sophia Ivanov, but she felt a sudden connection with her. Is this how she met her end? Leaving a party with a stranger, or was it something else as equally stupid?

Evan watched him drive with one hand. His eyes focused completely on the road. After just a few minutes, she saw that they were no longer in a familiar part of Paris. She spoke up. "I've never been to this part of town. We must be getting close to the outskirts of Paris. Is your hotel way out here?"

He smiled, but from where Evan sat, it looked more like a sneer. He didn't say anything. No words. No ticking.

"The only reservation I can find under the name Adam Dooley in Paris is at the l'Hotel Duo, downtown," Kirk whispered. "Right now, you're going the opposite direction."

She reached up and took Adam's hand and placed it firmly on her thigh, over a smooth section of the dress. She hoped this would work. "I just wish I knew more about you," she said.

"Good girl," Kirk said and remotely scanned the palm print. "Searching the databases now. I've sent him through facial recognition, but all I get is 'Adam Dooley, entrepreneur,'" Kirk said. "Smart to think of the handprint."

Adam's hand stayed parked on her dress, but he started to push her hem up slightly. Evan didn't want him to discover her Springfield, or anything else. She grabbed his hand in hers. "After the champagne," she insisted.

The road they sped over became more rural and winding. The buildings they did see were set farther back from the paving. The Ferrari picked up speed.

"I hope I have enough champagne for your friends, too," he said.

"What friends?" she asked.

Adam put both hands on the wheel. "The ones in the Jag behind us."

"Oh crap," Kirk whispered. "I'll tell Hedge."

Adam depressed the accelerator, and the Ferrari lunged forward, pushing Evan back in her seat. The silver Jaguar tried to match speed but began falling behind.

"I don't know what you're talking about," she said. "I wish you'd slow down, though. I'm not one of those girls who is impressed with riding in fast cars."

"Why don't you stop talking now," he said. It was not a question. Adam seemed to concentrate on the road ahead as he checked his mirrors in split-second glimpses.

As the speed increased, the turns became sharper. Gravel sprayed as Adam cut the curves. The tires squealed. Evan's heart pounded in her ears.

She tucked her right hand under her right leg, trying to discreetly unstrap her firearm. His pace pushed her from side to side in her seat. "You're scaring me, Adam. Let's just go to your hotel room and have some fun."

"I said to stop talking, now!" he shouted.

Evan felt the car move faster and faster. She could still see the lights of the Jag in the mirror, but they grew smaller with every kilometer. She watched him closely. He drove skillfully. He did everything smoothly. Her intuition told her that he was a pro. He could certainly be a killer, but not the strangle-and-slash type. He was too cool for that behavior. Adam was more of a two-in-the-chest, one-in-the-brain type.

Another thought flashed into her mind. He was a pro. But how could she tell Kirk?

Slowly she propped her elbow up on the door and began fingering her ear. Without saying a word, she tapped on the crystals in her earring. She started with two quick taps, and within just a few seconds had tapped out I-N-T-E-R-P-O-L in Morse code.

"Interpol, I gotcha, Evan," Kirk whispered. "Checking now."

"Mmmhmm," she hummed.

"Who are you communicating with? Are you wearing a wire?" Adam asked, groping at her with his free hand.

Evan tried to stay calm. She pushed his hand away. "Please stop. I haven't said a word."

"Double crap! Just hang on, Evan," Kirk said.

Adam put his hand into his jacket pocket and fumbled with something. A second later he placed his seemingly bare hand around the back of her neck.

She felt a pin-prick and turned her face away, crying out for him to stop.

She tried to push his hand away, but his grip was too strong, and she felt suddenly weak. The last thing she heard him say was, "This is for your own good."

CHAPTER FIFTEEN

"Hedge, we have to do something. Her heart rate spiked and then dropped to nearly nothing. She's out cold." Kirk was almost shouting into Hedge's earpiece.

Hedge clenched the steering wheel of the Jag and floored it, trying to maintain contact with the road around every curve. He could see the Ferrari's taillights but knew there was nothing he could do to keep up. The sky was dark and getting darker the farther from the city they drove.

Stanton Grey held tightly to the strap above the door with one hand. His other hand clutched at the leather armrest. His complexion was a pale green.

"I'm working on it, Kirk. Do you have any suggestions?" Hedge asked.

"Hang on, I'm getting a hit on the palm print with ... oh no ... this guy is one of us, Hedge. He's MI-6, and he doesn't have a clue who Evan is."

"Can you find out where he's taking her?" Hedge took another turn too quickly, sending the car into a fishtail. "There's no way I'm catching them." That fact didn't stop him from trying. He leaned forward in his seat as if it helped.

Hedge listened as Kirk tapped furiously at his keys.

"I can probably crack into his files, but it will take time that we don't have. He knows we're following him. Protocol won't allow him to go back to his place, anyway." Kirk panted. "We can't let him have her."

Hedge pressed ahead. A bead of sweat formed on his brow. She's more than capable. She's more than capable. Yeah, when she conscious. "What's on the dress that we can use? What do you have control of?"

"I have control of almost everything. She didn't shut it down before she— " Kirk paused and then said, "But I can."

"No. We need to keep contact," Hedge insisted. "We don't want to shut it down."

Kirk tapped at his keys for a second more. "Yes, we do. She's belted in safely. I think this can work. Hedge, keep after them and don't slow down. I'm going to activate the sonic pulse. From inside the car, it should be enough to shut off the car's engine. This year's Ferraris are equipped with hardened electronics to prevent a basic EMP surge, but our pulse is modified to compensate for that. It will cut the lights and airbags too, so watch closely. He should just coast off the road."

"Can't you do it without shutting down the dress?" Hedge asked.

"No, and it will have to be manually restarted. We're working on a shield for the dress, too, but it hasn't been perfected yet. The big problem is that right now her ear com is linked through the dress, not her earrings. We've never tested to see if the link will switch automatically. You'll have about five minutes of blackout with the car. If we don't find her in that window, she'll be gone."

Hedge huffed in anger and desperation. He scrambled to think of another plan. Anything but this one. "Kirk, are you absolutely sure this will work?"

"No, but it's our best bet, sir," Kirk said. He waited for a few seconds, and then prompted him. "Awaiting your go."

Hedge gripped the steering wheel tighter and gritted his teeth. "Go pulse."

"Pulse initiating." Seconds ticked away. "LBD is dark. No signal," Kirk said.

Hedge watched the road ahead but saw nothing. No taillights. No cabin lights. Only darkness. He drove on, dreading what he might find.

The road curved unexpectedly. Seconds slipped away with nothing but black asphalt and black sky.

"What are we looking for?" Grey asked Hedge.

"Any sign of Tyler or the Ferrari." Hedge scanned the sides of the road for the car.

"What about him?" Grey pointed to Adam, standing on the road's shoulder, aiming a pistol at their car.

Hedge assessed the situation instantly. He saw the Ferrari in the grass, resting at a line of trees that stretched infinitely into the night. Hedge pulled the wheel to the right with a hard jerk. He stood on the brakes, sending a shower of gravel and dirt into Adam's face. The Jag spun a three-sixty, and Hedge pulled off the road, positioning his car between Adam and the Ferrari.

A loud crack split the air as Hedge opened his door, and he ducked down. Another pop followed by the sound of shattered glass. He drew his weapon and steadied it, finding Dooley in his sights.

"Kirk, what do we know?" Hedge asked. He watched Adam step closer. Hedge fired a warning shot to keep him in place.

"His name is Robert Charles," Kirk panted. "I'm guessing that he's working Hrevic like we are, but from the other side." Kirk paused. "Do you have eyes on Evan?"

"Not yet," Hedge said. He wanted to run to the Ferrari, but he knew he couldn't turn his back on his challenger.

"Lay your weapons down," Adam called out. He moved his pistol from Hedge to the Jaguar and back to Hedge.

"I know who you are, Mr. Charles. We're on the same side here," Hedge answered. "You need to put your pistol down and listen to us. I don't want to hurt you, but I will to save my partner." Hedge inched toward the British agent.

"My name is Adam Dooley." The moonlight flashed on the side of his firearm.

"Your name is Robert Charles, and you serve King and Country. I'm a cousin from across the pond. So is Evan. Eve. My guess is that we all want to get the same man." Hedge held up his Glock and spread his fingers open to allow the pistol to hang on his index finger. "I'll put down mine if you do the same, Charles."

"Why should I believe you?"

"You don't have to believe me at all, but there's just one of you and four of us." Hedge cleared his throat. His chest ached from the tension.

Charles stood frozen, refusing to concede.

Hedge spat on the ground. "Listen, Charles. We don't have much time. Hrevic wired Eve with video. He may already know what's going on. In that case, you've blown both your mission and ours. Assuming you haven't hurt my partner, we might still be able to pull this off."

Charles lowered his sidearm an inch. "What if she is hurt?"

"Crap," Kirk barked in Hedge's ear. "What did he do to her?"

Hedge regained the grip on his pistol and stood up to square off against Charles. He leveled his aim at Robert Charles' head. "Did you hurt her?" he asked.

"No," Charles said. He didn't move from his stance except to lower his pistol another inch or two.

Hedge marched confidently forward, almost led by the muzzle of his Glock.

Charles began shaking his head. He dropped his weapon and kicked it toward Hedge. "No."

"We'll see," Hedge said to Charles. Moving forward, Hedge picked up the Brit's 9mm. He kept his sidearm leveled with Charles' eyes. "Tyler, I need you to give me a sign," he called out.

No response.

"Evan, report," Hedge barked. He marched to Charles' side and kicked his right foot out from under him. Charles landed on his butt in the gravel.

"What did you do to her?"

Facing the barrel of the Glock, Charles blinked. "I knocked her out with a micro-shot of sedative, that's all."

Hedge reared his pistol back to hit him but hesitated long enough for Charles to say, "This is my mistake. Let me fix it. I had no idea there was anyone else after Hrevic. The only reason I chose Eve was that she was new. I thought that maybe I could catch her before her loyalties were set."

Both men ran back to the Ferrari. Evan lay slumped in her seat, with no visible injuries. Hedge shook her shoulders and yelled to wake her. She didn't move. He pulled her out of the car and carried her to the grass where he laid her flat on her back. He pressed his fingers to her throat, searching for a pulse.

"She's barely breathing," Hedge said. "Can you defibrillate her?" he asked Kirk.

Charles shook his head. "I don't carry that equipment with me."

"Shut up," Hedge said, trying to listen for Kirk's instruction.

"The dress is shut down, so I don't have a reading on her heart or her breathing. We can't defibrillate if she's still breathing at all. That would stop her heart. I don't want you to do anything but bring her in." Kirk's voice shook.

Hedge picked her up and carried her to the Jaguar. "Come on, Charles. The Ferrari is out for a while. You'll have to ride back with us."

Charles followed and got into the back seat, cradling Evan in his lap. "How did you disable my car?"

Hedge glared at Charles. "Take care of her and keep your mouth shut."

Hedge jumped behind the wheel and scowled at Grey who was still hunched down in the floorboard, covered in shattered glass. "Get up."

"I've been shot," Stan said. He turned his shoulder toward Hedge. Blood soaked the edges of a hole in the sleeve of his jacket.

Hedge gave it a quick examination. "That's barely a scratch. Put on your seatbelt."

Hedge threw the car into gear and sped back to downtown Paris. His head pounded as he tried to reassemble a workable plan. His mind kept circling back to Evan's limp body in the back seat.

As they reached the edge of town, Charles muttered, "Eve, are you awake?" He tried to raise her head. "She's moving. She's trying to wake up."

Hedge looked up into the rearview mirror, and his cold stare met Charles' eyes. "You'd better pray Elle is okay, or I'll kill you myself."

The slip of the name wasn't lost on Grey or on Kirk. Kirk said nothing. Grey looked as though he would let Hedge have it, but all he could manage was another quiet moan.

"I thought her name was Evan," Charles said.

"Yeah," Hedge said. He slowed his speed as they reached the residential areas.

"You just called her Elle."

A thought popped into Hedge's brain, vaulting over his fury. His concentration was back on the job. He pulled the car to the closest curb and spun to face Charles.

"Where is your hotel? I think we can recover."

CHAPTER SIXTEEN

"You're out of your mind," Charles said, pacing circles around the slate-topped coffee table and taupe velvet chairs in the living room of his hotel suite. An accent wall covered in orange grasscloth wallpaper featured a sofa-sized print of a blurred black and white photograph. Between the rushing people in the photo and Charles' pacing, Hedge was starting to feel motion-sick.

"It's the only way to salvage this assignment." Hedge turned his attention toward the bedroom door, where Kirk and Evan were in the process of getting the dress functioning again. "We had everything under control until you put the moves on Evan."

Senator Grey sat on the black leather sofa with his head in his hands. His bloody shirt and jacket were in a pile on the floor. The room was cool, and though he wore only a bandage from the waist up, he was sweating. "I don't know. Can I call Eleanor about this?" Grey asked.

"Who is this Eleanor?" Charles asked, taking only a momentary break in his pacing.

Hedge scowled. "His wife." He turned back to Grey. "She sent you here as bait for this slime. She's the one who suggested we let him get compromising pictures of you so that we can see what he does with them. What could be more compromising than this?" His nerves wore thin. Kirk had been in the bedroom with Evan for nearly ten minutes, and he wondered if there was something wrong. Was Evan hurt during the car chase? By the drug? By this coward Brit?

Hedge turned his attention back to the senator and almost felt sorry for the man. He was between a rock and a hard place. Hedge knew how much a flesh wound hurt, especially the first one. But he was in charge of this mission, and they were all running out of options to save it. "We don't have time for you to call home."

The bedroom door opened, and the others joined them. Evan appeared shaken, but all right. Kirk looked worried.

"I've analyzed the camera on the necklace. It's designed to take still pictures every ten minutes while it's being worn. There are already six pictures in its memory now. The sonic burst shut down the processor, so it hasn't taken any more. We're lucky the pulse didn't fry it." He waited for Evan to take a seat next to Grey before he continued. "It's designed so that when the necklace is taken off, it will start capturing video with sound. Our problem is time."

Grey raised his head. With his hands still on either side of his face, he bore a slight resemblance to Edvard Munch's *The Scream*. "That's not our only problem."

"What do you mean?" Charles asked Kirk, without regard to Grey. He took a seat on the other side of Evan.

"We're already missing pictures. Every ten minutes we spend debating our next step is another picture we have to take with a false time stamp. I can do it, but the fewer, the better." Kirk shrugged and stuffed his hands into his pockets.

Hedge frowned for a second and then nodded respectfully to Evan. "Evan, Kirk and I have a plan that should fix everything, but these guys don't want to play." Hedge gestured to Grey and Charles as though they were spoiling a party.

Charles glared at Hedge. "A plan that you thought up. One that will have absolutely no adverse ramifications for you," Charles said. "I don't understand why you can't just take pictures and video of Evan and me and call it a night."

"That will keep you and Evan in Hrevic's graces, but I'll be out." Hedge said, taking a step closer to Charles. "And even if it worked, you would have to play along that Anton had the goods on you. We need more control than that."

Evan smiled, realizing the plan that Hedge had in mind.

"So, you propose that I get a twofer?" she said, nearly giggling. She put both of her hands on each of the other men's knees beside her and squeezed.

Charles and Grey both growled.

"I just can't imagine Eleanor thinking this is okay." Grey seemed more upset about this than about getting shot.

Kirk grinned. "Don't worry, Stan. Before I was a company man, I worked in Hollywood making indie pictures. I'll figure out angles and shots so that nobody gets hurt, or whatever. It will be my cinematic masterpiece," he said and then disappeared into the bedroom.

"Wouldn't we need some sort of script or something?" Grey asked.

"No time for that," Hedge said. "Let Evan do most of the talking. Just follow her lead."

"Then it's decided?" Charles asked. "I can't believe that everyone is on board with this plan."

Hedge shook his head and glared. "It's not that much different than what you suggested, man. He'll just be in the video, too," he said, motioning to Grey, who still held his head in his hands.

"Pardon my objection, but that is quite a lot different than what I suggested." Charles stood and resumed his pacing.

"I'm not kissing that man," Grey protested, pointing at Charles.

"If you do, I'll shoot you in the head," Charles said.

Evan seemed to stifle a laugh. "Look, we don't have a choice right now. And nobody has to kiss anyone but me. We don't have time for anything else." Evan stood up and walked to the bedroom door. "I'll work it all out with Kirk. You two be ready in five minutes."

Hedge glared at the men. "Strip to your shorts and grab a towel from the bath if you want. Grey, make sure your bandage isn't bleeding when you come in." He snorted and joined Kirk and Evan in the other room.

Kirk sat at the window, studying the monitor on his notebook. "We can make this work without much trouble at all." He motioned to the necklace on the nightstand. "The angle of this thing works to our advantage. We'll put Charles closest to the camera. Evan can be sitting in the center of the headboard, and then Grey can be on the other side. I don't want his bandage showing."

Hedge walked to the nightstand and back to the bed. He reviewed the rest of the room and then looked at Kirk's monitor to inspect the angle of the necklace camera. "How long does this video need to last?" Hedge asked.

Kirk and Hedge both looked at Evan and shrugged. She stood at the side of the bed, dressed in her corset and stockings. The dress hung in the closet, charging.

"No more than ten minutes," she said with a sly grin.

Hedge stared. She looked like something between a centerfold and superhero standing on the other side of the bed dressed in lace body armor with her fisted hands planted on her hips. He'd asked her to do the one thing he knew she most hated, and instead of taking sides with the opposition, she championed the idea. He knew what he wanted to do. What he couldn't do. He tried to fix a mask of appreciation over the expression he feared she could see. He turned back to Kirk.

"Do we need to take extra, so that you'll have enough to edit?" Hedge asked.

"Editing is not an option," Kirk said. "It's a timed static shot. We'll have to get it in one take. I'll give the men earbuds and direct them on the fly, so to speak." He laughed.

Charles and Grey entered the bedroom wearing towels wrapped around their hips. Evan nodded to them.

"If you can take direction," Kirk said, "I can get this in a matter of minutes. If you can't, we'll have to start over."

Kirk explained to the men how the scene would work, showing them on his computer monitor precisely what the camera saw. He gave them both earbuds, instructed them on their movements, and showed them how to use the bed sheets to their advantage. He adjusted the lighting in the room.

Hedge and Kirk gathered the computer and their gear and went into the living room to set up. Grey and Charles followed, leaving Evan alone in the bedroom. They were all set to begin.

"As you're ready," Kirk whispered into Evan's ear.

Hedge and Kirk watched the monitor, which showed feeds from both the necklace and the small camera he set in the corner of the room. Evan touched her fingers to either end of the necklace, as though she had just placed it on the bedside table.

As she leaned back against the headboard, she called out, "I'm ready, Adam."

Charles entered the room and rounded the foot of the bed to her side. He slipped between the sheets and began kissing Evan's arms and neck. Kirk, Hedge, and Grey all watched the monitor intently. Their breathing quickened, and they didn't blink.

They watched Evan pulling Charles' lips to hers and kissing him passionately. "Now let's have some real fun," she whispered to him. "Stan, are you going to join us?" Her voice sounded honey-sweet.

Grey glared over his shoulder at Hedge as he entered the bedroom.

Evan reached out to him as he entered the picture. "Come here, my darling," she said as he climbed into bed with her and Charles. She held the sheet up to cover the wrapping on his injured arm. Once Stan was in place, she planted a lusty kiss on his mouth as well.

The three worked together under the sheets to create the desired illusion for the camera.

"Eleanor is going to kill us," Hedge said to Kirk, watching the stream from the living room. He knew his former partner would blame him for this situation. Right now he didn't care.

"Charles, raise your shoulder a couple of inches to the right," Kirk said. He turned to Hedge and covered his microphone. "You think so? I was planning on giving her a copy for Christmas."

The two men laughed. They watched Grey's hands move over Evan's side and then squeeze Charles' shoulder.

"Oh yeah, we're dead," Kirk said. He played with the video feed sound and light levels and adjusted the signals on his small camera. "I can adjust the audio if I need to."

A few minutes later, with surprisingly little direction, Hedge nodded. "Tell them to wrap it up. I'm hungry."

"Twenty seconds, people," Kirk whispered.

The threesome frantically finished their improvisation with appropriate motion and volume. Afterward, the men each rolled over, and Evan sat up between them, breathing heavily and smiling. She shifted her corset back into place and smoothed back her red tresses. She leaned over Charles' exhausted looking body and picked up the necklace, covering the camera with her hand and ending the transmission.

"And cut," Kirk said. "Move it, folks. Every second matters from here on out.

Grey and Charles marched back into the living room quickly. Kirk retreated into the bedroom to gather his gear and work on the sound editing.

"What did it look like?" Grey asked, scooping his pants from the sofa.

"You don't really want us to answer that, do you?" Hedge shook his head.

Charles snarled. "You smug son of a ..."

"Face it, Charles," Hedge interrupted. "You were going to get screwed tonight one way or another." He threw Charles' pants to him. "Get dressed. We have some pictures to take."

Once Evan and the men were dressed, Kirk hacked into the necklace's camera program, adjusting it to allow him to force the snapshots. "Okay, just remember that everything is from the necklace's point of view. Step in front of mirrors when it's not awkward." Kirk directed them from across the room.

They spent the next several minutes setting up pictures with Evan and Charles talking, laughing and kissing. They set up a shot of Charles greeting Grey and Hedge at the hotel room door, and another with Grey and Evan reclined together on the sofa. The last two showed Grey and Evan leaving the hotel and getting into Grey's car, with Hedge waiting at the driver's door. Kirk took a few extra incidental random shots for authenticity.

Kirk quickly calculated the time stamps and added all the pictures to the storage chip on the necklace in the appropriate order.

"You think you can really pull this off?" Charles asked as the team said goodbye in the hallway of the hotel.

"Absolutely," Kirk said, offering his hand.

Charles just shook his head and closed his door. Grey, Hedge, Evan, and Kirk hurried down to the cars. Kirk climbed into the SUV, and the others got into the Jaguar.

"Remember, from now on, that camera is snapping pictures in real time. Good luck," Kirk said.

"Thanks," both Evan and Hedge answered.

"Can I go back to my hotel now?" Grey pleaded.

"We're dropping you off." Hedge motioned to his arm. "When you tell Eleanor about all of this, make sure you tell her you were shot. Tell her that first. Sympathy goes a long way with her."

Grey nodded.

As they pulled up to Grey's hotel, Evan leaned close to Hedge and whispered, "Kirk says we have about thirty seconds until the next picture."

Hedge watched as Grey got out of the car and Evan followed. She shut the car door and pushed Grey back against the car, pinning him against the silver sedan with one last kiss. She counted off the seconds in her head.

Grey stared at her with wild eyes. "Good night," he said, staggering inside his hotel.

Evan hopped back into the SUV, and they returned to Hrevic's party, which was just winding down. Hedge escorted her inside, where Anton greeted them with astonishment.

"What's this? You both left hours ago." A hint of anger tinged his voice. "I didn't expect to see either of you until tomorrow. Nothing bad happened, I trust?"

Hedge pushed out his bottom lip and shook his head. "I think you'll be pleased, Mr. Hrevic." He patted Evan on her shoulder. "Evie, why don't you see if you can find Mr. Brown. I need a minute alone with Anton."

Evan vanished into the party, and Hedge led Anton to a quiet place just beyond the foyer. "Eve's going to make you very happy, Mr. Hrevic. She's sharp as a pin, you know?"

Hrevic squinted. "You should speak plainly, Mr. Hedger. You see, I sent her away with Mr. Dooley, one of my richest and most influential clients. I expected her to spend the whole night with him." Anton stretched his shoulders and chin up and out to their full extent as if trying to match Hedge's physical capacity.

Hedge noticed and hunched down to give him the advantage.

"I know, and I'm sorry that we had a little miscommunication. I had promised Senator Grey a spin with Eve, and when Dooley stepped in, Grey got a little sad." Hedge smiled. "But Eve's brain is always working." Hedge tapped at his temple. "When Dooley told her that he wanted a bit of adventure, she called me, and I brought Senator Grey to them for a little fun."

Anton's face went sheet white and then flushed bright pink. "What?"

Hedge nodded. "I even snapped a couple of pictures with my phone's camera. Do you want to see?"

Hrevic raised his eyebrows. Hedge took that as a yes. He flipped open his phone case and pulled up the slightly blurred photos of Evan kissing Charles and then Grey. A stupid grin smothered Hrevic's face.

"You did this … tonight?"

"We aim to please, Mr. Hrevic. I had hoped to get her back here earlier, but Paris traffic is busier than you'd guess."

Brawn and Evan appeared behind them. "I guess we're ready to go," Evan said. "Anton, I left my jewelry upstairs in the dressing table. Thanks very much," she gushed, kissing Hrevic on the cheek. "Tonight was great fun."

"I'm glad you enjoyed yourself. Hedge told me about your adventure," Anton snugged her to his side. "Someday you'll have to tell me all about it, in detail." His lips curled greedily as he squeezed her waist.

Evan's face winced. "Oh my," she said. "If I don't get some sleep soon, I won't remember anything at all. But you will let me know when your next soiree is gonna be, won't you?"

Hrevic nodded. "I'm extremely impressed with you both. I'll contact you tomorrow, Mr. Hedger. I think we can come to an arrangement that will satisfy us all."

Hedge and Brawn shook hands with Hrevic, and after a minute of excessive hugs and kisses, Evan took the lead out to the car.

"Why is he waiting until tomorrow to make the deal?" Brawn asked. "If he's so pleased, you would expect he'd want us working on his next party immediately."

"He has to have time to review the pictures and video." Hedge laughed, helping Evan into her seat. "Are you alright? You've been through a lot tonight."

Evan met his gaze and nodded. "I'm actually real good, all things considered."

Hedge closed the door for her and slid into the driver's seat. He couldn't help but admire her. After all she'd bared to him last night, she didn't flinch in the face of duty. Tough woman.

They drove a long circuitous route back to their flat to ensure they weren't followed. Hedge and Evan were quiet for a full minute, but Brawn couldn't seem to hold back.

"Hmm," Brawn said. "I guess you got the scoop on Dooley? Xandra told me he was very powerful."

"Yeah," Hedge said. "You could say that."

Evan laughed. "Poor Brawny," she said. "For all your efforts and innuendo, you always miss all the fun."

Brawn looked at them with a confused and frustrated expression. "What did I miss this time?"

Hedge pulled up at the flat. "What didn't you miss? We had a car chase and a little gunfight. Senator Grey even got shot in the arm."

"What?" Brawn stared at Evan with raised eyebrows, obviously anticipating an interesting explanation.

"Evan got knocked out, and we had to set off a pulse to shut down

Dooley's Ferrari," Hedge said.

Evan interrupted. "I think you mean Charles' Ferrari. Adam Dooley is actually Robert Charles of MI-6."

They arrived at their apartment and parked the SUV in their secured garage. They walked back to the entrance and through the dingy lobby, trying to look like a small band of midnight revelers.

As they ascended to the third floor, Hedge continued. "We all went to the Brit's hotel room to shoot a movie. It was short, but I'm willing to bet you'd have enjoyed it."

Kirk greeted them at the door. "Get in here. Eleanor wants to talk to you, Hedge. And she's furious."

Hedge grinned. He wasn't about to let Elle spoil his mood.

"What is she angry about?" Brawn asked. He pulled off his jacket and let it fall on the sofa. He sunk down on top of it and propped his feet on the coffee table.

"Probably about the video." Hedge pulled himself free of his necktie and tossed it toward the bedroom door.

"What was on this video?" Brawn asked Evan. His gaze followed Hedge as he marched toward the phone.

"Senator Grey, Charles, and me, observing an old French custom," she said, sinking into the couch cushions next to Brawn.

Brawn shrugged. "What do you mean?"

Hedge rolled his eyes and shouted from across the room, purposefully holding the phone up so that Eleanor could hear. "They had a ménage a trois."

CHAPTER SEVENTEEN

Hedge stood in the corner near the kitchenette for his call with Eleanor. "You're just angry because he was wounded," Hedge griped into the phone. "I got him all wrapped up as soon as I could. He didn't even need stitches."

"My husband is a United States senator, and he received a gunshot wound to the arm while under your protection," Eleanor said with a manic tremor in her voice.

Hedge took a breath to respond but was cut off.

"I'm angry because when the situation changed, you neglected to inform me," Eleanor continued. Though she was an ocean away, she sounded like she was in the next room.

Hedge smiled. He knew this argument backward and forward. It was a dance they'd performed a hundred times before. But in the past, they had been on the same side. "I think on my feet. I thought that you *liked* that about me. I thought that's why you gave me my own team. By the way, it is *my team*. I report to you when the job is done, remember?"

"How could you put Stan in that position?" she argued.

"Oh no, you're not laying this one at my feet. You sent him here for this job. I didn't ask for your husband." Hedge looked around the flat. The rest of the team had put their gear away and assembled in the living room. Evan had washed her face and changed into her yoga pants and a tee. "Speaking of my team, they're ready for debriefing. I'll put you on speaker." Hedge pushed the button on the receiver, placing the phone in the center of the room.

Eleanor's voice rang loudly over the phone. "Don't you dare, Hedge. Not before we…."

"You're on speaker," he said, intentionally sounding like a radio DJ. He took a seat at the kitchen table, sitting back from the others.

"Hello, Eleanor," Kirk said. He tapped away at his keyboard, preparing to record the conversation to follow.

"Hello, Kirk." Eleanor's voice sounded stilted.

Hedge grinned as everyone greeted Eleanor. Her voice shifted to a more professional tone as she began her general questions. Each team member offered her their individual accounts of the evening.

Ramos began, detailing what he saw as he watched Hrevic's compound from just beyond the gate. He sent her a copy of his list of car plates from every vehicle that came or went during the party.

Brawn recounted the conversations he had with Anton, the models, and a few other guests. He included the description of the house and all noticeable security features, both human and electronic.

Evan reported the events she experienced, up to the point of being knocked out, and then afterward in the hotel suite. She used the most discreet terms when talking about Senator Grey. She made certain to credit Kirk with the quick decryption and results of her Morse code message.

Kirk related his account in a detailed sequence of events that sounded more like stereo instructions than a debriefing. His almost clinical statements lessened the sting of Grey's flesh wound and cinematic debut.

Hedge added another five minutes to the official report and then allowed Eleanor to ask questions.

When Eleanor finished her interviews, Hedge picked up the phone again and retreated to the privacy of the bedroom. "Are you ready for my two cents?" he asked her.

"I think I have a pretty clear picture of the evening," she said. "Do you have anything more to tell me?"

Hedge sat on Evan's bed and stretched his legs out in front of him. He leaned his head against the wall and pushed an overwrought sigh from his lungs. "Not much. You need to know that this team worked their butts off for you tonight. Evan didn't flinch at finishing the job after being drugged and wrecked. She uses the dress exactly as we intended. It's already become an extension of her person," he said. "You'd be proud."

"I am proud," Eleanor conceded. "I guess you are, too."

Hedge sighed again and rubbed his temples. Sitting on a bed in the middle of the night, talking quietly with her. It was so familiar that it hurt. "What do you want from me, Elle? What do you want me to say?"

"Stan told me that you called Evan by my name tonight."

"I did not," he lied. He hoped that it wasn't as obvious to Eleanor as it sounded to him.

"Kirk heard it, too." Her tone sweetened. "Was it just a slip of the tongue?"

"Maybe. I don't remember it. We were kind of busy, you know?" He raked his fingers through his short brown hair.

"Hedge, you know I don't blame you for my injuries." She paused for a second. "It's not your fault that I'm not the one wearing the dress."

His head ached. He didn't want to think about her right now. He could smell Evan's perfume all around him. She was his new partner, Elle was the past. Their partnership was the past, but she was still in his life. Present. Now. He balled up a fist and clenched it until his knuckles turned white. "Elle, I'm going to ask you again. What do you want?"

"I want you to finish the job." Eleanor sounded as though she had simply asked him to take out the trash. "And, though I'd like to have you drawn and quartered for what you did to Stan tonight, I know that your plan will probably work."

"You're welcome," Hedge muttered. He almost clicked off the line, but Elle continued.

"The only real problem we're finding is in Hrevic's financials. That is to say, there are no problems. We've scoured his personal records as well as the House of Alexei reports. Everything looks legitimate. We can't find any anomalies or discrepancies. The models all make reasonable incomes, and the records appear to be above board." Eleanor sighed. "We need a money trail, or we'll have to drop the whole investigation."

"He's getting compromising pictures and video for a reason." Hedge kicked off his shoes and let them fall to the floor. He hadn't slept in a bed for three nights now, and this felt good.

"Yes, but it could be solely for his own sick entertainment," she said.

Hedge chewed at his bottom lip, scouring his brain for an idea. He rocked back to his feet and returned to the living room with the others. He motioned for Evan's attention. "Hang on, Elle. I gotta ask Evan something." He covered the mouthpiece. "The women know that they're filming their dates, right?"

"Yes, at least...." She paused for a second with a look of deep thought. "They told me when to take off the jewels and where to place them, but they said it was to keep the necklaces from getting broken." She took a deep breath and shook her head. "I can't say with one hundred percent certainty that they know they're recording anything."

"Okay, Eleanor, Evan says that she's not certain the models are aware of the cameras or the bugs." His voice sped up as he spoke. "I saw the invitations that Hrevic and Templeton send out to their guests. They state that pictures may be taken on the premises. But when the women go back to their dates' hotels, they have an expectation of privacy. If the girls don't know, we can probably get at least some of them to turn on Hrevic."

"I wouldn't count on that," Evan said, shrugging.

Eleanor laughed, obviously hearing Evan's comment. "Have Evan pump the girls for what they know and what they don't know. The rest of you need to keep your eyes open for money. Favors and influence won't hold up unless we can get a victim to flip and tell us what's really going on in that place."

Kirk waved for Hedge's attention. "It's working. Hrevic is watching the video now. He's already downloaded the pictures." Kirk nodded. "Oh yeah, he's smiling ear to ear."

Hedge nodded. "We're in. We'll find the money, Elle."

"Very good," she said. She paused for a second. "Hedge, thanks for taking care of Stan. Honestly, I think he's excited about getting shot. I think he even enjoyed making the video, though he'll never admit it to me."

Hedge laughed and turned away from the others. "We'll make you a copy." He snapped the phone off and turned back to the room. "Okay, people, we've had a long night. Let's get some sleep. Lots more to do tomorrow."

Ramos and Brawn walked in from the kitchenette with bowls of popcorn, joining Kirk and Evan on the sofa. Evan sat at the end closest to the bedroom door. Once the others were sitting comfortably, she snapped the switch above her head to turn off the overhead light.

"After the movie," Brawn said, handing a bowl to Hedge.

"It's Evan's big screen debut," Kirk said, taking a bowl from Brawn. "Well, it would be if we had a big screen."

"I've already seen it," Hedge mumbled. "I'm going to bed." He handed the popcorn back to Evan and turned toward the bedroom, but stopped when Evan reached up and patted his hand.

Ramos turned out the table lamp, and the computer screen cast a blue-green haze over the shabby furniture. Hedge scooped up a handful of popcorn and sat on the sofa arm next to Evan.

She looked up at him and smiled. "I thought you were going to bed?"

"Well, I hate to miss your debut."

CHAPTER EIGHTEEN

Evan followed Hedge into the small apartment, glowing with perspiration from their morning run. She headed straight for the mini refrigerator and retrieved two bottles of water, tossing one to Hedge and opening the second for herself. She sat in the chair at the small dining table next to Kirk, who was busy at his computer.

Ramos and Brawn were in the middle of the living room floor, doing push-ups.

"I'm glad the rest of you are in such good physical condition." Kirk didn't look up from his notebook. "I do my work-out first thing in the morning."

Hedge drained his water bottle and nodded Kirk. "Yeah, what's your routine?"

"One hundred push-ups, two hundred fifty sit-ups and two hundred jumping jacks," he listed. "I've been doing the same thing every morning for sixteen years."

Evan grinned, sure that he was teasing. She had never seen Red do any more than a brisk walk. "You must do all of that before the rest of us wake up."

Kirk nodded. "I do it even before I wake up, in my dreams. It saves a great deal of time."

Evan wrinkled her nose and laughed. "And you don't get so sweaty." She took another drink and watched Brawn and Teo exercise. "But then, your physique is more self-sustaining than theirs."

Kirk reached for her arm. "I need to try something out if you don't mind. It will just take a second. It won't hurt."

Evan put her water bottle down and held open her hand. "Whatcha need?"

Kirk placed a small round piece of tape with a wire lead onto the inside of her left wrist and plugged the other end of the wire into a port on the computer. "I'm going to check your vitals."

Ramos and Brawn finished their sets and sat up on their knees to watch. Hedge shook his head and took the other chair at the table.

When Kirk seemed to realize that everyone was staring, he shrugged. "It's really not that fascinating. I'm just getting a base reading after an hour of sustained elevated heart rate. It's good to have different levels for comparison."

Evan sighed. "Not a big deal, guys." Everyone was watching everything she did now. Was it because of getting knocked out on the job, or because of the video?

Hedge exhaled loudly and turned to face Kirk. "Okay, so we had an interesting mission last night. I guess that we know a little more about it this morning?"

Kirk nodded. "A lot more, actually. We brought Senator Grey, Denny MacDonnell, and Marty Brassfield to the party. MacDonnell did his job and fed Tatiana a bunch of good stuff. From what I can tell, Hrevic has someone checking out all this information on a computer in the mansion, but not the one in his office."

"Is that important?" Teo asked. "I mean, that it's not the computer in his office?"

Kirk raised his eyebrows. "One can never tell what is or isn't important. I note everything, and then we'll know later."

Brawn nodded. "Okay. What else?"

Evan stared at the tape on her wrist. "What about Brassfield?" Marty Brassfield was a Hollywood celebrity with a mild activist following. His political clout was on the rise. "Hrevic might use him for influence, or just to give his muses legitimacy."

Kirk typed on his keyboard. "He had a ball. He spent the evening with little Maria. I think he really enjoyed feeding her the pack of lies we gave him. She's young, and he says that she spent most of the night in utter disbelief."

Evan laughed. "Don't be too sure about that."

Kirk began peeling the tape from her wrist after a quick beep signaled his input was complete. "What do you mean?"

"Little Maria knows a lot more than she'll ever let on. She was play-acting as much as Brassfield." Evan rubbed at the spot where the tape had been. "He may have two Oscars on his mantle, but she probably deserves one."

Brawn extended his arm across his chest and pulled on the opposite shoulder to stretch his back muscles. "Do you really think so? Last night you weren't sure that any of the girls knew what they were being forced to do."

Evan took another sip of her water. "I have no idea whether they know they are trafficking international secrets or what, but she's definitely not an innocent child. What she's seen by just being part of the fashion industry would put hair on your chest."

As if that was his cue, Brawn pulled his damp tee shirt off to expose his bare chest. His muscles swelled from the push-ups. He flashed a cocky grin.

Evan shook her head. Every time she thought she might be warming to Brawn, he did something like that. Cocky just wasn't her type.

Hedge rolled his eyes. "When you get a little older, you'll know what that's like."

Brawn seemed to bait him. "Why don't you get down here and join us, and Teo and I will show you what it's like to be young again if it doesn't kill you."

Kirk and Hedge exchanged a quick glance.

"So long as you go easy on me," Hedge sighed, moving the coffee table to make room for himself between the others.

"Hedge, you don't need to do that." Evan released a heavy breath when Hedge ignored her. She turned to Red in an attempt to ignore the challenge.

Kirk turned his computer to face the room, displaying a stopwatch. "Ready?" The three men grunted. "All right, then. Go!"

Evan slumped toward Red. "Not you, too." *Men.*

Hedge, Ramos, and Brawn began the contest. Their heads bobbed in rhythm as their arms and shoulders pumped them up and back to the floor. Long even breaths pulsed in and out of their lungs.

Evan began a casual conversation with Kirk. It was all she could do.

"What about the men that we didn't invite? What do we know about them?" She glanced down at the men on the floor. They weren't slowing. "We know about Charles, but what about the others? Did Hrevic invite them himself?"

Kirk nodded, with one eye on the timer. "Yes, it looks like it. I had three men on video from the party last night. I sent them through FRS and got hits right away."

"Big names?" Evan asked.

Kirk dragged the stopwatch to the corner of the monitor and pulled up another pane. After a few seconds of typing, he found the still shots of the men. He gestured to the first one. "This is Ian Carey."

Evan focused on a plump, middle-aged man wearing thick black glasses and holding a Sherlock Holmes pipe in his left hand. "What a prize."

Kirk laughed. "He's a fashion designer from Wales. Not big right now, but with the right connections and opportunities, who knows?"

Evan wiggled her eyebrows.

"I'm keeping tabs on him, but he spent very little time with any of the women. Spoke mostly to Hrevic the whole night. I could be wrong, but this looks like typical fashion party stuff."

The men on the floor began to huff, and their push-ups began to slow.

Evan blinked and sat up straight as Kirk pulled up the next photo. "Hello," she sang.

"I thought he might be more your type," Kirk said with a chuckle. "This is Michael Cooper. He is very rich, very sought-after, and completely unattainable. He owns property in nearly every civilized country in the world, and twice as much in the uncivilized ones."

"He's pretty, too." Evan cooed. She licked her lips as she focused on the hazel-eyed man in the picture. His sandy brown hair was cropped close on the sides, and he sported a chiseled chin with just enough scruff to make Evan take notice. She guessed that Cooper was about six-foot-plus and around one-ninety. She imagined all of that to be pure muscle. *Perfect.* "Are we worried about him? I could definitely follow him around Paris."

"Watch it," Hedge said from his place between the others.

"I'm tracking him, but judging by the short conversation I was able to read, this guy seems to have a standard monthly visit with Nastya. He may not be the Boy Scout you take home to meet the folks, but he doesn't seem to be anybody's puppet, either."

"And the third man?" Evan asked, listening as Teo's breathing became slower and deeper. "Take care, boys, you don't want to pass out."

"Thirty seconds," Kirk said as the timer counted down. He turned back to Evan. "This is the one I'm really watching closely." He brought up the third still. "This is Sergei Bershkov. He works in the office of the Russian embassy here in Paris. He spent the evening with Olga."

Evan considered the photo of the third man, and all she could think was how non-descript he was. Average build. Average looks. If the first two men were extremes on the one-to-ten scale, poor Sergei was a solid five.

She tossed a comment over her shoulder. "Hey, Brawn, I thought you were with Olga last night."

Brawn struggled to speak. "Can we talk about this in a minute? Kind of busy right now."

"Ten seconds," Kirk said, bringing up the timer.

"Y'all are doing great," Evan cheered. "Three, two, one."

Teo and Brawn collapsed on the floor and let their arms flop to their sides, but Hedge continued to pump.

"Ninety-eight, ninety-nine, one hundred," he said as he pushed himself back up and to his feet. "I hate to end on an odd count."

Evan watched his face as he crossed the room back to her side. He carried a confident smile and never lost eye contact.

"May I?" He picked up her water bottle.

"Help yourself," she said with a nod. "I'm done with it."

He finished off the last few swallows. "Thank you."

She raised her left eyebrow and watched him walk to the bedroom. "Thank you, sir."

Teo pulled himself up to a withered sitting position on the couch. He used his shirt as a towel to sop up the sweat from his neck and chest. "We shouldn't have challenged him so soon after finishing our last set of push-ups. He had that advantage over us."

Brawn managed to stand up but held his palm against his side. "That's true. We had already done our third set of push-ups this morning."

Evan patted Kirk on the back and looked Brawn over from head to toe. "Yeah, Hedge was still on his adrenalin high after running five K with me. That hardly seems fair."

Hedge returned to the living room carrying a bath kit and a towel. "I'm gonna grab a shower first this morning."

"Your privilege," Evan answered. She pulled her ponytail loose and went into the bedroom for her toiletries and clothes.

Hedge disappeared into the bathroom of the tiny flat and then emerged five minutes later wearing jeans and a golf shirt. His hair was wet but combed, and he looked ready for the day. Teo and Brawn argued over who would shower next as Evan slipped into the bathroom unnoticed.

After her shower, she trekked back to the bedroom. She noticed Brawn and Ramos' disgruntled expressions and caught a whiff of the aroma in the room. "Wow," she said, trying to speak and breathe through her mouth at the same time. "Had I known you guys would ripen so quickly, I'd have insisted you shower before me." She hurried into the bedroom.

Hedge sat on her bed with his fingers pressed into his lower back.

"How many push-ups did you really do?" she asked, startling him.

He turned to face her and smiled. "A hundred."

"You know, back in Texas, we have a term for that." Evan put away her stuff. "You don't have to show off, you know? You don't have anything to prove."

"I didn't keep count of how many I actually did, but I kept up with them."

Evan nodded as she tossed her laundry into the small basket in the corner. "You did great. You kept pace running with me. You can keep up with anybody on the team. You're Superman, Hedge." She noticed the way Hedge rotated his right shoulder and grimaced. "Are you hurt?"

"I'm not hurt. It's just an old baseball injury from school. It acts up sometimes," he said. He seemed to be trying to play down the pain.

Evan went to his side and began massaging his shoulder with her thumbs. "Good grief, Hedge. Are you carrying the weight of the world? Your shoulder is like a solid rock. You need to relax." She pushed the heel of her palm in firmly, making tiny circles against the muscle until it softened slightly under her touch. Evan worked slowly, partly because she was unsure of how he'd react, and partly because she was enjoying the feel of his shoulders. She wished her hands were under his shirt. She allowed her hands to linger for a moment.

She reached over his collar and moved her fingers to the back of his neck. His skin was warm to her touch as she kneaded a little more.

She could hear him sigh as she shifted her hands to rake through his hair.

"Quit kidding around," he responded, leaning away from her fingertips.

Evan took a step back and propped her hands on her hips. "What's wrong? You were fine this morning, playful on our run and showing off your stamina against the others, and now you're acting all defensive. I thought you were enjoying this."

Hedge drew in a deep breath and stood, facing her. He took a step closer, steadying his gaze on hers. "There's nothing wrong." He let his gaze rise from her knees to her eyes. "I'm sorry for being defensive."

"Then don't pull away," she whispered. Right now, all she wanted was to be folded into his arms. Evan held her breath as he inched closer to her. She felt a warm hum in her ears, and her fingers began to tingle. "It's okay," she heard herself say. It was more than okay.

"What's okay?" he whispered, just inches from her mouth. His hands slid around her upper arms, and he started to pull her body against his when the door pushed open.

"I need you both to come in here," Kirk said. "Sorry, but this is important."

They both took a step back from each other and blinked away any thoughts of what almost happened.

"On our way," Hedge said, gesturing for Evan to take the lead.

"What is it?" she asked, seeing Teo staring at the notebook. Kirk knocked on the bathroom door, and Brawn appeared, still wrapped in a towel.

"Look at this," Kirk said, pointing to his monitor. "Olivia Dresden was admitted to the hospital early this morning."

Evan looked at the photo on the screen and cringed. "That's Olga."

"Yes, it is." Kirk nodded.

"She's been beaten," Teo whispered. His tone was low, but nobody doubted the emotion in his voice.

"Yeah," Kirk said with a nod. "She has a black eye and strangulation bruises on her neck. The nurse suspected assault and took pictures."

Hedge furrowed his brow. "And how do we have this photo?"

"When I started the facial recognition search on the models the other day, I never closed the program. I keep it running until our case is closed. That way if there are any hits on any official channels, I get a notification," Kirk said.

"Did she press charges against anyone?" Ramos asked.

Kirk shook his head. "No, she told the hospital staff that she did this to herself. She just wanted painkillers for the black eye."

"How do you put strangulation bruises from a man's hand on your own neck?" Brawn asked.

Hedge crossed his arms over his chest and exhaled loudly. "It could have been a consensual act with a friend. There are a lot of people who take pleasure in doing dangerous things."

Teo raised his brows and turned to his team leader. "That's what we're going with here? That she's just kinky? We know what happened to the other model. We can't ignore this." He shook his head, looking determined. "This girl has been hurt, maybe violated. We need to see more of what's going on in Hrevic's house."

Evan let her fingers wander to her throat. "We're not going to ignore this, Teo," she assured him. "The fact that she's not talking to the authorities probably means that she's being threatened. If she's afraid of Anton, we could use that to get her to flip. This may be the best way to take him down."

Kirk nodded. "I've been watching the house feed. This didn't happen to her at Anton's place."

Hedge pointed to the picture of Olga. He looked as though he was working out something in his mind. The photograph revealed a dark purple crescent that spread from the bridge of her nose to the outside of her left cheek. Her neck showed a pink V-shaped line that ended in dark red bruises under each ear. "Is she still at the hospital?"

Kirk sighed. "Nope. She got her meds and went back home. Back to Anton's little chateau for safe-keeping. What's our next move?"

Hedge thought for a second. "Do we know where Bershkov is this morning? He was Olga's date last night, besides bachelor number two over here." He tilted his head toward Brawn.

Brawn scoffed.

Kirk tapped away at his keyboard. "Nothing showing up yet. We know he went to his own home last night, but from what I can tell; Sergei might still be in bed. I'll have him on a short leash."

"Good," Hedge and Teo said at the same time.

"I'm in contact with the nurse at the hospital. She thinks I'm with a battered women's shelter. She'll let me know if she gets anything more about Olga." Kirk nodded to the others.

Evan took a deep breath. "We can't act weird, either. As far as Anton and the muses are concerned, we don't know anything about this."

The others agreed.

She continued. "I'll check in after a while and see what Anton has in mind for me today. If I can manage a trip to the house, I'll go and find out whatever I can. The official report may be that her injuries were accidental, but women talk."

Hedge put his hand on her shoulder. Evan liked how it felt. Warm, reassuring. She wondered if there was any chance they could pick up where they left off.

"That's a good plan for now," Hedge said. "Kirk, you keep your eyes and ears peeled. Brawn, get dressed and then take a drive to Bershkov's place and make sure things are quiet there. Ramos, have Brawn drop you in Hrevic's neighborhood and make a wide circuit of the grounds. See what you can learn on site. Brawn will pick you up when he's done, and we'll all meet back here after."

Brawn combed his hair with his fingers. "And you and Evan?"

"We'll wait for Anton's call," he replied. "If they request her presence, I'll take her right over. If not, we'll formulate with Kirk on the way to get her over there anyway. No matter what happens, though, everyone reports in every thirty minutes. Understood?"

The team members looked at each other and nodded.

Brawn took a deep breath. "I'll be ready to go in ten minutes. Will that work with you, Ramos?"

"Absolutely," Teo said.

Kirk tapped Hedge on the shoulder. "Can I talk to you for a minute? I have something I want to check on." Kirk smiled at Evan and tugged on his right ear.

She understood the gesture and retreated to the bedroom.

"Sure. What's on your mind?" she heard Hedge say to Kirk through her ear receiver as she pushed her earring through her lobe. She didn't know why Kirk wanted her to hear his conversation. She figured it was another test.

"I'm going to pull the car up," she heard Teo say. The front door clicked open, then bumped closed.

She heard the bathroom door squeak and then close. Brawn must have gone in to finish dressing.

She heard Kirk inhale and then begin. "What is going on with you?"

Hedge paused before she heard his answer. "What do you mean? The push-up thing?" Another pause. "I was just showing them that I'm not as old as they think I am."

"That's not what I'm talking about, and you know it." Kirk sounded as though he was scolding Hedge. Evan felt a little guilty for being the cause. "I walked in on something between you and Evan."

"Keep your voice down." Hedge's voice sounded gravelly. Evan imagined him shaking his head and looking over his shoulder. "Nothing happened between Evan and me."

"Then why should I keep my voice down?"

"Because I don't want anyone else hearing this conversation and thinking that something did happen." She heard Hedge huff. She wished she could see what they were doing, too.

Kirk started again. "Well, something was about to happen, then. I've seen the looks you give each other, and I've seen them before, on both of you."

"You're being ridiculous."

"Listen, Hedge, you're a friend. So is Evan. I'd drop dead for either one of you." Kirk's voice softened. "I don't want to see you get hurt."

"Nobody's getting hurt," Hedge said.

Evan wanted to stop this conversation in its tracks. She was a big girl and didn't need anyone looking after her. She should just march in there and give them both a piece of her mind. But she also wanted to hear just a little more.

Another door click, and she could hear Brawn again. "Ramos and I are on our way." She heard sounds like things being picked up and moved around. Brawn said, "I hate it when Mom and Dad fight." The main door of the flat closed again.

Hedge sounded mad now. "I would expect this kind of thing from Brawn, but you?"

"Why not me? You were the one who instructed the entire team that Agent Tyler wasn't a piece of property or a prize to win. You didn't want anyone messing with her. I suppose I know why."

"You're jealous, old man." Hedge wasn't just upset. Now he sounded mean.

"Old man? I'm not that much older than you. Of course, compared to the rest of our team, I suppose we're both ancient." Kirk's voice remained steady. Evan imagined them standing face to face now. "Don't you think that's how Evan sees us?"

"Look, I didn't make a move on her. Without any prompting, she started rubbing my shoulder."

"With no prompting? Right. Did you tell her about your old baseball injury?"

"You need to stand down, Kirk."

Evan listened to the men go back and forth. She was about to storm the room when she heard Kirk start in again.

"Hedge, I understand how great she is. Believe me, I do. But I don't want to see a repeat of what happened with you and Eleanor."

She froze. She had to hear more.

"Now *you're* blaming me for what happened to Elle?" Hedge sounded as though he was speaking through clenched teeth.

"Not at all, Hedge. Elle saved your life. You saved hers. That's not what I mean. Ugh!" Kirk's energy faltered. "I just don't want Evan to feel like she's obliged."

"Now I'm pulling rank for a tumble?"

"Stop!" Evan yelled, rushing through the doorway. Hedge was holding Kirk's shirt collar. "You're both acting like complete idiots." She pushed her way between the men. "I want you both to sit down right now."

Kirk obeyed immediately, finding the chair behind him without looking. Hedge walked to the couch and lowered himself to the edge of the seat.

"How much of that conversation did you hear?" Hedge asked her.

"Well, since Kirk instructed me to turn on my ear receiver, pretty much the whole thing."

"He did what?!" Hedge seemed to explode. Evan was glad the men were out of reach from each other.

"Just breathe for a minute," Evan said, pointing an index finger at each of them. "Now I have no earthly idea as to why he would think that I should hear any of that exchange."

"I can explain in private," Kirk said.

"Oh no you can't," Evan continued. "You see, I don't intend to be in private with either one of you again." She let her hands settle at her waist and began an authoritative pace between them. "How can I? Little innocent thing that I am. You two big bad wolves might take advantage of me."

Hedge opened his mouth for a response but didn't get a chance to speak.

"Let me make this perfectly clear," Evan said. "I am a grown woman. I can take care of myself. Whether I'm dealing with you, or Brawn, or Teo or Anton, it makes no difference. I do not need a big brother beating people up for me." She glared at them both. "And yes, I said big brother and not father. I have a daddy, thank you very much, and neither of you ever want to meet him. Do you understand what I'm saying?"

"Yes," they both muttered, looking like whipped dogs.

Evan looked at Kirk. "I love you, Red, but I fully understand what a man is telling me when he complains about an old baseball injury."

Kirk seemed to stifle a laugh.

Evan faced Hedge. "And you, my friend, need to stop pretending that you're the same age as the other boys on the team. You keep that up, and you will hurt yourself. A lot worse than what you can do on a baseball field."

"I apologize," Hedge said. "I was out of line."

Evan looked like a contented cat. "You men really have no clue about women sometimes. We don't care how old you are. We know that most of you never mature past fourteen, anyway."

Both men smiled and released a sigh. The scolding was over.

Evan nodded. "I'm going to the bedroom to cool off. I don't want either of you following me in there. And I don't want any more arguing, either. Next time I have to get after you, I'll insist that you kiss and make up."

She tossed a sharp glance at both of the men and went back to the bedroom, removing her earrings as soon as she was alone. She stretched across her bed and growled to herself.

"Why do they have to act like selfish little children?" she asked the ceiling. "Why do they have to use stupid lines like baseball injuries?" She scrubbed her palms over her eyes. "Why is it wrong to just want to be kissed every once in a while, by someone who means it?"

A loud knock on the bedroom door pulled her upright.

"Yes?"

"Hrevic just called," Hedge said.

"Okay, I'll be ready to go in ten minutes."

"You have five," he answered.

Evan gasped in exasperation. "Yessir."

CHAPTER NINETEEN

Hrevic's office looked much different in the daytime with the sunlight flooding through the expanse of French doors. The ornate furniture and knick-knacks seemed to recede when challenged by the bright blossoms of the garden outside. Hedge listened carefully to Hrevic's request, focusing on the man's tone and body language, eager for any signals of desperation or suspicion.

"Of course, Olga will be all right soon enough, but until then, I'm short one muse," Hrevic said, peering at Evan over his laced fingers." He leaned over his desk and sighed. "My problem is that I have a private show tonight for my most important buyers. I could rework the whole thing and divide up the ensembles that Olga was to wear amongst the other girls, but that would take time and effort and a great deal of trouble. It would be a tremendous favor to me if Eve would just take her place."

Evan smiled her sweetest grin and tilted her head. Her lashes fluttered. "I am sorry to hear about poor Olga's accident, and I would love to walk in one of your fashion shows, but really, Anton, I doubt I'll fit into anything that Olga was going to wear. She's your tiniest muse, bless her heart."

Hedge watched Evan work her magic on the other man. She spoke very differently to Anton than she did to him. With Hrevic, Evan's voice dripped of honey. When he was alone with her, it was more like moonlight. Soft and subtle, but real. He had already forgotten the fire in her tone from the hour before.

Hrevic nodded as if he was prepared for this challenge. "I can shift the outfits about without too much worry. Xandra is the closest to your figure, dear. I'm sure that she won't mind squeezing into something smaller to let you wear her wardrobe. The timing for the show is more important than who wears what."

Evan nodded. "It sounds as though you have it all worked out." She turned her chin to face Hedge. "What do you think, Mr. Hedger?" She batted her lashes for him as well.

Hedge smirked. "I'd like to talk to Monsieur Hrevic for a moment, in private, if that's all right, Evie."

They both regarded Hrevic, who nodded and stood. "Perfect," he said, reaching out for Evan's hand and leading her to the door. "Don't worry, mon cher, we will work everything out."

Evan smiled over her shoulder to Hedge and then turned her attention back to Hrevic. "May I go up and see Olga? I'd just love to wish her a speedy recovery."

Hrevic furrowed his brow as if he were speaking to a child. "Not now. I'm afraid she is resting. But Nastya is out in the garden, and she will be happy to entertain you while I talk to Mr. Hedger."

"Of course," she chimed. "Come find me when y'all are all done."

Hedge stood as Evan left the room and returned to his seat when Hrevic resumed his chair.

"Anton, I appreciate that you like Evie. She's a great girl," Hedge began.

"A great woman," Hrevic corrected. "We should be plain in our talk. She pretends to be innocent and charming. No, she is certainly charming. But she is not innocent, is she, Mr. Hedger?"

Hedge shifted in his chair. "What do you mean?"

"I mean simply that she knows how to handle a man. She plays the role of ingénue, but she is not naïve. She looks to you for guidance. She looks to me for opportunity. In the end, though, Eve gets whatever she wants. It is true, isn't it?" Hrevic asked.

Hedge wondered how to play this card. Hrevic spoke with purpose, but Hedge wasn't sure he knew which direction he might wander. "I suppose she appears…." He let his words trail off, hoping Hrevic might cut in. He did.

"But that's exactly what I mean. The way she appears. Eve is everything I want. She is manipulative, intuitive, and sophisticated, yet she *appears* to be none of that. She casts a spell on men, and they believe that they are completely in control. All the while she is pulling their strings." Hrevic moved his hands in a pantomime of a puppeteer.

Hedge watched as Hrevic's face delighted in the whole idea. He decided to give him the upper hand. "Are you saying that you like that about her?"

"Oh no, like is not nearly a strong enough term. I am in love with her. I would like to swim in an orgy of Eves. She is the perfect woman for my needs."

Hedge blinked in shock. "Your personal needs?"

"No, certainly not," Hrevic said. "Well, if we were to be honest, I would say yes, but that would then squander this gift in front of me. This gift that you *pretend* to offer." He leaned forward an inch for emphasis. "That I *pretend* to accept."

Hedge took a deep breath, contemplating Hrevic's explanation. He didn't seem suspicious. Eager, maybe. Hedge waited for another beat. Evan wasn't the only one who could pull puppet strings.

Hrevic laughed. "I am merely saying that Eve is giving us these moments to talk and to feel like we are making this decision. We both know that she wants to model for me. We both know that you will ask for a nice commission for her services. We both know that I will pay it because I want her. We go about this little charade because we know that this is what we all want, and this is how it must be done."

Hedge laughed. They were in.

"Then terms are not a problem?" Hedge asked. He noticed Evan and Nastya walking past the French doors. The women smiled and waved.

Hrevic waved back. "Numbers are only hurdles to step over, Mr. Hedger. We want our girl to be happy." He stood up and gestured to the doors leading to the gardens. "Why don't we join them? I believe we're finished in here. Eve can walk in my show tonight, and tomorrow we can discuss a more permanent arrangement for us all. Does that satisfy you?"

Hedge stood and offered a firm handshake. "That suits me just fine."

The men found the women surrounded by roses.

"The beauty is overwhelming," Hrevic said, gesturing to Nastya and Evan. "I imagine a spring collection of floral patterns and rich, rosy hues." He kissed both women on the cheeks. "With lots of translucent fabrics. I want to see your glowing skin through it all."

Hedge saw the way Hrevic looked at the women, undressing them in his mind. Hedge wanted to punch him in the throat. "Are you enjoying the morning?" he asked instead. He kissed Nastya's cheeks and took a protective position at Evan's side.

"Very much so, Mr. Hedger," Evan said. She raised her shoulders in anticipation. "What did y'all decide? Do I get to walk in the show?"

Hrevic glanced at Hedge, who nodded back. Evan waited.

"Of course you can," Hrevic said. He scooped his arm around her waist and pulled her to his side. Evan threw her arms around his neck in a warm hug.

"Thank you," she chirped. She turned back to Hedge. "Thank you, both."

Hedge took a step toward Nastya. "You look radiant out here this morning, Nastya."

"How sweet to say," Nastya replied. "I am glad that Eve will be a part of the show tonight. It will be fun to walk with her."

"I'm just so sad that Olga can't be with us. Do you think I can give her a hug after a while?" Evan asked.

Nastya nodded. "I'm sure we can all wish her well before the show."

"And where will the show be?" Evan asked as the foursome rounded the corner of the estate to the back terrace.

"It will be here in the private gallery upstairs," Hrevic said. "I am having it prepared for a small crowd."

Hedge nodded, looking around the yard. He noticed a truck from the market at the kitchen entrance.

Hrevic continued. "We will have a banquet for my clients, and then the show. Afterwards, we will have dessert out here, and the muses will wear their best pieces and allow the buyers to touch and enjoy the merchandise up close."

"It's going to be magical," Evan said. "I just know it will."

Hrevic offered his hand again to Hedge and gestured to the house. "I'm sorry that you won't be able to stay for the evening, Mr. Hedger. I'm sure you understand, though. I ordered only enough meals for my guests."

Hedge shook his hand again. "Not a problem at all. What time should I drop Evie back here?"

Hrevic shook his head, and Nastya laughed. "She is here, Mr. Hedger. She doesn't have time to leave and return. Nastya will take her upstairs to get ready right now."

Hedge shot a quick glance to Evan, concerned that this adjustment might upset her strategy. She bounced to his side and kissed his cheek.

"Don't worry about me, Hedge. I'll be having the time of my life." She started inside after Nastya, but turned back to the men, appearing to have thought of something. "You come pick me up at midnight, alright?" Evan looked to Hrevic as if she were asking for permission. "That way I don't turn into a pumpkin."

Hrevic raised an I-told-you-so brow in Hedge's direction. "That will be suitable, cher," he said. He watched the women go inside, and led Hedge to the front door. "You see, she knows exactly how to get whatever she wants from us. She is utterly dangerous to a man unaware and entirely beguiling, to the few of us who truly know her."

Hedge opened the door to leave, taking a quick appraisal of the mansion. His gut told him to figure out a way to stay, but he knew that Evan was capable of performing her duties without him. "Good luck tonight. Take care of our girl," he added.

He walked to the corner and down a few blocks, giving Kirk a short debriefing of the situation through the earbud transmitter. Ramos and Brawn picked him up in the car about a mile from the house.

"Where is Evan?" Ramos asked.

Hedge answered with a cold, hard fact. "In bed with the enemy."

CHAPTER TWENTY

The plush dressing room was busy with activity as all the muses prepared for the show. The glittering chandelier and vanity tables reflected light from every angle. Like Tatiana, Maria, and Nastya, Evan was dressed in a fluffy white robe, sitting at her dressing station, and staring at her reflection in the mirror. The others listened to Debussy's *Girl with the Flaxen Hair*, and she listened to Kirk's admonishment.

"How could you let him leave you there? You don't have the dress. You don't have any back-up at all. All you have is me, and you are constantly surrounded by the other women. You won't have any real means to communicate with me," he said. "You can't do this all by yourself, you know."

She wanted to respond to his harsh reproach. She wanted to remind him that until this week she'd never even known of a tool like the dress. She wanted to remind him that he'd always considered her more than capable before. But at the moment she was being watched. No talking to voices in her head. If she couldn't sass back, the silent treatment was the next best thing.

She reached up to the huge plastic curlers in her hair. Still slightly damp. *Wait a little longer before pulling them out.*

Evan slid open the jewelry tray in front of her. "Let's see what beautiful gems I'm going to wear tonight."

Kirk continued. "Don't even think about taking out your earrings. If you do, I'll have no way to talk to you or hear you."

The shallow drawer was empty.

"Oh dear me," she said with a lilt in her voice. "My jewelry is all gone. I suppose I just have to wear my own."

"Good," Kirk said.

Evan breathed a sigh of relief but hoped that Kirk didn't notice. She could handle herself, but having an extra ear wouldn't be so bad, either.

"Don't be stupid," Tatiana said with a scoff. She shook her head at Evan, and one of her curlers started to pull loose. As she reached up to secure it, Nastya finished her thought.

"This is a real fashion show, Eve. All of the accessories have been paired with the outfits. On each hanger is a pouch that holds everything you must wear." Nastya pointed to the small portable clothing racks against the wall. "One of those is yours. You will pull it over to your station once your hair and makeup are finished. You will change your clothes between your runway walks at your station so that you can touch up if you need to."

Evan raised her eyebrows. "The shows I've done before haven't been as organized as this one, I guess. We mostly just stripped and changed right backstage and got right back in line."

Nastya nodded and smiled.

Tatiana laughed. "That is how most big shows are, but Anton loves us. He built this room just for us."

Evan nodded, imagining all the places there might be hidden cameras. Yep. He loves us, alright.

Nastya added, "Tonight we will model just as we did the other day, but for this show, we have the makeup artists and dressers to help us."

"How fun," Evan said with an enthusiastic punch to her voice. *More people to poke and prod. Yay.*

Tatiana patted her pinky finger at the corner of her eye. "The dressers will make sure that you are wearing the correct earrings and bangles with each ensemble. You don't have to worry."

Kirk's voice sizzled in Evan's ear. "It's too dangerous. Make yourself throw up or something."

Evan stifled a laugh. She leaned toward Nastya and said to Kirk, "You know, it's been a little while since I've modeled in a real fashion show, but I know I can do it."

"Evan, I know you can model." Kirk's voice softened and trailed off.

"You will be fine," Nastya said. She nodded to Evan for encouragement.

"At least give me some warning before you disconnect," Kirk requested.

"I will," Evan said, answering both of them.

Just then Xandra burst through the dressing room door like an erupting volcano, followed by Anton. "Absolutely not!" she shouted.

"Xandra, be reasonable," Anton said. "You are the nearest one to her dress size. I couldn't rework the whole show at the last minute." He chased her as she marched to the middle of the portable racks.

"I cannot help it if she is fat!" Xandra said, gesturing to Evan. "These clothes were designed for me! Now I will have to squeeze into Nastya's dresses, and she will have to squeeze into Tatiana's and so forth." Xandra's face flushed red with fury. "It's stupid. Make her squeeze into Olga's dresses. Then she can see just how fat she really is."

Evan listened to the outburst. If Xandra was closest to her size, and she was fat, what did that make Xandra? She wanted so badly to ask that question out loud.

Anton shook his head and pleaded. "That would be ridiculous. She would no more fit into Olga's gowns than you would."

All of the women froze in place at Anton's remark. Xandra began to tremble from head to toe. Evan half-expected to see lightning bolts shoot from her fingertips. Evan didn't like being called fat, but she somehow felt sorry for Xandra.

Evan stood and took a step toward the unstable situation. "Anton, I don't mind trying on Olga's wardrobe if you want. I don't want to make any trouble."

Kirk's voice hummed in her ear. "Be careful. This doesn't sound like anything you want to be at the center of."

Xandra glared at her and twisted her lip. She walked to Olga's rack of clothes and picked an outfit, holding it up and out to Evan. "You think you can fit into these? Do not make me laugh."

"How will I know if I don't try it on?" Evan said.

She started to reach out for the gown, but Xandra snatched it back. "That is ridiculous. I will wear Nastya's rack of clothes. You cannot make a fool of us, Eve."

"I'm sure sorry, Xandra. That was never my intention," Evan said.

"But you certainly succeeded," Kirk whispered.

Anton and the other girls seemed to relax, happy that a nuclear meltdown had been averted. Anton cajoled Xandra for a few more minutes, making an exaggerated effort to promote the outfits from Nastya's rack. When it looked like Xandra would no longer be a problem, Anton pushed the individual racks behind each girl at her station.

Evan sat back in her place and pulled the hair rollers from the top of her head. Her brilliant red tresses cascaded down in wide coils. Her personal hairdresser jumped to her side and began spraying her hair for volume.

Anton shooed the little man away and stood behind Evan. He pulled the neckline of her robe open and settled his hands on her bare shoulders. Evan knew this move and quickly clasped the robe front closed to avoid giving Anton too much inspiration.

His fingers caressed her neck for a second, and then he leaned his lips close to her ear. "Thank you for saying what you did back there," he whispered, staring at her reflection in the mirror. "Xandra can be cruel, but I don't want you to take what she said to heart."

Evan appreciated his words but despised the touch of his fingers on her skin. She wrapped the fleece robe more tightly closed. "Maybe she's just afraid of being replaced."

He took a step back, as though he was contemplating something important. Evan noticed that he didn't seem to be insulted by her subtle rejection, merely perplexed.

She wanted to right any misunderstanding quickly. She turned her head to smile at him over her shoulder. "I just can't wait to get ready and get out there on that runway. Modeling for your buyers is gonna be so much fun!"

Anton beamed. He motioned for the little dresser to resume the hair teasing. Evan winked as he paced to the middle of the dressing room.

He clapped his hands for attention. "My muses, you all look marvelous. Make me proud tonight." He returned the wink and mouthed the word beautiful to her.

"Is everything all right now?" Kirk asked her.

She winced as the dresser pulled and raked at her hair. "Everything is just wonderful," she said.

After several more minutes of teasing, spraying, and pinning her hair, the dresser picked up his bag and gestured toward the clothes rack. The short man barked at her in a language she couldn't quite recognize, and Kirk translated efficiently. He told her that her little friend spoke Catalan, and explained that it was like a cousin of both French and Spanish.

"He wants you to get out of his way," he said.

Evan nodded at the man and took a step away from her dressing table. As she did, he swooped in and pitched all of his brushes, combs, and accessories into his satchel. He retrieved a small cloth from the kit and began wiping the vanity area until it sparkled. Evan saw the other dressers go through this same routine with the rest of the muses.

She turned to her clothes rack and began surveying her wardrobe. She took a quick inventory of the clothes on her rack for Kirk. Tatiana and Nastya worked through theirs as well, examining the different pieces and inspecting the accessories. They seemed thrilled with their new attire. Evan wondered why Xandra was so angry about switching dresses, and then she picked up the last gown on her rack. White silk chiffon with a blue-white lace bodice. "It's a bridal gown," she whispered.

"Xandra is planning to marry Anton?" Kirk asked.

Evan coughed, amused at his assumption. "No," she whispered under her breath. "A bridal gown is a signature piece of a designer's collection."

Kirk whispered. "Oh. Reserved to be worn only by your best model."

"Mmhmm." Evan fondled the silk between her fingertips. "I gotta fix this."

Evan inhaled a deep breath, grabbed her rolling rack, and dragged it across the room to Xandra's station. She took advantage of the squeal that the rack wheels made and said, "I don't want her to think I'm usurping her crown."

"Do what you gotta do," Kirk said.

"What are you doing?" Xandra asked.

Evan held her palms up and shrugged. "I shouldn't have accepted your wardrobe, Xandra. You are Anton's top muse. You should be wearing the signature pieces."

Again, the other women stopped their chatter and stared.

Xandra raised her chin. "What do you suggest?"

"Just let me wear Nastya's. You can have your pieces back. You will be dressed just as Anton envisioned." Evan nudged her dress frame in Xandra's direction.

"And you think that I will just do what you say? Do you think that Anton will not mind? He is the designer, not you." Xandra's tone was dry and bitter.

"I just thought," Evan began. "This was what he planned from the beginning. I don't think he'll be angry." She let herself appear flustered, hoping for Xandra to initiate the next move. "Let's face it; these pieces will look much prettier on you than on me."

Xandra surveyed the faces of the other women, especially Nastya's. She accepted Evan's offer with the slightest curve on her lips. She pushed the other rack away, and Evan wheeled it back to her station.

"You're taking some chances, making these kinds of decisions." Kirk's voice had a warning tone. "Don't you think this will make Hrevic angry?"

Evan smiled at the other girls. "Don't care," she whispered through her teeth.

"What did you say?" Tatiana asked.

Evan grinned broadly. "I sure do like my hair."

Tatiana laughed. "It does look wonderful. Your little worker is talented."

Evan's dresser nodded to both women in appreciation for the comments. "Gracies," he said.

"What is your name?" Evan inquired. With a little coaching from Kirk, she asked again. "El nom?"

He smiled and patted his chest. "Peter."

Evan squeezed his hand and then pointed to herself. "I'm Eve."

Peter nodded and plucked the first dress from the rod and removed the pouch of accouterments from the hanger. He carefully laid out the necklace, earrings, and bracelets under the vanity lights. Evan dropped her robe and stepped into the navy-blue frock. Peter circled his finger, and Evan turned away from him. He tried to raise the zipper, but it slowed halfway up the back.

"No," he said and lowered the zipper again.

Evan raised her finger and removed the dress. She turned her back and pointed to the hooks on her long-line bra. "Tighter," she said.

He moved the hooks from the last position to the first, cinching her waist at least an inch smaller. Once all the hooks were adjusted, they tried the dress again, and the zipper slipped in place easily. She turned for Peter to inspect. The dress was short, well above her knees, with a tight bodice over a knife-pleated skirt. Instead of sleeves, a stiff ruffle fit over each shoulder like butterfly wings. Peter nodded. This was going to work.

Evan smiled at him, and they shared a look of relief. She studied her reflection in the mirror and reached up to her ears. "Good-bye, my beautiful earrings," she said.

"Take care," Kirk whispered.

Evan dropped the pair of small platinum hoops into a shallow crystal bowl on the dressing table, a little sad to lose her Big Brother.

Peter draped a choker of yellow gemstones around her throat and secured the piece at the back of her neck. He handed her the coordinating earrings, and she put them on.

Peter began a long series of instructions, complete with hand motions and wildly twitching eyebrows. Evan picked out approximately four words that she thought she understood.

Nastya noticed the confusion on her face. "He's telling you to come straight back to your place after each trip. He will have everything ready for you here. He says you should run so that you will have plenty of time."

Evan nodded to Peter. "Gracies."

Nastya smiled. "Do not be so nervous, Eve. You look good in this dress. The blue is right with your hair. Very red-white-and-blue American."

Evan smoothed the dress at her sides. "Maybe I should have tried all of these on first, to make sure I could fit."

Nastya tugged at the hem of Evan's skirt. "If you can wear this one, you'll be fine with the others." She adjusted the straps on her own floral chiffon sundress. "We are all going to be a little bit tight in our clothes tonight. The buyers will like the narrow waists and overflowing bosoms."

Evan laughed. "Anton should sell every piece."

"You are brave, you know?" Nastya said.

"How do you mean?"

"Changing Anton's orders like that." Nastya shook her mane of gold curls as she looked in the mirror.

"Will he be mad? I didn't want to make him mad. I just didn't want to hurt Xandra's feelings." Evan studied Nastya's expression carefully. No perceptible change.

"He might be angry at first," Nastya answered. "If he does well with the buyers, everything will be all right. And he likes you."

Evan smiled. "I like all y'all, too."

Nastya laughed. "You try too hard with Xandra," she whispered. "Xandra is certain that Anton will be furious with you about this. That's why she agreed to exchange clothes. She doesn't care what she wears, you know."

"Oh, I'm sure you must be mistaken," Evan said. "We all just want the show to be a success."

The hallway door pushed open and in rolled a cart with a tray of champagne flutes filled with the requisite mineral water, a spread of raw vegetables, and a bowl of ice. The women barely looked up until a familiar, but hoarse, voice chimed.

"You weren't going to come see me before the show?" Olga asked. "I have good luck kisses for each of you."

The muses surrounded their petite friend and bathed her in smiles and air-kisses. Evan examined her closely. Olga's eye socket still showed the bruise under a generous layer of make-up. She wore a long-sleeved tee shirt and a scarf around her neck, though the room was warm. Evan suspected that under the sleeves her arms would show grabber bruises that the hospital snapshot didn't include.

Olga looked at each of the women in their gowns. "You are all beautiful." She took a step to Evan. "And aren't you lovely? I am so happy that you could come and take my place tonight." She gestured to her face. "I couldn't model with a face like this."

Evan tilted her head, sympathetic to Olga, but furious with the man who did this to her. "Anton told me that you had an accident. It doesn't really look too bad, though."

"You are kind. I was stupid. I was not looking ahead of myself and walked into the side of the door. Without my make-up, I look like a blue whale." Olga seemed to over-explain.

Evan sighed. 'I walked into a door' is the universal translation for 'a cowardly jerk punched me in the face' "I hope you feel better soon," Evan said. She wondered if the other girls knew about Olga's other injuries.

Olga kissed her cheek. "Do a good job tonight," she whispered. "We can model together in the next show."

"Bless your heart," Evan said with a winsome dip in her voice. "Y'all are all so nice."

After a few minutes of munching on carrot sticks and ice chips, the muses took their places at the draped door. From her position at the front of the line, Xandra coached.

"Do not be nervous. Just do what you do best. If a buyer makes eye contact, you may smile, but not too much. And remember to keep your mouth closed. An open mouth makes you look stupid." Xandra nodded to the others. "Do not get out of order. This is important."

Evan stood tall, pushing her shoulders back. "I just hope I don't take a tumble in these heels."

Nastya squeezed her elbow. "You must keep your chin parallel to the catwalk and lift your knees slightly with each step, like a march. That will keep your toes and your heels from catching on the rug."

"You're just so smart," Evan said.

Xandra glared. "No more talking. It is time."

The deep-thumping music began playing in the gallery, and the room lights went dark. For a split second, Evan flashed back to the private show for Anton. Her skin crawled. Focus, girl. She pulled herself back into the moment.

Peeking from behind the drape, Evan scanned the room. A row of stage lights on both sides of the runway shone, and a series of spots centered overhead cast a brilliant glow on the whole catwalk. A fog machine puffed at the draped entrance, cueing the first model.

Xandra stepped into the room, and the small crowd of buyers cheered. She made her way to the other end, smiling at Anton as she turned. Evan watched from out of sight, wondering about his reaction to the adjustment to his line-up. He smiled at his blonde, and she strode back to the velvet curtain.

Evan stepped out confidently and started her first walk. Her fingertips caught the fullness of her skirt, causing it bounce as she walked. The buyers grinned as they saw the potential. She offered just enough twirl at the foot of the platform and remembered to smile at Anton. She noticed that his broad smile was beginning to wane.

He just realized what happened. *Good.* She winked and walked back.

Behind the curtain, the dressing room became a madhouse. Peter leaped to her side as soon as she cleared the other women, and began unzipping and tugging as Evan raced back to her station. In less than a minute, she wore another outfit, complete with all new accessories. This one was a slim green gown with a flounced hem. *Great, now a mermaid.* She got back in line with at least ten seconds to spare before her next trip down and back.

Evan watched Anton's expression change a little each time she walked. The buyers in the room all beamed enthusiastically with each new ensemble. Anton nodded with pride at each one but offered only a cold stare to Evan at her sixth presentation.

"One last gown," she chirped to Peter as he shifted the pink sequined bodice into place. Pink is not usually the best color for a redhead, but Evan was determined to make it work. Peter layered pearls around her neck and clipped emeralds on her earlobes. His forehead glistened with perspiration. His smile grew weaker, and exhaustion crept into his eyes. "This is it."

She stood at the curtain and took a deep breath. Xandra was just making her way back with an icy look of determination in her eyes. Xandra still had the bridal gown to model before the show ended.

Evan strutted to the end of the catwalk and shifted her hips. She made one last attempt to evoke a smile from Anton by fluttering her lashes and pursing her perfectly curved lips. He raised his gaze over her head.

Evan lingered at the end for an extra second. Someone caught her eye. Standing just to the side of Anton was Sergei Bershkov, grinning like a child in a toy store. Evan wanted to throw her shoes at him but decided to finish her job instead. *Time for that later,* she hoped. She walked back to the curtain, turning behind it with a flourish. She figured that if she was going to get a scolding, she might as well make it a good one.

She went back to her station where Peter waited with a kabuki brush loaded with mica dust. As soon as she sat down, he swirled the highlight powder over her cheekbones and across her neck and shoulders. He dabbed a rosy stain on her lips with his fingertip and showered her with another cloud of hairspray. Once finished, he pushed her back toward the curtain.

She was ready for her encore and then for the dessert on the terrace. Xandra was nearly back to the drape after her triumphal display as a beautiful bride. One by one the other muses joined her on the runway. The audience took to their feet and applauded.

Anton jumped to Xandra's side and kissed her cheek, obviously basking in the adulation. When the buyers finished their cheering, Anton instructed them to make their way downstairs to the terrace where cocktails and pastries awaited. They took turns pumping his hand in congratulations and then emptied the room.

Xandra gestured for the muses to wait on the catwalk for Anton's instructions.

"My darlings," he began. "You were marvelous, almost perfection." He straightened a ruffle on Maria's purple gown. "I want you all to attend to my guests in the garden. Mingle and say lovely things about me. About the clothes."

He nodded to Maria, Nastya, and Tatiana. He waved his hand to release them to the party, and they left the room in turn. He stared at Xandra and Evan with a stern, twisted grimace on his mouth. "And what did you two do?" His tone was sharp and menacing. "I thought that we had the wardrobes all settled."

Xandra fixed a pitiful expression on her face. "Eve insisted I switch with her. Maybe she could not fit into the gowns. I do not know. She refused to wear them."

Evan stood silent. Xandra fixed her lips into a thick pout. "The show was a success, I think," she said.

Anton slipped his index finger under the tip of her chin and glared into Xandra's eyes. "You may join the others downstairs."

She hesitated for a moment, but Anton asserted himself. "Go downstairs now."

Xandra left the room, and Evan swallowed her rising nerves. She waited for him to make the first move. He circled her, studying her body and attitude.

"Why would you disobey my specific instructions?" he asked.

She calculated her best response. "I wanted the show to be the best it possibly could be," she said softly. "Some of the gowns on Xandra's rack were very tight, while most of the clothes from Nastya's were more flowing. They fit better. They looked better. I wanted to show your designs in the best possible light." She let her chin drop. "I apologize for disobeying."

"What hand did Xandra really play in this exchange?" he asked her.

"None at all. It was my idea. I take full responsibility. Please don't blame her for my mistakes." Evan lowered her chin even more and fluttered her lashes.

Anton pressed his lips into a thin straight line and exhaled through his nose. A deep red flush rose in his cheeks. "You cannot ignore my instructions as though they are mere requests!" he yelled, only inches from her face. "You belong to me, now. You are not your own. You cannot do as you please!"

Evan blinked at his sudden fury. She watched him clench his fists until his knuckles turned white. She inched half a step back from him as he continued a series of concussive outbursts. She was ready to defend herself if this became physical, but she wasn't going to be the aggressor.

"I am the designer! I put the gowns in order for the show." With each statement, his volume rose, but Evan guessed from his hunched stance that he was more bark than bite. "I see them as they should be on your body. You cannot see this. You are the model. You walk. You turn. You smile. You do as I say!"

Evan expected him to at least shake a finger in her face, but he kept his hands clenched and at his side. Evan let her chest rise and fall beneath the pink sequins. She manufactured a tear in each eye, ready to release them with a well-timed blink. She waited for Anton's full attention before she coaxed her chin to quiver. "I'm so sorry, Anton. I'll never disobey again."

Anton slumped even more at Evan's submissive response. Not what he's accustomed to.

He seemed to calm his temper and reached for her hands. He rubbed tiny circles on the backs of her hands with his now-gentle thumbs. "I appreciate that you wanted to help make the show successful. That was a wonderful thought," he said. "But next time you must obey."

Evan made a little sniffing sound and let her gaze rise to meet his. "Does this mean you'll let me model for you again sometime?" she asked.

A slow smile crept across his lips. "Of course I will. You are my newest treasure, Eve."

"And you're not too mad at me?"

He shook his head. "Just disappointed that I didn't get to see you in that wedding gown."

Evan bit her bottom lip, aware of what her next move should be, but wishing for a better option. "Will you allow me to make it up to you?"

Anton grinned and squeezed her hand. "We should get down to the gardens. You can help sell my designs tonight. That will more than settle me." He started to lead her from the room.

Evan took two swift steps to position herself in front of him. She threw her arms around his neck and kissed him. His initial shock dissipated quickly, and he returned the kiss with a full-bodied embrace.

After several seconds their lips parted. "Now we really must get down there. The clients will ask where we've been, and I'm not a good liar," Anton explained.

Evan pushed her hair back from her face. "Maybe I shouldn't have done that?" She blinked innocently and shrugged.

"That was fine. Better than fine, cher. We will visit with our guests now and talk about this later. But do not regret this kiss," he said. "There will be many more."

Evan took his hand and followed him down the hall and to the head of the stairway. Before they descended, he motioned for her to take her place in front of him. She tossed him a questioning glance as she released his hand. "You're coming too?

"I am right behind you. Let's not show too much affection in front of the other girls," he admonished. "We should celebrate the show tonight."

Evan floated down the steps and into the fiery glare of Xandra. "What do they say about a woman scorned?" she whispered to herself.

CHAPTER TWENTY-ONE

Rowan Kirk sat at the dinette table with one eye on his notebook computer and one eye on his work. He was busy gluing a short piece of fiber-optic material to a black curve of wire. His left knee bounced in a rapid, nervous pattern of dots and dashes. He didn't like the situation. He was supposed to be at Evan's side. Well, in Evan's ear. That's where he preferred to be. That's where he was comfortable.

Hedge paced and checked his watch several times each minute. "I can't believe she took out her earrings. How are we supposed to keep an eye on her?"

Kirk nodded to his monitor. He had just witnessed his partner kissing Anton Hrevic, and now she was following him down the hall to join the other women. "Eyes we have. Ears, not-so-much."

Hedge cleared his throat. "You know what I mean."

Kirk grimaced. He was still replaying his argument with Hedge over in his mind. Hedge Parker was one of his oldest friends. He didn't like these kinds of confrontations. He especially didn't like being dressed down by Evan. Fieldwork. Just put me back at a desk. But then there's Evan. She needed him. He focused on the job at hand. "When I'm done with these, we won't have this problem again. I hope."

Hedge stopped his march and sat down across from Kirk. He pointed at the arrangement of curved wires in front of him. "What is all this?"

Kirk laid the one in his hand alongside the other nine identical curves. "These are the pieces of my latest invention for communication with Evan. Well, the latest one that I've been able to get materials for." He picked up the first wire and carefully handed it to Hedge. "Be careful. The adhesive is still tacky."

Hedge took it and examined it with squinted eyes. "Is this what I think it is?"

Kirk shrugged, glancing down at the monitor. Evan was smiling at one of Hrevic's guests. *She's okay. No problem.* "Do you think it's an underwire for a bra?"

Hedge placed it back on the table with the others. "Yeah."

Kirk laughed. "That's what it is. I made them of carbon fiber. They won't bend or break, and they have curved edges, so they won't pinch, either."

Hedge shook his head. "And how…?"

"I attached a micro-receiver and transmitter at each end with a wire that connects and relays all sound information. I have them set up to sync with her ear receiver. This will keep her connected to us even if she doesn't have the dress or the earrings. I can replace all of her underwires with these. If she gives me the go-ahead." Kirk smiled and sighed. "Of course, it still won't help us if she's nude, but it's the best I can do for now." He shot a quick glance back at Hedge. He didn't want to appear flippant when regarding Evan's nudity. "Not that she's going to be nude very often. I mean, on the job." Hedge hadn't seemed to hear him.

Hedge pressed his lips into a long thin line and sat back in his chair. "I just wish we'd hear something. Can you tell anything from the video feed?"

"Not much," Kirk explained, turning the monitor to face Hedge. "The fashion show is over, and the guests are returning to the garden again, I think. The tables are all set for cocktails and dessert."

"How'd she do in the show?"

Kirk nodded. "Perfect." His mind wandered back to the first time he saw her in Milan. A genuine smile crept across his lips and up into the corners of his eyes.

"What?" Hedge asked.

"Just remembering when I met her."

"Oh yeah?" Hedge propped his elbow on the edge of the table. "What was she like?"

Kirk positioned the computer where both men had a good view of the feed. He scratched his jaw and began. "I was on a lead in Milan, chasing a guy all over Europe. He was trading drugs and guns and who-knows-what with every man on our most wanted list. I tracked him down to this dump of a hotel in the worst part of town. It should have been a quick tag job for me. Another team was going to trace his moves, find his boss, and pick him up later."

"Basic assignment," Hedge said.

"Yeah, so I went up to his room, dressed as a courier, which we were told he was expecting. But when I get there, his door is wide open. I go in. Who knows, right? I find him on the floor of his closet, his throat slashed from ear-to-ear. He's been dead for a half an hour. I had to watch my step if you know what I mean."

Hedge cringed at the picture in his head. "What did you do next?"

Kirk continued. "I left. I called in, and my contact told me to head to the embassy to meet with the other team. They were having some kind of paperwork problem, so I waited. I parked myself at a free desk and did a little bit of work while the rest got sorted out upstairs. That's when Evan walked in."

"And?" Hedge leaned forward a fraction of an inch.

"Looking like a glowing marble sculpture, with those eyes that defy human proportion, she walked right up to my little station and asked if I could help her. She shook like a leaf, and sat down across the desk from me before I had the chance to answer her." Kirk saw her face in his mind's eye. "Just a kid."

"What brought her to the embassy?" Hedge asked.

"Me. She'd followed me from my guy's hotel to the embassy. It turns out that she was the courier he was expecting."

"What?" Hedge scoffed. "Evan worked for a drug dealer?"

Kirk shook his head. "Not exactly. She told me about how she was a student, and how she was in this study exchange. Her modeling agent had found her a job through their Milan office, but right off the bat she knew that something didn't feel right."

Hedge nodded. "She has that natural gut instinct."

Kirk agreed. "Her boss asked her to take a package to my suspect. He gave her the address of the hotel and sent her on her way. When she got there, she couldn't go in. She knew something was wrong. She waited across the street for nearly an hour, watching people come and go. She saw a man go into the hotel and come out shortly before I arrived. She said that he changed clothes but had blood specks on both his arms. When she saw me go in and then come right back out, she followed me. Tailed me all the way to the embassy without me knowing."

"Impressive."

Kirk grinned. "Very impressive. She waited for me to settle at my desk before she approached me. After she told me her story, she handed over the package of cocaine and asked if I wanted her to describe the man that she believed killed my suspect."

"Wow," Hedge said. "Quite the first impression."

"I haven't gotten over it. At first, she was scared. Who wouldn't be? But when we caught the killer, she was all in. Wanted to help us get the next man up the ladder." Kirk turned to study the monitor. "Oh, great."

"What's wrong?" Hedge asked.

"Look who's enjoying the party." Kirk pointed to a man talking to Nastya.

"I can't make him out. Who is that?" Hedge stared at the picture, but the image was in fuzzy shades of gray. "Why is this so grainy? Your cameras are better than this."

"Mine are. We're piggy-backing on Hrevic's system, remember?" Kirk twirled his finger, waiting for the man in question to face the camera again. "If he'll turn around again, you'll see that it's our friend, Sergei Bershkov."

Hedge studied the video feed closely. "He's talking to Nastya and someone else. Someone across the table from him. Can we get another angle?"

Kirk nodded. "Give me a second. I'll grab the view from the camera on the doors." He typed in a code, and the picture changed. "Crap. It's Hrevic, and he's showing off Evan like a prize."

"Maybe this is a good thing. Maybe she's working out a way to investigate that slime." Hedge shrugged.

"It won't be a good thing if she doesn't have back up." Kirk shook his head and talked to his computer as if Evan could hear him. "Don't go with him if I'm not in your ear, Evan." He worried and willed her to be cautious.

"We just talked about her instincts." Hedge patted his shoulder. "She won't do anything stupid, right?"

Kirk sighed. "I haven't told you how stubborn she can be when she's on a scent, have I?"

"Where are Brawn and Ramos? Could they tail her if she leaves with him?"

Kirk brought up another screen with a map of Paris, punctuated with two red blips. "They're still making rounds to all of the locations we have on our suspect locations. They've left Hrevic's mansion, and they're on their way to Bershkov's apartment. Do you want me to call them in or send them back to Hrevic's?"

"No, let's just keep watch on Evan and make sure that she doesn't need us for anything else. Where is she now?"

Kirk flipped back to Hrevic's soiree and found the right camera feed. "It's okay, she's with the rest of the girls, and it looks like things are winding down."

Hedge nodded again. "Good. Good girl. I'm going to get my gear. She wanted me there at midnight."

"I'll check in with her as soon as she gets her earrings back." Kirk tapped at his keys. "It looks like another long night."

CHAPTER TWENTY-TWO

Evan meandered between tables in the garden as the buyers and guests ate Crème Brulee and chatted about the designs. Champagne poured everywhere she looked, but not a single glass waited for her. This was a business show. She modeled the merchandise. She was not to be seen eating or drinking anything by anyone.

She felt slimmer by the second. Her stomach growled, but the sound was muffled by the layers of pink sequins and chiffon.

Her ears sparkled with emerald chandelier drop earrings. A pendant of brilliant green surrounded by diamonds lay in the notch between her collarbones.

"A red-head in pink," she heard a woman with a raised brow whisper.

"But she looks stunning," the man at her elbow replied.

Evan smiled and paused at his side. He reached out with a discerning finger and examined the ruffles at her waist.

"High-quality silk," the man said with a nod. "And the paillettes seem secure." He regarded Evan. "What is your name?"

"Eve, sir."

"Eve, does this gown fit comfortably? Do the sequins bother?" he inquired.

Evan smiled. His voice sounded very proper and stuffy, but his eyes appeared kind and sincere. "No, sir," she answered. "I mean, yes, it's quite comfortable. No, they don't bother at all."

"You're American," the woman said, with a very French accent. "How charming. Lucas, dear, add this pink one to the list. It's a good transition piece." She grinned at Evan and dismissed her with a wave of her hand. "Merci."

Evan nodded and strolled to the next table. Nastya winked at her from the other side. "And this is Anton's newest muse, Eve," she said, gesturing to Evan.

The man with whom she spoke turned to face her. It was Sergei Bershkov. Evan swallowed hard and forced a smile.

"Good evening," she said, dipping her chin. "Are you enjoying yourself?"

His Russian accent fell heavy in the delicate twilight. "I am. I saw you last night at the party. You did not stay long, no?"

"No, sir. I had an engagement to attend to," she said with a sigh.

"Maybe next time I can be your engagement?" He pushed his chair from the table and patted his knees.

Evan hoped his open lap was not intended to be an invitation. She fluttered her lashes and tossed a glance over her shoulder. Anton was nearby and overheard Bershkov.

He slipped up alongside Evan and wrapped his arm around her waist. "You met my prize, Sergei. Eve is a special one. New to my fold." Anton kept his voice low as if it was a cue to Bershkov.

Sergei nodded and lowered his tone. "Anton, she reminds me of my Trina, you know?"

"Yes, I notice a likeness, now that you mention it." Anton looked into Evan's eyes. "Sergei's wife, Trina, passed away many years ago. He's a very lonely man these days."

Evan wondered what she was supposed to say to this. She looked at Sergei and back to Anton. "Will you be at Mr. Hrevic's next party?"

Sergei spread a broad grin over his lips. "I like her very much."

"Why don't you take her home with you tonight?" Xandra suggested as she approached from behind the average-looking man. "Anton owes you a favor. It is good for business."

Anton furrowed his brow and shot Xandra a scowl. "Eve has had a very long day already, Xandra. Sergei can certainly wait another day or two."

Sergei shook his head. "I will make sure that she gets a good night's sleep."

Evan blinked, trying to maintain her best poker face. She turned her head and leaned her lips close to Anton's ear. "May I talk with you for just a tiny minute?" she whispered sweetly, employing her drawl judiciously.

"Just a moment, Sergei," he said, nodding to Evan. "Excuse us, s'il vous plait."

Evan took Anton's arm, and they walked casually to the corner of the porch.

"Anton, thank you for looking after me like that," she said. She tilted her face to within inches of his. "But is Xandra right about Sergei? Do you owe him a favor?"

Anton appeared frustrated. "Mr. Bershkov does a great many things for me, but he doesn't get to order me around. This is a show for my buyers, not a party. I cannot have him taking you home."

"Is it because of me, or because of the show?" she said, with a pouty lip. "What do you mean?"

"Are you still angry about before?" Evan didn't have a concrete plan in mind, but the idea of gathering information about Bershkov had her excited.

"I am not angry with you, Eve," he said. "I just need you here for the evening."

She nodded. "I understand." She noticed that his eyes focused on her mouth, so she licked her lips and pursed them. "Would it be helpful to you if I met him later? Nobody else at the party would have to know about it."

Anton quickly raised his gaze to her eyes. "You worry about helping me?"

She smiled. "Of course, Anton, I'll do anything for you." She placed her hand on his shoulder and offered a demure giggle.

He shot a glance to Sergei, and then looked around the party. "I will talk to him. I will let you know in a short while. We still have guests to greet." His tone was business-like.

Evan decided not to push the subject further. She nodded. "You're the boss."

As if that was all the affirmation necessary, Anton made a discreet signal to Sergei with his hand, and the two men adjourned to the corner of the terrace to talk.

Evan made another circuit of the buyers and joined the other girls near the doors as the event approached a close. Xandra explained that they should stand at the exits to ensure that all of the guests got one last look at what they might purchase before retiring for the night.

"Bonne nuit," Evan said as the company filtered through the doors and away from the party.

Nastya squeezed Evan's hand as the last visitor disappeared. "Wasn't that wonderful? I think every ensemble was sold tonight."

Xandra nodded. "Yes, Anton should be pleased. Now we should all go upstairs and get everything ready to go back to the studio. He will come up for congratulations shortly."

They all climbed the stairs to the dressing room where Peter and the other dressers waited to help them out of their couture and back into their robes. As quickly as she removed the designer jewelry, Evan put on her own earrings, eager to reconnect with her team.

Before she could get any kind of word to them, though; Anton strolled into the room. He beamed like a proud papa, hugging and kissing each girl, and shaking hands with each of the dressers.

"You have all made me very happy tonight," he said. He positioned himself between Xandra and Evan to address his harem. "Every piece of my collection sold. Every single piece. This is the first time that has happened in one night."

The girls all cheered and hugged each other.

Anton swept his arms out in a broad, inclusive gesture. "I thank you all for your work. And I want to especially thank Eve for stepping into Olga's shoes, quite literally, tonight. I ask that you all welcome her as your new sister-muse."

He took Evan's hand in his and raised it overhead in a show of triumph. The other models clapped and offered smiles, but Xandra just stood silently with a placid expression in her eyes.

"Congratulations, Evan," Kirk finally whispered in her ear. "You're the belle of the ball, I suppose."

Evan thanked her new circle of friends and spoke cryptically to Kirk. "I'm just so excited about everything. I feel like this night might not ever end."

She looked at Anton with raised brows, and he nodded back. "Ladies, I want you all to get a good night's sleep tonight. I have a little business to discuss with Eve for now." His tone was professional and firm. He gestured for the others to hurry on to their rooms and then turned back to Evan. "Get dressed and meet me down in my office in five minutes."

"Yes, sir," she answered. As he left the dressing room, she went back to her station, changed into her day clothes, and brushed out her hair. She wanted to talk to Kirk, but Peter still waited on her hand-and-foot until she had everything back in place and was ready to leave.

"Is something going on?" Kirk asked. "Hedge is just leaving to come get you."

"Wait!" she almost shouted. Peter froze in place as he held the door open for her.

"Qué es?" he asked.

"What is it?" Kirk asked as well.

Realizing her abruptness, Evan took a long deep breath. "I know that soon I'll be in my own dress all by myself, but I just want one more look at this dazzling room before I head down to talk to Mr. Hrevic." After a few seconds of Peter's bewildered expression, she kissed him on the cheek. "Merci, Peter. Gracies."

Evan whispered under her breath as she bounced down the stairs. "Tell Hedge to bring the dress. This night might not be over."

"Roger that."

CHAPTER TWENTY-THREE

Anton and Evan waited outside at the front door for Hedge to arrive. Evan inhaled a deep breath of the cool night air. *Refreshing to be outdoors. Ready to really work.*

"Is there anything special I should know about Mr. Bershkov before I see him tonight?" Evan asked, fishing for information about the man.

Anton grazed his fingertip up and down the back of her arm. "You just be yourself, and he will adore you."

She smiled and leaned closer to him. "What about his wife? How did he lose her? He said that I reminded him of her."

"Yes, Trina had red hair like yours. That is really where the similarities end, though. She died after an illness, I believe."

"They were married for a long time?" she asked, noticing Hedge approaching.

"A few years. I am not sure about that." He turned to greet Hedge with a handshake. "Mr. Hedger, good evening. Eve did very well in the show. So well, in fact, that I have given her another assignment for the evening. I hope you won't mind."

Hedge shook his hand firmly. "If she's up to it, I'm good."

Anton grimaced and turned to face Evan, though he spoke to both of them. "Mr. Bershkov is a very important associate of mine. He helps me take care of a great deal of my business. He is expecting you to spend the entire night with him. I don't want you to leave his side until he takes you home. Do you understand?"

Evan nodded. "I understand."

Hedge agreed as well. "I won't be picking her up. Got it."

"And there is no need to snap pictures, either," Anton added, regarding Hedge. "Bershkov is not that kind of friend."

Hedge nodded again.

"He might take you for drinks," Anton suggested. "Be careful not to drink too much."

Evan patted Anton's chest. "Don't you worry about me. I know how to take care of myself."

Anton shot a knowing glance to Hedge. "Of that, I am perfectly aware."

Evan kissed Anton quickly on the mouth and shrugged her shoulders with coy flirtation. "I'll call you tomorrow and let you know how I am."

Hedge and Evan waved as Hrevic went inside and closed the door behind them. As they reached the black SUV, he opened the back-passenger door for her, and she hopped inside.

"Hi, Red," she said to her friend in the front seat, planting a kiss on the back of his head. "I sure missed you tonight."

"I missed you, too. Let's not do that again, okay?" Kirk gestured to the pile of folded clothes on the seat next to her. "I brought you something."

"Thanks a million," Evan said as Hedge pulled out into traffic. "Before I change, though, can we please stop somewhere and pick up something to eat? I'm starving."

Hedge handed her a paper bag from the front seat. "Thought of that, too. We got you an apple and peanut butter."

"And some milk to coat your stomach before this drinking binge you're about to go on," Kirk added. "Don't let him get you drunk, kid."

Evan bit into the apple with enthusiasm. "I won't even have a whole drink, not even if it's a margarita." She dipped her finger into the peanut butter and put the whole dollop into her mouth. "I love peanut butter," she said with sticky lips.

"Hang on, what?" Hedge said, staring straight ahead. He put his hand to his ear to steady his earbud. "Say again."

"Yeah. It's fine. I'm putting you on speaker," Hedge said, signaling Kirk to switch the reception. "What's going on?"

Brawn sounded worried. "I dropped Ramos back at Hrevic's house to make sure he wasn't having any late-night meetings with anyone else. I came back to the apartment to pick up a spare flashlight, and when I got here, the door was open a crack, and the dress was gone."

Kirk and Hedge exchanged concerned expressions. "The door was open?" they both asked.

"Yeah. Not much, maybe an inch. But it was open. I searched the flat, and nothing looked out of place, but I noticed that the dress wasn't here. Do you have it?" Brawn asked.

"We have it with us," Hedge answered. "We just picked up Evan, and now we're taking her to Bershkov's home. She has a date with him, and she needs the dress."

"Good. What do you want me to do? Should I stay here or pick up Teo or meet up with you?" Brawn asked.

Hedge raked his fingers through his hair and sighed. "Sweep the place for wires and make sure we haven't been compromised. The building is old, maybe the latch didn't catch when we left. Just be certain. After that, pick up Teo and let us know whether it's safe to return or if we need to find another hole."

"Yes, sir."

Evan wiped the peanut butter from her mouth and took a long draw on the bottle of milk, finishing it with a satisfied sigh. "How bad is this?" she asked.

Hedge shook his head. "I guess we'll see. You get changed. We're almost to Bershkov's house. Don't worry about the apartment right now. You keep your mind on what you need to do tonight."

Evan kicked off her shoes and started changing from her day dress to her black strapless. She trusted the men to keep their eyes on the road while she shimmied into the fashionable weapon and zipped herself up, but she watched the rearview mirror just the same.

"What exactly do you need from me, Red?" she asked.

"If you can get his hands flat on your dress, I should be able to scan his prints and measure the spread of his fingers."

Evan laughed. "I don't think that will be a problem."

Kirk nodded. "I know. From the measurements, I should be able to determine if he is the one who strangled Olga."

"Once you scan his hands, how long until you can feed me the results?"

"If it's close, it might take as long as an hour. A negative I'll know pretty quickly. What's your plan to occupy him all night?" Kirk shifted in his seat to face her.

"If he starts with drinks he won't be a problem at all. I have a little kicker in my purse that not only incapacitates but provides the subject with all sorts of wild hallucinations, the good kind." She laughed. "I just hope he's a heavy drinker. It takes about three cocktails before you can't taste the mickey."

Hedge nodded. "I doubt you'll have any trouble with that, either." He pulled up to the curb. "Redo your lipstick and check your bag to make sure you have everything you need."

Evan took a quick inventory of her clutch and spread a fresh coat of Pink Pearls over her lips. "I need my Springfield," she said after everything else was in place.

Hedge retrieved her sidearm and thigh holster from the console. "Anything else?" he asked as he gave Evan her weapon.

She snugged the strap to her leg and pulled the skirt down to cover the pistol. "I think I'm good to go."

Hedge faced her squarely. "Until we hear back from Brawn, we'll hang close behind you and Sergei. Just give Kirk a signal if you have any trouble or need us to step in."

Evan tugged on her earrings. "I got you right here," she said.

"Loud and clear," Kirk responded.

Evan took a second to summarize the plan for the evening. "Drinks, maybe dancing, whatever it takes to get his handprints. Then I bring him back home and tuck him into bed where he'll dream the night away. I'll search his place until I hear back from you about whether he stays in bed or goes into custody. If he stays, I'll wake him up in the morning with a home-cooked breakfast and have him bring me home."

Hedge raised his eyebrows. "What if he wants more than eggs for breakfast?"

Kirk shook off the suggestion. "He'll get a call from his office. No problem."

"Thank you, Red," Evan said, giving Kirk another kiss, this time on his cheek.

"Aren't we kissy tonight?" Hedge raised his brow.

Evan rolled her eyes. "You're just jealous because you didn't get one."

Hedge nodded. "That's probably it. Now get your butt out there."

Evan laughed and slid out of the black SUV. She looked up and down the quiet street and walked past the dark green sedan parked in front of the gate. She discreetly peeked inside.

"That's Sergei's car," Kirk whispered to her. "It looks like he is planning on taking you out for a nightcap, with it on the street like that."

"Good," she said, walking up to the intercom. She pressed the buzzer, and Sergei responded immediately.

"Hallo, Eve, I've been waiting for you," his Russian accent contained a bounce already. "Come up to the door."

"I'll be right there," she sang into the receiver.

A hum of electricity and a metallic clang alerted her that the gate would open. She pushed her way through and walked carefully up to the front door of the estate, navigating the uneven flagstone path with her stiletto heels. Sergei waited for her at the open wooden door with a broad grin. "I'm glad Anton said you could come."

Evan greeted him with a kiss on the cheek. "It's good to see you again, Mr. Bershkov."

"Please, you must call me Sergei."

"Of course," she replied. "Are we going out?"

Sergei pulled on his sports coat and closed the door behind him. "I know this wonderful little place. It's very dark and very quiet, but they make wonderful, wonderful martinis. Do you like martinis?"

Eve nodded and looped her hands around his arm. "It sounds wonderful."

They walked back to the gate, and Sergei was just about to open it when he stopped and turned to face her with his back against the iron barrier. "I want tonight to be fun, Eve." He placed his hands on her bare shoulders and moved his thumbs in small gentle circles at her throat.

"I hope it will be," she said, forcing an unnatural calm. She took his hands in hers and wrapped his arms around her body. She set his hands firmly on her waist and walked her fingers up to his chest. "I think we'll both have a good time."

He pulled her close, and she kissed him full on the mouth.

"Clean scan," Kirk whispered.

At that second Sergei's green sedan exploded into a ball of fire, sending a concussion blast in every direction. Sergei was thrown against Evan, and the two flew several feet before landing in his yard. Sergei's body shielded her from the explosion, and he lay heavily on top of her as she struggled to regain her senses. Shattered glass and twisted metal from both the car and the iron gate lay all around them.

All she could hear was a hollow ringing. She called out for Kirk, but she couldn't even hear her own voice. She realized that Sergei's hair was on fire. She pushed him off of her and rolled him in the grass to extinguish the flames. His eyes were wide open, and his face was misshapen. Blood ran from his nose, eyes, and mouth. She turned him to his side and saw that the back of his head was peppered with pellets of glass and shrapnel.

She kicked herself away from him and managed to get to her hands and knees before she vomited. The smells of burnt flesh and machine stung her nose and churned her stomach. She staggered to her feet just as Hedge appeared at her side.

She could see his lips moving, but couldn't hear anything but the ringing. He scooped her up and took her to the SUV. He sat her in the back seat and wrapped a lightweight blanket around her shoulders before he began examining her for injuries.

She watched as Kirk worked furiously at his computer. He talked to someone, but Evan was deaf to his voice. Hedge patted Kirk on the shoulder and ran back to Sergei's side to check out his situation. Kirk jumped out of his seat and came around to attend to Evan. He placed the little pieces of tape with wires at her wrists again and smiled to reassure her. He knew she couldn't hear, so he didn't try to speak. He took her right hand and examined her fingers, then moved to her left. He looked over her legs and feet and, apart from a few scratches on her ankles, was satisfied that her wounds were only superficial.

Kirk lifted her hair and looked at her neck and shoulders. He looked into her eyes and nodded. He opened a small bag from behind her seat and pulled out a white cloth which he used to wipe her face and arms and legs. Evan knew he was collecting specimens of blood and explosive residue for examination. He dropped the soiled cloth into a baggie and sealed it.

Evan let her gaze wander back to the ruined car. The flames were gone, now. So was Sergei. She swallowed hard. *What next?*

Kirk checked his computer monitor and gave her a quick "thumbs up" before removing the leads from her arms.

A few neighbors appeared in the dark street and began asking questions. Hedge had covered Sergei's body and directed attention back to the automobile. Evan watched both Kirk and Hedge explain to the bystanders that the car's engine had caught fire and that the authorities had been called. She realized that her hearing was returning when she recognized that both Kirk and Hedge were speaking fluent French.

She stayed in the car, shivering.

A large black van arrived on the scene, and four men with official black suits took statements from everyone on the street. Once each person offered their account, which was requested for their benefit more than for the investigation, the men in the suits sent them all home. In an efficient ninety minutes, the street was clear, and the men in the van collected Sergei's remains into a zippered black bag.

She watched the men talk to Hedge and Kirk in muffled, business tones. She filled her lungs with cool air and released it again slowly. Her throat rasped, and her ribcage ached. *That could have been me.*

A wrecker pulled up and soon the skeleton of the green sedan was piled up and hauled away. Evan knew that by sunrise, the yard and street would be clean, the gate would be replaced, and the house would appear as if nothing at all had happened.

Kirk returned to her side as Hedge finished up with the cleaning crew.

"Can you hear anything yet?" he asked.

Evan nodded. "Yes. My ears are ringing, but now I can hear a little over that."

Kirk patted her cheek gently with his palm. "Do you want me to ride back here with you?" he asked.

"No, I'll be okay. You stay up front with Hedge. He needs you right now." She squeezed his hand.

Hedge slapped Kirk on the back, tagging himself into the conversation. "I need you, too."

Evan tried to smile. "I'm not going anywhere."

"Good to know," Hedge said. He closed her car door and got back into the driver's seat. Kirk was in his place, checking in with Teo and Brawn.

"Teo says that he's good. Nobody coming or going at Hrevic's and the last light just went out," Kirk summarized. "We should probably swing by and pick up Ramos."

Hedge raised his chin and focused on the street. "And Brawn?"

"Brawn says he can't find anything out of place. No wires, no bugs. All he can figure is that the latch slipped. He thinks we can come back."

"What do you think?" Evan asked the two men with her.

"Hedge kept his gaze straight ahead. "I suppose if he's satisfied, we can go back to the flat."

"Was the bomb for Sergei or for me?"

Kirk sent a worried glance to Hedge, his expression asking the same question.

Hedge took a deep breath and swallowed before answering. "The other team is going to study the fragments to see who built the device. Once we know that, we should be able to determine who the intended victim was."

"Anton asked us not to take pictures. He said that Bershkov wasn't that kind of friend. Did he say that because he figured Bershkov would be dead? Do you think Anton intended to kill us both?" Evan's voice scratched its way out.

"We can't discount that idea," Hedge said, sounding as noncommittal as possible.

Evan's mind kicked into high gear as they approached Hrevic's estate. She reviewed every word that Hrevic had said to her earlier that night. Did she push too hard to see Sergei? Did he realize who she was? She couldn't think of anything that might make Anton want her dead.

"What's the plan?" she asked as Hedge pulled the car to the curb.

Hedge parked and turned in his seat to face her. He paused for a moment while Kirk gave the signal for Ramos to join them.

"I'm not much of a seat-of-the-pants-er, but we may need to play this one by ear for a while. Let's watch Anton for a reaction." Hedge waited as Teo got in the back seat next to Evan.

"I heard what happened," Teo said. "Are you okay?" he asked Evan.

"Yeah, I'm good."

"What did the blast look like? Was there a flash and then fire, or just a ball of flame, or was there smoke first?" Ramos' curiosity seemed to displace any etiquette.

Evan shook her head. "I didn't see the explosion. Sergei was standing between me and the car, and then I was knocked to the ground after that."

"Oh." He sounded disappointed.

Hedge preempted any more questions. "Kirk and I can give you our details when we get back to the flat."

"Great. Did Brawn give the all-clear?" Teo asked.

"We're good," Kirk said with a nod.

Hedge let a pleased look settle onto his face. "Do we have a feed on Hrevic's personal phone?"

Kirk brought up the appropriate program on his notebook. "Yes, I have both his private land line and his cell."

Hedge cleared his throat and said, in his best Russian tenor, "Do I sound enough like Sergei to fool Hrevic?"

The other three team members were impressed. "Yeah," Kirk replied.

"I need this to come from Sergei's number," Hedge instructed as he picked up his phone and handed it to Kirk.

"No problem."

After a minute Kirk handed the phone back. "All set."

Hedge punched in Hrevic's phone number. "I'm putting this on speaker for you all to hear. Just keep quiet, though." They nodded and watched from the parked car as a single light came on in the house.

"Bonsoir," Anton's groggy voice answered.

Hedge began. "Bonsoir, mon ami. This is Sergei. Did I wake you?"

Anton's voice showed no unusual reaction. "No, I was just about to get into bed, though. Que voulez-vous? What do you want?"

Hedge continued his impersonation. "I want to thank you for the lovely Eve. She is quite magnificent, is she not? Magnifique?" He raised his eyebrows and smiled at Evan.

"Yes, oui. Why are you calling me?" Hrevic's tone sounded more annoyed than surprised.

"I just dropped her back at her tiny apartment. Anton, you must really provide a better place for her than that."

Anton's manner changed as his agitation became more apparent. "Why did you take her back? I told her to stay with you all night. Elle ne peut pas suivre les instructions?"

"It is all right, my friend. She follows your instructions very well, indeed. It was I that had the trouble." Hedge nearly laughed out loud.

Anton calmed his attitude. "What do you mean?"

Hedge continued. "I received a call from my office. I have a family emergency back home in Russia," he said.

Kirk quickly scanned Sergei's file and mouthed the words *brother in Kasimov* while pointing to the file. Hedge nodded.

"My brother in Kasimov has suffered a heart attack. The doctors do not know if he will survive. I must go to him right away." Hedge squinted to get a better look at Sergei's information.

"I am sorry, Sergei. Is this your older brother?" Hrevic asked.

Hedge scrambled. "No, Vladimir is still in Lyuban. Ilia is the one who is sick."

Kirk nodded with encouragement.

"Je suis désolé," Anton apologized again. "Are you leaving tonight?"

"Yes, I have a plane waiting now. I hope to be back in Paris next week, but I won't know for certain until I see my brother," Hedge said, still maintaining the Russian accent.

"Call me when you know, then," Hrevic said. "And give your brother my best wishes."

"Thank you, Anton. Bonne nuit."

"Good night," Anton said and disconnected.

Evan and Teo both exhaled in relief, but Kirk and Hedge kept their eyes on the notebook and the mansion, respectively.

"He sounded okay," Evan whispered.

"We'll wait for a few minutes. Let's see if he makes a call to anyone else," Hedge suggested.

After a few seconds, Hrevic's light went out again. The house was completely dark. Kirk shook his head. "No calls on the landline or his cell. Nothing on the main house line, either."

Hedge let a few more seconds tick away. "I think it's safe to say that he's down for the night. He started the SUV, but before he pulled out, he turned back to face Evan. "His reaction was minimal. He wasn't surprised to be talking to Sergei. He didn't act as though he thought he should be dead. If I were placing bets, I'd wager that Anton was not the one who set the bomb."

Evan couldn't decide whether to be relieved or not. "If Anton didn't plant the bomb, then chances are it wasn't meant for me." Her ears still carried a hollow ringing. "Is that the general consensus?"

Kirk smiled and nodded. "That's what I would say."

Teo patted her shoulder. "Car bombs on lonely streets are pretty specific. The owner is almost always the intended target. This is my expertise."

Evan pushed a grin over her lips. She felt overwhelmed with trepidation, not only about the explosion and Sergei's death but also about returning to the apartment.

"Are we sure that the flat is secure?" she asked as casually as she could manage.

Teo tapped Hedge on the shoulder as they reached the front of their building. "Why don't you let me go up first and check things out?"

Hedge parked and turned to the demolitions expert. "That would be great, Ramos. We'll make the block and then be right up."

"No," Evan insisted. Her voice sounded louder than she expected. "The dress is our best tool for sweeping the place for wires, isn't it?"

Kirk raised his eyebrows. "She's right, Hedge."

"You need to take it easy, Evan," Hedge said.

"I need to do my job," she asserted, gathering her things from around the seat. "Let's get up there and see if we get to stay."

All four of them carried their gear inside, riding the dubious elevator to the third floor. Brawn waited for them at the door.

"I pulled the knob and checked it over. It looks like the spring mechanism gave out. It's about a hundred years old." Brawn gestured to the handset with the screwdriver in his hand. "I heard that you all had a bit of a blow-out. Glad you made it back in one piece."

Evan began her stroll through the tiny habitat. Kirk followed her, adjusting the settings on his notebook. "Sergei wasn't so lucky," she said as she passed in front of Brawn.

Hedge regarded the door. "Did you check the room for prints?"

Brawn nodded. "I took several samples. They're in that file on the table. I figured Kirk could scan them into his little reader thing."

Kirk flipped open the file. "Good job." He placed his computer on the table and began feeding the samples into his scanner.

Evan made a slow and precise trip around the bedroom and the bath, still searching for stray signals. When she returned to the main living room, Kirk shrugged. "I haven't picked up anything."

Hedge closed the main door and secured the bolt. "Prints?"

Kirk shook his head. "Just ours. And there's no sign of anybody wiping anything clean." He scratched his head and twisted his lips. "I guess we didn't pull it tight enough when we left."

Hedge growled. "This is ridiculous."

Evan sunk into the couch and stretched her feet out in front of her on the small coffee table.

Brawn sat down next to her. "Tell me all about it."

Evan sighed and shook her head. "I can't." Her voice trembled hoarsely.

"Sure you can," Brawn said. "Start where you were naked in the back seat."

Evan cracked a smile and elbowed Brawn in the chest. "I wasn't naked in the back seat."

Brawn shrugged. "Sorry. I misunderstood when they told me you changed clothes in the car. My mistake. So start from whenever was the last time you were naked. Don't leave anything out."

She sighed and released an exhausted laugh. "You've been through workplace training, right?"

"Right."

Evan dipped her chin. "I know we work in very different conditions, but you make a lot of suggestive comments. Maybe some find it endearing, but…."

"But not you. Got it." Brawn's voice was clipped.

Hedge gestured to the bedroom door. "Go clean up and let me know when you're ready. Kirk and I will come in, and we'll talk a few things through, and then you can get some rest." He gave Evan just a few seconds and then reached down for her hand. "Come on, I don't want to be up all night, either."

Brawn made a sweeping motion as Evan walked to the bedroom. "You all take care of the grown-up business while us kids camp out in here."

Evan tilted her head to address his sarcasm. "It's not like that, Jarrett."

"No, I get it," Brawn snipped. "I understand. Don't let the left hand know what the right hand is doing. What I don't get is why I'm always the left hand."

"Look," Hedge said with authority. "We've all had a tough night. We need to work out a plan to get Evan back into Hrevic's house. We need to make sure that nobody is onto us, or trying to kill us. Any of us. If you have any suggestions, I'm open."

Kirk and Teo pulled snacks from the refrigerator while listening to Hedge.

Brawn tucked his chin.

Hedge nodded. "I thought so." He waved Evan into the bedroom. "We four can go over our details now while she's unwinding."

Evan closed the bedroom door. The ringing in her ears still crowded the sounds from the other room. She didn't care. She unzipped her dress and changed into her yoga pants and a tee shirt. She pulled her brush through her hair several times.

Her head ached. When she closed her eyes, she could plainly see the image of Sergei's face with a fiery halo around his head. Evan winced at the picture. She couldn't imagine falling asleep again, but her body refused to perk up. She opened the door to the living room.

"I'm as ready as I'll ever be," she said.

CHAPTER TWENTY-FOUR

Evan and Hedge sat across the desk from Anton, waiting for him to complete his phone conversation. Evan glanced out the French doors casually, though, in reality, she was constantly assessing the room for escape routes and security features to avoid.

She crossed her legs, bumping her foot against Hedge's leg. He looked in the direction her finger pointed, catching Anton adjusting the pens on his desk precisely. He smiled.

"Evie," he said quietly. "What was the name of that flower shop you wanted to visit this afternoon?"

Evan twitched her lips back and forth. As if she suddenly remembered, she sat straight in her chair and took a deep breath. "I think it was called *Aquarelle* or something like that. They had such pretty roses," she gushed.

Hedge snatched one of the pens and clicked the end a few times while he reached into his jacket for something on which to write. He found a paper scrap and began scribbling as Hrevic looked on with frustration.

"Bonjour," Anton finally said and replaced the phone in its cradle. He took the pen from Hedge's hand and realigned it on his desk. "And how are you both this morning?" Anton asked.

"Frankly, I'm a little tired," Evan said with a giggle. "I had a busy night."

Anton smiled and nodded. "I heard that Mr. Bershkov was called back to Russia last night. He told me that you gave him quite a send-off. Thank you for that."

Evan took a deep breath, pushing Sergei's image from her thoughts.

Hedge patted her hand and leaned forward with a professional smirk on his face. "How are you, Mr. Hrevic?"

"I'm quite pleased with all you've shown me in this last week. I am pleased with you both, Mr. Hedger." He let his elbows rest on the arms of his leather chair and laced his fingers together. He extended both of his index fingers straight and let them rest together against his chin.

Evan decided that he must imagine this attitude made him look more intelligent. He held the pose for several seconds.

"I'd like Eve to move into my home. I have a room all ready for her, so she'll have plenty of privacy. Xandra will take her under her wing and instruct her about our little traditions and routines." Anton nodded to Evan. "What do you think of that, Eve?"

Evan nodded with raised eyebrows and a quick gasp of excitement. "I'd just love that. I already feel like I've made friends with the other girls. Will that be okay, Mr. Hedger?" she asked.

Hedge inhaled slowly, expanding his chest to capacity, and raised his chin. "I'm sure Mr. Hrevic and I can come to a mutually beneficial agreement of terms." He turned to Anton and stared him directly in the eyes. "Can we discuss our terms in private? You gave me some fine assurances the other day, and I'd really like to get those down in writing."

Anton stood and reached for Evan's hand. "Of course, we'll just find Xandra, and she can take you upstairs to see your new room."

Evan feigned a look of uncertainty toward Hedge.

"Run along, Evie," he said, patting her on the hip. "I'll take care of things down here."

As Hrevic opened the door, Xandra appeared in the hallway.

"Take Eve up to her room, please," he said, passing Evan's hand to Xandra.

Evan and Xandra made their way up the stairs to the room at the end of the bedroom wing. "I hope you like red," Xandra said, opening the door.

Evan walked into the suite with wide eyes. The walls glowed with a pale yellow-white, but everything else in the room screamed color. The bed, dressing table and armoire were constructed of highly polished cherry wood. A red velvet comforter covered the bed, and a dozen pillows of every shape, size, and animal print topped that. On the wall opposite the bed sprawled a red leather camel-backed sofa that resembled a giant pair of lips.

The walls held paintings of Parisian landmarks and flowers. The chandelier above matched the crystal one from the dressing room down the other hall. Despite the gaudiness, Evan found that she liked the room's whimsy and eccentricity.

"All of this is for me?" she asked.

"Of course." Xandra pulled her into the center of the room. And there is your closet," she said pointing to the first door on the left. "That one is your bath."

Evan couldn't resist. She opened the closet first and stepped into a room roughly the size of a third-world country. One side contained shelves and drawers, while the other offered rods with empty hangers. At the other end of the closet sat a tufted bench in front of a full-length triple mirror. Another crystal chandelier finished the look.

"Oh, my gracious!" Evan said. She somehow added an accent to her gasp of delight.

Xandra laughed. "You Americans are easily impressed."

"Now I just gotta see the bathroom," Evan pulled open the door to the bath and blinked. Everything was white or reflective and sparkly. A claw-foot tub held court in the center of a bay window overlooking the gardens behind the house. A spotless glass shower stood beside it, and the other wall mirrored the natural light all around a glistening lavatory.

"Does every girl in the house have a bath this nice?" Evan asked. She touched her fingernail to the mirror to see if a camera lurked behind it. She suspected one did.

"This whole suite is probably the smallest of them all. Being a model for Anton has many rewards," Xandra explained.

"I wanted to ask you about that," Evan said, using the opportunity to her advantage. "How exactly does he pay us? Is it just in room and board?"

"Certainly not," the model said. "We get a regular salary for our work. After each show, we get a nice bonus, and after every party, we get another bonus."

Evan knew about their bank deposits. Everything appeared above board on paper. "What about gifts? You know, from the gentlemen?"

Xandra laughed. "We can keep just about anything they give us except cash. We give that to Anton, and he manages that for us."

"Oh, like in a special account or something?"

"Don't be silly. Anton invests it back into the company. We get shares of his stock. We all reap the benefits," the blonde explained.

Nothing. Evan sighed and tried to play dumb. "I guess I never thought about it that way," she said.

Just then the other models burst through her door. "How do you like your room?" Nastya asked.

"It's amazing!" Evan replied. "I can't believe how spacious it is. My flat in town could fit entirely in the bathroom."

Olga giggled. "It's wonderful to be rich." She still wore a scarf to cover the bruises on her throat, but Evan could see some discoloration behind her ear.

Xandra crossed her arms. "I need to talk to Anton about Eve's pictures."

Evan swallowed hard. "What about my pictures?" she asked.

Xandra shook her head and left the room. Maria grabbed Evan's hand and pulled her to the leather sofa. "Today you will have your pictures made." She put her fingers through Evan's auburn hair and piled it up on top. "All of Anton's women have their pictures made."

Olga nodded and plopped down on the other side of Evan. "We will fix your make-up, and you get to wear whatever you want."

Tatiana sat down at the dressing table and gazed at herself in the mirror. "If you are lucky, Anton will let you wear something from the private jewelry tray."

Nastya frowned. "You shouldn't get her hopes up. Anton hasn't let any of us even see those since Sophie got married and left."

Evan's ears pricked. "What happened when Sophie got married?" she asked. She widened her eyes and reached out to Nastya.

Olga and Maria pulled Nastya onto the sofa with them.

"When Sophie told us that she was getting married, of course, Anton was very happy for her. We all were. The man was a very wealthy businessman from Egypt." Nastya paused as if she waited for a response.

Evan shrugged. "And then what?"

"Anton took her to the vault. That is what he calls the room with the private jewels. He gave her a pair of earrings with priceless pink diamonds." Nastya held her breath. "They were beautiful."

Evan smiled. All of the models sighed romantically. She wondered. "What do you mean when you say, 'priceless'?"

"Maybe I say the wrong word." Nastya apologized for her English. "Does priceless not mean worth more than money?"

"It does, but…. Well, I mean, they're just diamonds, right?" Evan asked. She started doubting her logic. *Diamonds are incredible, but they aren't priceless.*

Tatiana blinked at her with an obtuse grin. "You haven't seen these diamonds."

A knock at the door sent all the women into gasps of laughter.

"Come in," Evan said.

Anton and Hedge stood in the hallway. Hedge peered into the room with a raised brow.

"You see how I take care of my ladies," Anton said.

The models formed a line at the door, and Evan decided to join them. Hedge nodded to her. "How do you like these accommodations, Evie?" he asked.

"Who wouldn't love this room?" she responded. She pulled him inside as Xandra appeared behind Anton. "I have tons to show you."

Anton held up his hand. "That will have to wait, I'm afraid. You have much to do to get ready for your photo shoot."

Hedge put his arm around her shoulders. "You can show me another time. You have pictures to take. This is the big break I promised you, Eve. Anton's going to make it all happen for you."

Evan turned on an electric smile for both men. "I'm awfully grateful to you."

Anton directed the models using few words. "Hair. Make-up. Wardrobe.

Shoes." He pointed to the blondes.

Hedge patted Evan's hand. "I'll bring in your dress."

"We have plenty of clothes for Eve to choose from," Hrevic said.

Evan immediately pushed out her bottom lip in a full pink pout. "Oh, I don't mean to be rude, Anton, but after last night I consider that my lucky dress. Maybe Sergei told you about it? I've just gotta have my picture made wearing that one." She fluttered her lashes at him and tilted her head.

Anton tucked his chin to his chest.

"You've got him," Kirk whispered in her ear.

Kirk had been so quiet all morning that Evan nearly forgot he was there. His voice startled her, and she jumped.

Anton reached out for her hand. "I didn't intend to upset you, Eve. Of course, you may wear your own dress for these pictures."

Evan threw her arms around his neck to reward his concession. She hugged him warmly. "Thank you, Anton!"

Hedge quickly went to the car and got the dress from Kirk. He checked the other men's positions on the street. Brawn jogged in the park across the street from Hrevic's compound. Ramos read a newspaper at the end of the block.

By the time Hedge returned with the dress, Evan was in a makeup chair being worked on by others from every direction. In a matter of minutes, she was ready to dress.

She took the dress from Hedge's hand. "Excuse me for a minute, y'all," she said. "I need to go to the ladies' room for a sec."

Evan retreated to her bathroom and put the dress on in private. She stared at herself in the mirror and sighed.

"You look good," Kirk murmured. "I've got your vitals coming in loud and clear. Just stay focused."

Evan nodded to him. "This mirror is lovely," she said, as though talking to herself.

"Two cameras. One on either side of the lav," Kirk advised. "Nothing in the chandelier. The bedroom has one over the headboard and one at the dressing table. The closet has one in the triple mirror. The good news is that there will be some weird electrical surges in the neighborhood this week. Most of his cameras are going to experience technical difficulties."

Evan primped at her hair and smiled. "Fabulous!"

When she returned to the others, Xandra grinned and motioned her to follow.

Nastya grabbed her hand and walked with her down the hall. "Xandra says that you get to wear some jewels for the pictures," she whispered. "You are very lucky, indeed."

Xandra opened the door to a small sitting room at the head of the stairs. To one side rose an eight-foot-tall painting of two women in a garden with a cherub over their heads. Xandra pulled on the frame of the painting. It hinged open like a door, revealing another room beyond.

Xandra went right in and began tapping at a small keypad on the side of a wall cabinet. A drawer slid open, and Xandra motioned for Evan and Nastya to join her.

"You may pick anything that you like," Xandra said. She spoke softly, with a marked reverence for the gemstones.

"Slowly," Kirk hummed. "I'm not picking up any signals from them at all."

Evan picked up the first piece and examined it carefully. She held the canary diamond ring just below her neckline to allow the cameras to capture it from every angle. She turned it from side to side, allowing the light to filter through each facet. She slipped it onto her right hand. A little loose for her ring finger, but a perfect fit for the middle.

She gently scooped up a pair of chandelier earrings. Nastya raised her eyebrows. "Do you think they will be alright? The other day you said that you were allergic."

Evan nodded. "These are twenty-four karat gold. They shouldn't cause a bit of trouble. Anyway, they're so beautiful that I just can't resist."

Again, she held them up for Kirk to scan them before placing them into her earlobes. No feedback. Good so far.

Lastly, she picked up a strand of white diamonds with a substantial pendant drop of gold filigree and pastel-colored gemstones. The mere weight of the piece impressed Evan as she let the cameras have a look. She felt the stones glide around her collarbone and then fastened the clasp behind her neck. "All done," she chirped.

"Are you sure that's all you want?" Nastya asked.

"Oh, heavens, yes. I don't want to look gaudy for the pictures," Evan said.

Xandra approved. "You look nice."

Evan spent the next hours being posed and prodded for smiles, pouts, and distant gazes. The photographer spoke to her in a punchy French and English combination. He shot several dozen pictures in the runway room first. They moved from room to room around the house, using stone fireplaces, antique chairs, and artwork as backdrops and props.

Every time the shoot switched rooms, another touch-up on her hair or lipstick was called. The last venue was the garden. An entirely new box of gear emerged for outdoor lighting and glare. More makeup.

During the photo session Hedge and Anton watched from a short distance, making comments and suggestions to each other. The other models offered Evan tips from just beyond the lens' view. She remembered the months she spent as a college student shooting pictures for magazine advertisements and clothing catalogs. She grew tired just thinking about it.

When the photographer packed up his gear, everyone was more than ready for the event to end. Evan followed Xandra back to the vault where she carefully removed the jewelry.

"It was a pleasure to wear such exquisite things," she said gratefully. She excused herself to her bedroom and changed back into her day dress. She scrubbed her face clean and gently combed out the teased knots in her hair.

She joined Hedge downstairs in the foyer, carrying her garment bag over her shoulder. Hedge took it from her and squeezed her shoulders.

Anton reached for Evan's hand. "You did a marvelous job today, Eve. Now Mr. Hedger will take you back to your flat to pack up. Tonight you will sleep in your new bed."

CHAPTER TWENTY-FIVE

When Hedge and Evan returned to the apartment, Kirk led them through the door with his notebook in his hands. "You two need to see this." He crossed the small room in two long strides and landed in a seat at the dinette. Kirk spun the computer to face the others, and they joined him at the table.

They studied the pictures of the models that were lined up across his monitor.

"I ran Facial Recognition Scans on all of the girls the other night, going back ten years. Everything came back pretty slim because ten years ago, most of these women were still in school, and all in Russia. The two exceptions are Xandra and Nastya, who were both beginning their modeling careers, together as a matter of fact."

Hedge nodded. "They do seem more mature than the others."

"Most of his women don't use their real names, either," Kirk added.

"That's not unusual for models," Evan said with a quick shrug.

"No, it's not. We can come back to that." Kirk punched the keys of his computer. The pictures of models vanished, and Anton Hrevic's face filled the screen. "Hrevic isn't his real name, either."

Hedge's eyes became slits as he focused on the photo of Hrevic. "Anton Hrevic has been in the headlines for at least a dozen years. His fashions have always caught the critics' eyes."

"Yes," said Kirk, "but if you go back just fifteen years, Anton Hrevic doesn't exist. Hrevic isn't even a real last name. There is nothing on this man or any man with that name anywhere. Even WITSEC leaves more of a trail than what this guy has."

Evan furrowed her brow and stared. "So who is he?"

Kirk nearly bounced with excitement. "I have a suspicion. Look at this." He switched photos to zoomed-in images of the jewelry that Evan wore earlier. "He pointed to the ring. Look here." He punched the zoom button again and traced along a tiny line that appeared to be a fracture or occlusion in the stone.

"What are we looking at?" Evan asked.

"An imperfection. All of the stones have these little scars in them." Kirk shifted to the next picture and the next, pointing out flaws in each stone until he looped back to the picture of the ring. "These would never be considered priceless stones…"

"What's this blur?" Hedge asked, pointing to a smudged area of the picture.

"That's my big find." He rotated the image of the ring. "Lots of jewelers mark their diamonds with a laser signature. All of these stones have this same microscopic engraving." He punched the zoom one more time. A laser-cut image of a crowned, two-headed eagle holding a scepter and a censer appeared.

Evan exhaled. "I've seen that heraldry before."

Hedge shot a concerned stare at Kirk. "This is the mark of a famous jeweler?"

Kirk shook his head. Evan reached out and squeezed Kirk's hand. He knew that she recognized the seal. "Hedge, that's the crest of the Romanov family," Kirk said.

"The Russian Imperial jewels have all been accounted for," Hedge said. "Even if these were stolen, who would mark them with laser signatures? That would be like sending up flags for them to be found."

Evan nodded. "That's almost true. There was one collection of Romanov gems that was never recovered. When the tsar and his family were slaughtered, eyewitness accounts stated that the daughters did not die right away. The Bolsheviks' bullets glanced off their bodies because the girls had sewn jewels into their dresses. Even the bayonet blades didn't penetrate. Like mine, their dresses protected them from attack. The revolutionaries had to shoot them in the head to kill them." She paused and shook her head. Kirk saw another expression of realization light up her face.

"What is it?" Hedge asked.

"Of course, the names of the Romanov daughters! That's where he got the names for his muses. Olga, Maria, Tatiana, and Anastasia. And the Tsarina's name was Alexandra," she said.

Kirk continued. "The stones sewn into their bodices were never recovered. Historians assumed that the soldiers that carried out the executions kept them for souvenirs and trophies. Insurance for rainy days. If these jewels really are Romanov, they are indeed priceless pieces of history."

Hedge squinted. "How can we verify this?"

"I did a genealogic search on Yuri Yakovsky. He was one of the leaders of the Bolshevik troops who carried out the execution orders. I'm still working on the branches of his family tree. It would be easier to start with today and work backward, but since Anton's lineage is a mystery, we'll do what we can." Kirk patted the tabletop. "I suspect that someone is marking these diamonds, which would otherwise be considered low quality, in order to verify their place in history."

"Are these imperfections natural, then?" Evan asked.

"If they're authentic, these microscopic fractures may have been caused by the bullets." Kirk raised his eyebrows. "Gemstones have grain, like wood. When they are impacted against the grain, it can show the imperfections."

"How do you know this stuff?" Hedge asked.

"I have a poker buddy who happens to be a gemologist." Kirk raised his hands and shook them for emphasis. "That's not even the best part. The muses told you about Sophie's wedding gift of the pink diamond earrings?"

"Yes."

"Ten days ago in Vienna, a highly sought-after hitman deposited two million dollars into an account after spending three months in Paris. He is known for his surgical strikes against men, such as the recent 'mugging' death of Egyptian media mogul, Ehud Kharu. His attacks against women are not so generous. His MO includes strangling and stabbing his female victims." Kirk bit his lip. "Kharu was a recent guest at Hrevic's home."

"Do we have an ID for our hitman? Can we link him directly to Hrevic?" Evan asked.

"Not yet. The guy is good. Never lets a camera catch a glimpse. Never leaves a trace of anything at the scene. He's a real pro." Kirk shrugged. "But I'm working on it, too. We'll figure him out."

Hedge crossed his arms. "Let's get this all to Eleanor. If we can link the earrings to an exchange for two million, we have our money trail."

Kirk clapped his palms together. "I'm on it."

Evan helped Kirk search for possible transactions by known fences. They watched the clock, knowing that Anton would become suspicious if Evan failed to return soon.

"I have something," Kirk announced. "A less-than-reputable jeweler in Belarus transferred just over two million dollars from his bank to an account in the Caribbean. He has ties to our hitman. The jewelry shop is ... wait for it ... Yakovsky's. Tell Eleanor we have the trail."

Evan released a heavy sigh. "What do we think? Is Anton the hitman or the employer?"

Kirk shook his head. He wondered the same thing. "What does your gut tell you?" He watched Evan's expression grow more serious as she seemed to evaluate her own question.

"That's tough to say." She twitched her lips from one side to another. "I can't really see him wanting to get his hands dirty. I think he'd be the employer. But I don't know. He doesn't seem like much of a chess player. I'm not saying he's not smart, but maybe he's not clever enough to play the long game, you know?"

"Well, I know one thing for sure; Sergei wasn't our strangler. His handprints weren't a match to the bruising on Olga's throat," Kirk explained.

Hedge punched in Eleanor's number and immediately set the receiver to speaker. "What do you have for me?" she asked without a greeting.

"We have the money trail, complete with at least two murders for hire." Hedge said.

"I'm sending you details now. It's big," Kirk added.

"What's our next step?" Hedge asked, pacing the carpet.

Eleanor paused on the line. Kirk knew she was scanning the information he'd sent. "I want Evan to go back to the house, as planned."

"Yes, Ma'am," Evan answered.

"Good. Do you think you can get Anton out of the house by yourself? Without a defined link to the other women, I'd prefer a quick extraction."

Evan nodded and said, "I can get him out."

Eleanor continued. "Good. Our top priority is getting Anton Hrevic into custody. Hedge, you work out your plan to get Anton's models into custody as soon as we know that Hrevic can't hurt them. Report back to me at midnight."

"Yes, Ma'am," the team said together.

"Listen up," Hedge ordered as he disconnected from Eleanor. "We only have about an hour before Anton's going to get antsy." He looked at Evan. "This one will be all you."

Evan smiled at Kirk and dipped her chin. "With my Springfield, the dress, and the little voice in my ear," she tugged her earlobe, "I have everything I need to take on the world."

CHAPTER TWENTY-SIX

Evan wore her gray suit jacket over the black strapless. She pulled her red suitcase behind her as she walked up the front steps to Hrevic's door. She inhaled a deep cleansing breath and pressed the buzzer. *You've got this.* She wasn't sure whether she heard Kirk's voice or just her own thoughts.

Anton greeted her right away. "You live here now, Eve. You don't have to ring the bell," he said, wrapping his arm around her shoulders. "I'll walk you up to your room." He took her bag.

"Thank you, Anton, for everything. I just know that I'm going to love it here," she said. The chandelier in the foyer sparkled brightly overhead, but the other rooms were dark and quiet. Anton gestured to the staircase, and she started up. She felt her host's gaze roaming her body as she climbed the stairs in front of him. "Where are the others?" she asked.

"They are all out having an early dinner," Anton replied. "I wanted to be here for your arrival."

She walked to the end of the hallway and reached for her bag.

He held up his hand in protest. "I'll carry it inside for you."

"I've got you," Kirk whispered. "You can handle this creep."

Evan gestured, and Anton placed her bag at the foot of the bed. "We're all alone in the house?" she asked.

Anton nodded. "My security man is downstairs, but he won't bother us unless he's called. What do you need?" He took a few steps toward her.

Evan guessed that he was trying to look both innocent and helpful. He laced his fingertips together in a mid-air bridge, which gave him the look of a greedy child about to grab whatever was offered and more.

"I was just a little bit hungry," she sighed. "I suppose I can find my way around the kitchen for a salad or something." She took a deep breath and removed her jacket. "Unless you want to go out somewhere?" She would offer a little and hope that he would become careless.

Anton smiled. "You are certainly dressed to go out. You are wearing your lucky dress."

"I was hoping...." She took a step closer to him. She shifted her hips and shoulders seductively. "But if the others will be back soon, maybe I should just fix my own dinner."

Anton shook his head. "My muses only just left. They'll be gone for at least another hour. I could take you to a quiet place for dinner, and then we can come back here and ... talk."

Ticking began in Evan's ear. She expected as much.

Evan smiled and nodded. "Of course. I can leave my unpacking for when we return. Where shall we go?" She took his arm, and they ambled back downstairs. "Nothing too fattening, I hope?"

"I always look out for my muses," he said. More ticking. "Let me get my jacket and my keys, and we can decide in the car." Hrevic left her alone in the foyer.

"Just let me know where you are going, and Hedge and Ramos will meet you there," Kirk said. "Any other sign of trouble? Besides his lies."

"No." She cloaked her response with a sigh.

"Try to make him tell you where the models are eating. Brawn and I could pick them up before they return. Taking people into custody is always easier if you're not on their home turf."

Evan heard the sound of glass breaking from Anton's office. "Heads up," she whispered. "Anton, is everything alright?" she called down the dark corridor.

No response.

"Anton?"

Still nothing. Evan started down the hall. "A strange sound from his office, Kirk. I'm going to check it out," she whispered.

She swallowed hard and listened. She couldn't hear anything. Before she reached the office, she pulled her Springfield from the strap on her leg. "Kirk, I'm going in. Kirk?" she said under her breath.

No response from Kirk.

Evan's heart pounded. The sub-compact felt like it was pulsing in her hand. She held the pistol behind her back as she turned into the opened doorway. Anton stood at his desk with a frustrated expression.

A small lamp lay on its side across his desk. The green glass shade was shattered. "Clumsy," Anton said.

Evan sighed. Still half in the hallway, she turned to slip the Springfield back into hiding. Before she could, she glimpsed a figure in the hall.

For a split second she felt panicked, but then a bolt of electricity seemed to shoot through her brain. Then nothing but blackness.

CHAPTER TWENTY-SEVEN

Static hummed in Evan's ear.

Her eyes fluttered open, and a flood of pain rushed down her spine. She was in a dark room, with only a strip of light seeping under the door. She thought she heard a voice, but in the dim light she couldn't make out anyone. Evan moved her hand to the pain in her earlobe. It had been ripped in two, split from someone pulling her earring out.

She pushed herself upright to a sitting position on the floor. Blood covered her face and stuck at the corners of her eyes. She was cold and naked.

The buzz again. She saw a glint of light reflecting from something on the floor at her knee. She picked up a mangled earring and bent the wire back into place.

Sliding the jewelry into her other ear, she heard, "Evan! Evan, where are you?"

She whispered, "Kirk, is that you?"

"Evan! Are you there?" The voice was Hedge's.

"I'm here," she said with effort. Her eyes blurred as she tried to look around again. "What happened?"

"I'm working on that," Hedge replied. "Are you hurt?"

She reached up to the knot rising on the side of her head and the gash swelling at her temple. She checked the rest of her body for injuries but found none. "Goose egg on my head. Not much more than that."

"We lost your signal. Can you reactivate the dress?"

Evan sniffed. Her head felt as though it might explode. "No. The dress is gone. Someone knocked me out and took it." Her hands trembled. She searched the shadowy room. She saw her underwear discarded just a few feet away. She grabbed them and pulled them back on.

"What?!" he screamed. "Who took it?"

163

"I don't know, Hedge." Tears filled her eyes. "I heard a noise." She froze. As her eyes adjusted to the dark room, she saw a man sitting in a chair, watching her. She did her best to cover herself with her arms. "Who are you?" she asked.

There was no reply.

Hedge waited. "Is someone with you, Evan?"

She swallowed hard. "Yes," she whispered.

"Who is it?"

She crawled toward the man. He didn't move. As she inched closer, she saw that it was Anton. "Anton?" she asked. "Anton, what happened?"

He didn't answer. Evan raised up to her knees, keeping herself covered, and inched closer. Every move sent another pain through her body. She was shaking. She approached the chair and saw a pool of blood on the floor.

Anton Hrevic, or whoever he was, stared into eternity with a bullet hole between his eyes. Evan scrambled back to the other side of the room.

"He's dead, Hedge. He's dead. Shot in the head." She struggled to keep breathing. Every muscle in her body ached. Her mind cranked slowly. Her eyes were adjusting to the dim light. "I don't know for sure, but I think I'm still in the house," she said. "The walls look like the same pale yellow. Where's Kirk?"

"He and Brawn went for the other girls. Kirk said you told him that they were at a restaurant. Brawn said that they lost your signal on the computer. They couldn't find you."

Evan tried to recall. "I can't remember where the women were going."

"Can you get out of the room you're in?" he asked her. She stood up and found the door. "Locked," she said. "Give me a second."

She looked around the room for something to use on the lock. There was nothing but Anton's body and the metal folding chair that held it. Evan took a deep breath and pulled Anton's jacket from him, searching the pockets. She found a set of car keys and a handkerchief. She pushed her hands into his pants pockets. Nothing.

She wrestled to remove his bloodstained shirt from his body. She slipped into it to stop her shivering, and when she did, a cufflink dropped to the floor with a loud plink.

Evan picked it up quickly and examined the design. Struggling to focus, she popped the front off and bent the hinge bracket out straight. "I think this will work," she said.

She dropped to her knees to work on the door lock. Within seconds the knob turned. "I have the door unlocked. Let me check the hall."

Evan pushed the door open a fraction of an inch and looked out. "I'm definitely still in the house. The carpet is the same. I may be in the basement. The ceiling is low." She opened the door wider and looked down the hall in both directions. "I don't see anyone."

She heard Hedge growl. "Ramos and I are on our way to you. Brawn and Kirk haven't checked in, and with your situation, I'm worried. Anton isn't calling the shots now. Maybe he never was."

"Why are you on the com?" she asked. "Kirk never leaves it."

"I know." Hedge's calm sounded forced.

"How long until you'll be here?" Evan tried to sound strong, but her nerves were catching up to her.

"Hang on, Evan. Ten minutes, tops. Just stay put where you are."

She looked back into the small storage room where Anton's body sprawled. "Sir, I'd feel better if I did something to help. May I look around the house to see what I can find?"

Hedge grunted. "Stay where you are."

"If Ramos were in my situation, would you ask him to stay put?"

"Absolutely," he spat out.

"I don't even need the dress to know that you're lying. I'm going to find out who's in charge of this circus."

"Just keep me in the loop."

"Yessir," she said. "Thanks, Hedge."

Evan peeked into the other two rooms off the hall. The first was another storage room. Empty. The next one was obviously the security station. The monitors sat dark. The computers were off. She didn't wait for someone to return.

She found a stairway at the end of the narrow corridor. She climbed silently to the door at the top. Holding her breath, she opened it a crack.

She saw the darkened foyer, but nothing else. "I was in the basement. I'm at the front door right now."

"Just get out," Hedge ordered.

Evan listened. She heard rustling from somewhere upstairs. "I'm not alone. Give me a few more minutes. I'll come right out if I don't find anything."

Hedge conceded. "Five minutes. I should be there by then."

Evan started up the next flight of stairs. She searched for whatever made the noise. She didn't detect any light coming from beneath the bedroom doors. She stared at the door beyond the head of the stairs. It led to the sitting room that concealed the vault.

Evan glided to the dark paneled door and placed her aching ear against the wood. She couldn't hear anything from within. For a moment she doubted herself, wondering if her hearing had been permanently damaged by the earlier explosion or if she was just impaired by the concussion she knew she had. She listened again. She had to risk it.

The door handle turned smoothly in her hand, and she pushed it open and went inside. "So far so good," she whispered to Hedge. "I'm gonna try to get into the vault room."

"Be cautious," he answered.

She tried to remember exactly how Xandra opened the painting door. She didn't want to set off any alarms. As she touched the frame of the artwork, the door swung open. Evan quickly retreated behind a chair.

She waited for a few seconds, but no one came through the doorway. No light on the other side, either. All she could hear was the thumping of her heart.

"Somebody left the vault door open. I'm going inside."

"I'm almost to the house. Can't you wait?" Hedge asked.

"Would you wait if our positions were reversed?"

"Go in. Be careful."

"Yessir," she said.

She entered the room, closed the vault door, and turned on the light overhead. The brightness caused her pupils to scream shut. Her head pounded as she adjusted to the light. She went to the cabinet with the jewels and studied the electronic keypad. "I sure wish I had the dress," she muttered.

"Me, too," Hedge said.

"Sorry," she said.

"You've got to be kidding me," Hedge snorted.

"What is it?"

"I just got a message from one of Kirk's colleagues, Dr. Ronald Merrill. He says that Yakovsky has three descendants still living. A seventy-year-old nephew in Moscow, a fifty-five-year-old granddaughter in Zurich, and a thirty-year-old great-granddaughter in Paris named Alexandra Yakovsky." Hedge growled.

"Xandra."

"Get out of the house, Evan."

"I will. Just get here soon." She tried not to think about Kirk or Brawn. She'd already seen Xandra's handiwork on Anton.

She blinked away the pain and tears. She stared at the jewel case. She didn't dare tap on the keys. She knew without a doubt that an alarm would blast if she did. She instead examined the cabinet itself.

The construction was of solid wood, but the grooves on the side betrayed a dozen shallow trays that probably contained jewelry. Evan breathed hard. "That's a lot of buying power," she gasped.

"Yes, it is," said a female voice from behind her.

Evan spun around to see Xandra standing in the doorway, wearing the little black dress.

CHAPTER TWENTY-EIGHT

Hedge dropped Ramos at the back gate and circled the house to the front. He sprinted from the car to the door with his Glock drawn. He noticed that the house was dark except for the solar yard lights at the perimeter. He listened at the door for any signs of trouble.

He hadn't heard Evan's voice in over three minutes. He couldn't hear anything now.

"Papa in position," he said quietly.

"Romeo in position, awaiting your *go*," Ramos responded.

"Go, Romeo."

Both men shouldered their way into the house. Hedge went through the front door, and Ramos entered through the French doors in Hrevic's office.

"Foyer clear," Hedge said.

"Office clear. Broken lamp on the desk. Nothing else out of place."

The men continued room to room until they met at the gallery hall between the main gathering room and the dining room. Hedge motioned for them to proceed together. Hedge rounded the long dining table while Ramos entered the kitchen.

Hedge's earbud crackled. "Papa, I have Kilo. Kilo is down."

Hedge hurried through the door to the kitchen and found Ramos on his knees next to Kirk's slumped body. Ramos held his finger to Kirk's throat.

"Condition?" Hedge asked, expecting the worst. He turned on the light.

"He's breathing, but just barely." Ramos examined Kirk and found two bullet wounds. They both had ripped through his right shoulder. Blood drenched Kirk's clothes and covered the floor and cabinet behind him.

Hedge knelt down to help. Ramos packed the wounds while Hedge wrapped them as quickly as he could. "I want you to take him to the hospital," Hedge said. "Call en route and have the doctors waiting for him. I'll let you know if you need to send out medics. Alert Eleanor to send back-up."

A loud thump from behind them sent Hedge and Ramos spinning, weapons raised. They saw nothing. Hedge stood slowly and inched toward the back of the kitchen.

Another thump, but no movement.

Hedge looked into the short hall that led from the kitchen to a servants' area. To his right was a glass door with a stocked pantry. He turned to his left just as another loud bump pounded. It was a walk-in freezer.

He opened the latch to find Nastya bound and gagged. Her shoulder was scraped and covered in blood from ramming into the door. She fell into his arms, and he pulled her into the warmth of the kitchen.

He removed the gag from her mouth, and she began crying. She sat on the floor, shivering violently and sobbing.

"Ramos, help me. The others are in here, too," Hedge said.

One by one they carried each of the women out and removed their bindings. Nastya and Tatiana cried and trembled. Olga and Maria both lay unconscious with no pulse. The men began CPR right away. Maria responded almost immediately. Olga took longer. The bruises on her throat were a dark purple.

Hedge gave Nastya a severe glare. "Where are Xandra and Eve?"

She shook her head. "I don't know. We were having a drink before dinner, and I started to feel sick. I woke up only a few minutes ago. I pounded on the freezer door."

Hedge looked at Ramos. "Take them all to the ER. Have them checked out. Tell the police to hold them in custody," Hedge said. "And keep them warm," he added.

"Yessir."

When Ramos had them all safely away, Hedge went back inside to find Evan. He started up the steps to make sure the second floor was clear. He checked the bedroom wing. No signs of struggle. No lights. Nothing amiss. He crossed to the other wing and found the runway hall empty. He peered into the dressing room, seeing a faint orange glow from the far end.

His chest ached and pounded. The unmistakable smell of burnt hair stung his nose. As he stepped to the end of the dressing tables, he saw the glow. One of the girls had left her curling iron turned on. He sighed with relief.

He heard a static hiss.

"Evan," he whispered. "Are you there?"

The hiss faded. Silence.

He went back to the hall and went around the edge of the loft, to the sitting room behind the stairs. The door stood open.

He looked around the room, seeing nobody. The painting with the cherub looked like any other piece of art in the house, except for the bloody handprint on the gold-leafed frame. The image of Eleanor face down in a pool of blood flashed in Hedge's brain. He wiped the sweat from his brow.

First Eleanor, now Kirk. He let his friends down again. He wasn't going to lose Evan.

He raised his weapon to the ready position. He pushed the painting door open and backed to the wall beside it, waiting for a response. Nothing. He lowered his sidearm to chest-level, prepared to meet the devil himself.

The room was empty. He couldn't see anything out of place until he turned on the light. Another handprint smeared across the top of the jewel cabinet. Blood spattered the side, too. The dark stained wood hid most of the spray, but the droplets shone brightly on the white keys of the electronic security pad.

Hedge's adrenaline pumped furiously. His mind scrambled for the next move. She was gone. He pushed a breath out and pulled another in. It tasted stale and metallic.

His vest and gear weighed heavy. His ears rang with the stillness that surrounded him. He wondered where she might be. Probably with Xandra.

Hedge went back to the balcony and looked over the railing to the foyer below. He moved down the stairs like a cat burglar. He stood at the front door and peered out the glass. "Where is Anton?" he whispered to himself. He knew he could find him in the basement, but he wasn't sure where the basement stairway was.

Too many things went wrong. How did Xandra know about Evan? About the dress? Kirk had patched into their signals, and there had been no chatter that their cover was blown. Ramos had followed the plan to the letter. Evan hadn't slipped even once.

Where is Brawn?

CHAPTER TWENTY-NINE

"Xandra," Evan said with an icy tone. Every inch of her body ached, and her brain was still misfiring. She clenched her fists, preparing for battle. She eased her body two steps back, placing the jewel cabinet between her and Xandra.

"You are scared, I see," Xandra replied. She looked satisfied that the jewels were still in hiding. She stared back at Evan. "You know that you will die soon."

"You're wearing my dress."

Xandra laughed as she took another step into the small vault room. "Yes, but I will have to take it in. You are much fatter than I."

Evan took a long slow breath, assessing the situation. The vault room had one exit, which Xandra blocked. Xandra wore the dress, and probably had her Springfield strapped to her thigh. Evan wore only a dead man's bloody shirt and her underwear. No shoes, no protection at all.

"You should have killed me when you had the chance," Evan said. "Maybe you thought you would leave me to answer for Anton's death?"

"You spoiled years of hard work. You *will* answer to me." Xandra jumped at Evan and grabbed her hair before Evan could escape her reach.

Xandra yanked Evan's moving body back quickly, and Evan's shoulder crashed into the side of the cabinet. Evan held her hand on her arm, wincing at the pain. Still grasping Evan's hair with her left hand, Xandra slapped Evan's face with her right.

Evan spun, stopping only by throwing herself across the top of the cabinet. Her palms pushed flat against the top. Evan felt as though the tiny room tumbled around her.

"You are so eager to die," Xandra said with a laugh. "I need you to tell me about this dress. I need to know everything."

"I'll tell you one thing. The dress is useless to you. You can't control it."

Evan lifted her gaze to meet Xandra's cold stare. She held to the cabinet for balance.

"Perhaps you refer to the remote monitor computer. I assure you that I have those controls."

Evan squinted through her pain. "You can't."

"I can, and I do. I took them from your white-haired friend earlier. He was reluctant to part with them, but I can be persuasive." Xandra pulled at her hair again. "I killed him like I killed Anton."

Rage took over Evan's brain. She pushed herself off the cabinet and threw her head back into Xandra's face. An explosion of pain blinded Evan and a spray of crimson shot from Xandra's nose and mouth. Evan darted from the room.

She made it to the door of the sitting room before something hit her back, sending her crashing to the floor.

Xandra pulled her upright by her injured shoulder. "I didn't tell you that you could go. You Americans have no manners."

Evan swung her right arm around and landed her fist squarely in Xandra's stomach. Punching the LBD body armor was like punching a wall. Xandra exhaled sharply but didn't release Evan's arm.

"I'm stronger than you," Xandra spat out between gulps of air. She pulled Evan to the head of the stairs and pushed her head down level with the handrail.

Evan's eyesight blurred. The floor from the foyer below seemed to rush at her. The second that her eyes focused Xandra pulled her to standing again. Evan felt her body being dragged down the stairs. She struggled for control, but the dizziness sent waves of pain and nausea to every inch of her body.

When they reached the foyer, Xandra pushed her down to the cold marble floor. The frigid tiles acted to revive Evan's equilibrium and clear her mind for a moment. She raised herself and watched Xandra look out the glass at the front door.

"We need to get somewhere with more privacy," Xandra said. She walked deliberately to Evan and grabbed her under her injured shoulder. "Come on."

Evan tried to kick and punch, but her blows seemed to miss her target. The concussion affected her more than she expected. Xandra pulled Evan to the back of the main gathering room, through the dining room and into the kitchen. She shoved Evan down against the cabinet and reached for something on the countertop. Evan stared at the dress, wishing she hadn't let it be stolen. *How could I be so careless?*

Xandra turned on the light and found the object of her search, a roll of duct tape.

Evan tried to make her feet run away but slipped on something slick.

She tumbled over something and fell back to the floor. She backed away in panic when she realized that she fell over a bloodied body. She forced herself to look. It was Kirk.

"Nooo!" she screamed. She launched herself at Xandra who blocked her rage-driven blows.

Xandra grabbed something from the countertop behind her and smashed it into the side of Evan's head. Blackness took over again.

When Evan awakened, her hands were bound together behind her with tape, and she had another strip secured over her mouth.

She was in the trunk of a car. Her head pounded over every bump and dip. *My stupidity cost Kirk his life. I lost my nerve and failed. Who else was dead?*

The car stopped with a jolt. Evan decided to run as soon as she had the chance. Better to be shot in the back than to make any more mistakes. She feared giving anything more away. She heard Xandra's footsteps.

The trunk lid opened and Xandra grabbed Evan by the hair before she had the chance to move.

"You're walking on your own this time," the blonde said. "You will answer my questions about this dress."

Evan tried to pull away. She dropped to one knee and rolled, but Xandra's grip was secure. Her muscles grew weaker and less coordinated. Her stomach churned.

Looking around, Evan saw that they had come up a freight elevator and were inside a warehouse. Bolts of fabric leaned against the far wall and dress forms stood like a jury behind a long cutting table. *We're in Anton's design workshop, probably upstairs from the House of Alexei shop.* Her thoughts scrambled for clarity. *Do I run or play this out? Hedge will be here soon. If he's still alive.*

She looked at the tools on the near wall. Dress weights, cutting wheels, and scissors lined the pegboard. She speculated which could be the best weapons against her opponent's assault.

Xandra pulled her into a metal folding chair in the center of the large room. As soon as Evan sat down, Xandra slapped her. "You have to tell me everything that this dress does," she demanded. She ripped the tape from Evan's raw lips.

"I won't tell you anything."

"I know that the dress sees and listens. It will make my job a great deal easier. I know that it's bulletproof, among other things. I just want to know what else it does," Xandra said.

"Why don't you just start experimenting?" Evan suggested.

"Your friend told me that could be extremely dangerous."

"My friend didn't tell you any such thing," Evan growled. Rage grew in her gut. She couldn't let Kirk's death be for nothing. She would take this woman down. She began working on the tape at her wrists. "Who was

Anton?" she asked.

Xandra smiled. "He was nobody. He was a broke nobody who liked to draw pretty pictures of women. I made him rich. I gave him his name. I gave him his success."

"Where did you find him?"

Xandra dropped her hands to her hips. She paced back and forth in front of Evan and glared at her with a menacing grin. "He was a street artist in Moscow. He sold drugs to keep himself fed. He has no family to miss him, so you don't have to worry."

Evan nodded. "But you invested a great deal of money into him. The house, this shop, the business? Such a waste to kill him."

Xandra stopped her pacing and faced her squarely. "You're the reason I had to kill him. He thought you were some sort of angel. He wanted to tell you all about me in exchange for letting him continue his design. He thought he was good enough without me." She scoffed at the idea.

"Maybe he was," Evan replied. Her right hand was almost free.

"You know nothing about couture," Xandra said.

"I know more than you might think." Her right hand worked at peeling the tape from her left. "I knew enough to find another career before I was dropped by my agent. You had to find your own personal designer to keep you in the fashion industry."

Evan was about to attack but hesitated when Xandra began talking again.

"Why do you think I decided to collect information? Powerful people love to surround themselves with beauty. To rich and powerful men, a beautiful woman is merely a possession. We are property to admire and wear like an expensive gold watch. They talk about their business and their political plans around us as though we can't hear or understand." Xandra spit out her words like bile. "I got sick of it. I decided that if I couldn't change it, I would use it."

Evan nodded. "You're right."

"I began collecting the men's words, their conversations, and plans. I listened to their business deals and their political maneuvers. I gave them women to play with and blackmailed them with pictures to get their secrets and influence their business and politics. I used them to get what I wanted. People pay good money to keep their secrets. Money I used to regain my family's rightful place in the world."

Evan drew a deep, painful breath. *Rightful place? What in the world is she talking about?* Evan's brain processed too slowly.

Xandra tilted her head and raised her right brow. "You do the same thing, but you aren't as profitable as I am. I have power and money and fame. Soon I will have a voice that every world leader will hear." She made a dismissive gesture toward Evan with her hand. "You have nothing. No friends. No home or family to speak of."

"You know nothing about me," Evan muttered. "I have friends."

"And I take them away."

Evan's rage filled her with fire. She grabbed the front legs of the metal folding chair, and as swiftly as she could, stood, and swung the chair into Xandra's side.

Xandra fell and rolled another three feet across the tile floor. Evan leaped onto her, and the two women began tumbling in a whirlwind of hair and fingernails. They bit and scratched and pulled handfuls of hair. Evan wrapped her hands around Xandra's throat to throttle her, and Xandra slammed Evan's head into the floor. Nothing was off limits.

Evan tried to get to her Springfield, but Xandra continued a barrage of head blows. As they rolled toward the sewing tools, Evan managed to get to her knees, lunge away from Xandra, and reach for a large scissors. She swung the blades at Xandra's torso, hesitant to make a stab at the dress.

She wanted Xandra to keep talking, hoping that the dress was recording their conversation.

"Where did you find the other girls? On the streets as well?" Evan fished.

"You don't find world-class fashion models on the street corners," Xandra said with a gasp, dodging the point of the scissors. "But if you know what to look for, you can find and polish a young model into something special."

"Someone who can twist a man around her little finger and get him to talk. Get him to do anything?" Evan suggested.

Xandra twisted at the waist and reached under the dress for the sub-compact firearm strapped to her thigh. She raised the pistol in her trembling hand. "Enough talk about my work. Tell me about the weapons in the dress."

"Wearing my dress does not make you invincible. That dress is mine. The team that comes with it is mine," Evan said, wiping blood from her freshly split lip. A surge of pride energized her.

"You don't have a team anymore. After tonight you will just have a pile of bodies, all killed with your gun. I like it, by the way. It has a nice weight. Wouldn't you agree?" She swung her arm in a full right hook, trying to smash the pistol into the side of Evan's head.

Evan ducked and turned. The butt of the grip grazed her forehead as she spun a three-sixty. The heel of her foot crashed into Xandra's side. Again, the body armor absorbed most of the force and only knocked the pistol from Xandra's grip.

The Springfield slid across the floor and under the worktable. Evan raced to catch it, but Xandra grabbed her ankle and pulled her down beside her. Hitting the floor, Evan lost hold of the scissors, and they spun out of her reach.

They again wrestled face-to-face, slapping and punching and kicking furiously. Evan was determined not to let this go further with Xandra. She evaluated her position and decided to give up the defensive stance. The sharp pains had quieted to a dull ache. Evan knew that tomorrow she would probably be immobile. She sustained her fight fueled only by the fumes of adrenaline.

She wedged the heel of her left palm under Xandra's chin and pushed up until her opponent's face was about eighteen inches over hers. She jerked her right arm free and brought her elbow down on Xandra's left collarbone with as much force as she could muster. A sharp snap indicated her success.

Xandra screamed suddenly into the quiet of the warehouse. A door from the other side of the room flew open, and the silhouette of a man filled the space. Evan pushed Xandra's injured body away from her and sat up to focus on the man. Jarrett Brawn.

"Hello, Tyler," he said. He spoke in hushed tones that were barely audible over Xandra's sobbing.

"Brawn." She managed to stand, but her legs felt weak and unsteady. "Jarrett, please help me."

He crossed his arms and shook his head. "Now you want to be friends?"

Evan drew long slow breaths, trying to renew her energy. The dried blood in her nostrils made it difficult to breathe without hissing. *Make them talk.* She was desperate to carry out her mission.

Xandra gasped and cried in between fits of Russian curses. At that moment Evan was glad that her Russian was terrible. Brawn pulled off his belt and strapped it at Xandra's waist, cinching and immobilizing her left arm.

Evan wondered how long they had been working together. *The first party? No, they've been playing us all along. She's had him on her leash for a while.*

Brawn turned away from Xandra and approached Evan. "You are going to tell us about the dress. We need you, it's true," he said. He pulled his knife from his boot. "But we don't need all of you."

Evan staggered away from him until she was almost against the wall. He charged her, taking a firm grasp of her neck and hitting her head against the plaster. Everything around her blurred into a swirl of bright green and yellow. His fingers tightened on her throat. He held the flat of his blade against her cheek.

"You'll talk. You don't want your pretty face messed up," he whispered.

She tried to pull his hands away. His muscles felt like steel.

Evan struggled to suck in enough oxygen to stay conscious. Her mind flashed back to her first self-defense training class. She moved her hands from his arms to his face, scratching at his face and trying to poke her fingers into his eyes. He dropped his knife and released her throat to grab her hands.

She gulped in the air, filling her lungs to capacity.

Brawn held both of her wrists with his left hand. He pressed them against the wall over her head. He groped roughly at her side with his right hand.

"You know, when you fight like a girl, you remind me that I'm a man," he growled into her ear.

"Yes, you are," Evan answered. She punched her knee up into his groin with all her might.

He doubled over and fell backward. Evan turned a back-roundhouse kick and landed her heel on the side of his head. He collapsed in a moaning heap, out cold.

A bullet flew past Evan's shoulder, ripping a hole in her shirt, but not touching her skin. "Stop," Xandra shouted.

Evan froze in place. She studied Xandra's stance. Her opponent was shaky, visibly in pain. She held the pistol with her free arm straight and her elbow locked.

Evan raised her hands slowly. "Xandra, you don't have to do any of this. You have the dress. You can just walk away."

Xandra screamed at her. "You don't know about anything. My family should have been given all kinds of power in Russia. My grandfather should have been honored for his actions. For the millions of lives he saved. His great work brought down the family that oppressed the poor. They should have made him a leader. Instead, the people hated him."

"And you're just taking back what the people stole from your family?" Evan asked. "You make these powerful men tell you their secrets. That is how you take their power?"

"It's mine, now. I have more power than the Romanovs ever had," Xandra boasted. "It's what my grandfather wanted for me. It's why he saved the pieces of the shattered jewels."

"You had them re-cut and marked." Evan inched toward her, staying out of Brawn's reach, in case he regained consciousness. "But why engrave them with the Romanov crest?"

"Still so stupid. To remind me of the power. To remind me that sometimes the blood of innocents is required for change." Xandra pushed the pistol forward another inch. "I warn you to stop. I will shoot you again."

Evan shook her head and took a short step closer. "You missed." She saw Xandra's arm shaking. "You're in bad shape, Xandra. You need to be careful. If you get upset, the dress can be deadly to you."

Xandra's breathing became angry huffs. "You stay away from me," she said, adding a Russian curse.

Evan took another step. "There are only a few other dangers that can be deadly. But then perhaps I'm lying. Am I lying to you, Xandra? You know the dress can tell when someone is lying."

Xandra blinked nervously. She sniffed. Sweat began to form on her lip and brow. "Shut up!" she yelled.

"I wouldn't get over-excited if I were you," Evan warned. She took another step.

Xandra's whole body began to shake. Evan watched the Springfield tremble in her grip.

"Calm down."

"You are lying to me," Xandra huffed.

"Of course, I am," Evan said in her most soothing voice. "I'm sure you can tell. Does the dress feel tighter? Is it getting warm?"

"Yes."

Evan lunged at her, and Xandra fired another shot. This one missed Evan completely. She grabbed the pistol from Xandra's hand and pushed the blonde away with her foot. Xandra hit the wall with her injured shoulder and howled in pain.

"Just relax," Evan said. "It's over."

Evan spun around with her pistol ready just as the door opened and two men burst in.

CHAPTER THIRTY

Hedge found the door to the basement stairs and descended as quietly as possible. He listened for any sign of others but heard nothing. He searched the short hall at the bottom of the stairs, peering through the open doors. The rooms were empty. Only one door remained closed.

He took a deep breath and readied his weapon. He pushed open the door, leading with his Glock. The small storage room flickered with the dim light of an overhead fluorescent.

"There you are," he muttered to Anton's body, sprawled shirtless in the center of the floor. The dead man's jacket lay to one side, and a folding chair stood at his feet. A small pool of blood under the chair indicated that he'd died quickly.

Evan was missing.

Hedge's brain shifted into high gear. He called Ramos.

"Kirk is in surgery now. No prognosis by the doctors. Did you find Evan?"

"Not yet," Hedge answered. "I have Anton's body. When will back up be here?"

"Soon," Ramos assured him. "Hedge, check something for me. As I was leaving the house, I thought I saw a black Ferrari parked up the block."

"On it," Hedge said. He took the stairs two at a time and plowed through the front door. He skirted the yard and driveway, hiding in the shadows of the iron fence and the shrubs that lined it.

Through the bushes, he could see the black sports car as well as the man behind the wheel. Robert Charles.

Hedge snarled and marched through the gate and right up to driver's window. Charles rolled his eyes as his window came down.

"What do you want, Mr. Parker?"

"How long have you been here?" Hedge asked.

"What do you mean? Tonight?" Charles shrugged.

"Where is Evan? Did you see her leave? Who was she with?" Hedge barraged him with rapid-fire questions.

"I haven't seen Evan since she arrived an hour ago. The only person to leave, besides your friend in the SUV, has been Xandra, but I assume you know that. She left the garage about a minute after you arrived," Charles said.

"Where did she go?"

Charles cocked his head to one side, apparently preparing a snide remark, but then seemed to realize Hedge's urgency. He tapped on the keys of his tablet. "It looks like her car went downtown to the fashion district. Probably to Anton's shop. She was alone in the car."

Hedge ran around the front of the car to the other door and pushed his way in. "Take me there. She was not alone."

"My orders are to wait for Hrevic to come out and then take him into custody," Charles said.

"Anton's not coming out. He's dead in the basement. Now drive me to the shop." Hedge gripped his pistol.

"Did you kill him?" Charles asked, starting the engine.

"Xandra shot him in the head. She has Evan with her."

Charles raced through the narrow streets to the dress shop. The storefronts were all dark and empty. The House of Alexei shop was dark, but a light shone through the second-floor windows.

The men checked for security cameras on the doors but found nothing visible. A muffled pop sounded from upstairs.

"We have to risk it," Hedge said, breaking through the front door in seconds. He pushed into the store, and together the men scoured the lower floor before finding the stairs to the second level.

"Most of these places have a front office and a workroom in back," Charles whispered as they climbed the steps.

"Xandra's armed, and Evan is injured. I'm not sure who else we may be up against," Hedge informed Charles. "Be careful."

Charles nodded as they reached the metal door at the top of the stairs. Hedge turned the lever handle slowly and waited for any reaction from the other side. Nothing.

They pushed the door open and again heard nothing. As they entered the small front office, a gunshot popped loudly from the back room. Both men instinctively ducked and then positioned themselves on either side of the adjoining door. They held their weapons at the ready.

Charles nodded for Hedge to take the lead.

He pushed handle and rushed through the door. Side by side, both men faced the raised muzzle of Evan's drawn pistol.

"What took you so long?" Evan asked.

CHAPTER THIRTY-ONE

"I hope y'all brought flex-ties," Evan said, releasing a breath and lowering her weapon.

Hedge exhaled in relief and scanned the room. Jarrett Brawn's crumpled body rested a few feet from one wall, and Xandra's slumped figure leaned against the cabinets of another. Evan stood in the middle of the huge room, dressed in nothing but a man's ripped and bloody dress shirt and underwear. Tough. Beautiful. He couldn't be prouder of her.

"Sorry we're a bit late to the party," Charles said. He pulled out a handful of nylon restraints from his jacket. "Who gets the prizes?"

Hedge marched across the space and motioned to Brawn. "Him first," he muttered gruffly. He didn't even look back at his former team member. He couldn't see anyone but Evan.

He took her into his arms and hugged her as tightly as he dared. She pressed her face into his neck, he could feel her shiver in his embrace.

"Are you alright?" he asked once he'd finally released her.

"Yeah," she said. Her voice was weak and scratchy. "But I want my dress back."

Hedge turned toward Xandra. She spat at him and glared. She swore in Russian, and Hedge raised his eyebrows.

"Tch, tch, tch. That's not very lady-like," Hedge said. "But then, I don't suppose that's your goal, is it, Ms. Yakovsky?"

Hedge unbuttoned his shirt and handed it to Evan. "Get that dress off her. I don't want to see it on anyone but you," he ordered. He looked around the room and saw a changing screen to the side of the dress forms. "Take her back there."

Hedge walked to Charles' side and helped him pull Brawn upright. He grabbed the metal folding chair from the floor and pushed it under the traitor.

Brawn hissed a long string of expletives and began flexing against the bindings at his wrists and ankles. "You know you had to tie my feet, too, because I'd kill you both otherwise."

Hedge didn't hesitate. He made a fist and punched Brawn squarely in the mouth. The chair in which Brawn sat rocked back on two legs and then crashed down hard with a jolt.

"I'd take that as a compliment if I were you," Charles said to Brawn with a laugh. He turned to Hedge. "What next?"

Hedge looked back at the door to the office. "If you can watch him for a minute, I need to check the other room for something."

"My pleasure," Charles answered. He paced a tight perimeter around Brawn. "If you keep your mouth shut, I might just pull you upright again."

Hedge called over the screen to Evan. "I'm going to search the office for Kirk's notebook, Evan."

"It has to be here," she answered. "I doubt Brawn would have let it out of his sight."

Once in the small office, Hedge shuffled through the paperwork on the pale green metal desk. He found the typical utility bills and invoices for fabrics and equipment. A desk calendar noted dates for incoming shipments, fashion shows, and parties, but little more. The cheap desk phone showed no messages or recordings at all.

He pulled open a file drawer to the right of the desk. The files in the front were labeled with the five models' names. Behind those were three more folders marked with other names: Sophia, Xenia, and Nikki. Hedge snapped a picture with his camera phone. He started to email it to Kirk, and then realized Kirk wouldn't receive it.

An idea flashed through his mind. "Maybe Kirk won't get it, but his notebook will," he said to himself. He punched the buttons on his phone, and within a few seconds, a faint chime and a dull blue glow emanated from a black canvas bag to the side of the door. "Found you," he said with satisfaction.

Before Hedge could open the laptop, he heard the sounds of a scuffle and another shot from the workroom. He raced back in, dreading what he might find.

Charles lay on the floor with blood seeping from his chest. Evan, again wearing her dress, lay face-down on the collapsed dressing screen. Xandra howled in pain, holding her left arm. Blood oozed from between her fingers. Brawn was gone.

Hedge started to Charles' side but saw immediately from the huge gashes in his chest that he was dead. He ran to Evan and rolled her over.

He felt for a pulse but found nothing. He took her pistol from her hand and tucked it into the back of his waistband. "What happened?" he asked Xandra.

"He aimed at her, but the bullet hit me," she cried. "Help me!"

Hedge scoffed at the blonde and focused all his energy on Evan. "Come on, Evan. You're okay. Remember, just a hiccup." He started chest compressions. He backed off for a second, waiting for the dress to fibrillate, but nothing happened. "It's shut down," he complained to himself, resuming compressions.

He closed his mouth over hers and pushed two heavy breaths into her lungs. He waited for half a second to listen. Three more compressions. "Evan, stay with me," he ordered. A few seconds ticked by. Too long. He took another deep breath, ready to start again.

Before his lips were over hers, Evan's eyes fluttered, and she coughed.

Hedge sighed in relief. "Breathe for a second before you try to sit up."

"My Springfield," she whispered hoarsely.

"I've got it," Hedge reassured her. He scowled at Xandra. "Where did Brawn go?"

"He disappeared," she said bitterly. "That's why I hired him in the first place. He vanishes. You won't find him."

Hedge helped Evan sit upright and regain her composure. She'd been through hell, and he wasn't about to leave her side until she was steady again. Xandra glared at both of them from where she moaned in the corner.

"Can I please shut her up?" Evan asked. She pulled herself to her feet using the end of the long cutting table. "She's giving me a headache."

Hedge laughed. She was back. He nodded and said, "You take care of her, and I'll call Agent McKinnon-Grey."

He called Eleanor and explained the situation. She ordered a BOLO for Brawn while Hedge was still on the line. "I'll be in Paris tomorrow," she said.

"Find out what you can about Brawn," he replied. "We'll get what we can from Xandra."

"Your job is done, Hedge. You don't have any team left to work with. You clean up and come home," she said.

"I still have Evan and Ramos. We're more than capable of finishing this job." Hedge nodded to Evan, and she smiled through swollen lips.

"The job is over," Eleanor said.

"We'll talk when you're here." He clicked off before she could respond.

Xandra whimpered as Evan bound her wound and then re-wrapped her shoulder and arm to limit movement.

"I took one knife from Brawn, but he probably had several on him," Evan said. "I didn't have a chance to search him before you got here."

Xandra smiled as she cast a casual glance at Charles' body. "He learned the hard way. Too bad. He was handsome," she hummed.

Evan looked as though she was going to slap Xandra. "She killed Anton. And she killed Kirk."

Hedge pushed his chin up and shook his head. "I found Anton. But she didn't kill Kirk. He's in surgery. She's no better aim than Brawn."

They waited for ten minutes before the authorities arrived. Hedge quickly debriefed them and waited for Xandra to be taken into custody. "Don't take your eyes off of her," he warned. "She's dangerous. She's already murdered one man tonight and attempted to kill another."

The officer guarding her glowered. "She won't charm me."

"See to that," Hedge barked. He motioned to the men attending to Charles' body. "He was MI-6. Treat him with respect." Charles had earned it.

He grabbed the notebook and escorted Evan down to the street. They drove the Ferrari around to the back entrance of the building, looking for clues to Brawn's whereabouts. All they found was an ear receiver that had been smashed on the pavement.

"He's in the wind," Hedge whispered.

CHAPTER THIRTY-TWO

Ramos called from the hospital. "Kirk is going to make it. They're taking care of Xandra now, too," he said. "I'll head to the flat for a sweep. I doubt Brawn's stupid enough to go back there, but I don't want to assume anything."

"Let me know if you hear something," Hedge said before disconnecting. He sighed as he waited in the upstairs hall at Hrevic's mansion. "You need to go to the hospital and get checked out, too," Hedge called through the bedroom door.

"I will. But I'm not leaving this house without some record of who all they were blackmailing." She stepped from her to-be-bedroom at the end of the hall, cleaned up and wearing the dress.

Hedge eyed his partner from head to toe. Evan's red hair covered the cut in her forehead and the knot on the side of her head. Her bottom lip swelled in the center at the split. Her right eye started showing signs of blackening. Hedge cringed at the sight of her torn earlobe.

He reached his hand to brush back her hair from her neck. He saw Brawn's thumb and fingerprints on her throat. The scrape on her shoulder ran down and joined an abrasion on her elbow. Her fingernails were ripped and chipped from the attacks. Her knees and calves were covered with bruises and small cuts from the stiletto heels she now wore.

His heart swelled and thumped with admiration as his gaze met hers.

"Do you have any idea where we might find all these records? Our officers seized all of the computers and the other jewelry. If there's anything on them, Kirk will find it." Hedge patted Kirk's notebook and followed Evan down the hall.

"I do," she answered.

They entered the sitting room and stepped into the small vault room.

"I just gotta know," she said.

Hedge opened the computer and brought up the LBD program. Evan pressed the top button on the waistband, and the monitor flashed to life.

"This may take a minute or two," Hedge said. "But if this works, it'll sure make Kirk happy." He enabled the encryption decoder.

Evan stood next to the keypad and let the dress scan the device remotely. Hedge pulled a pair of gloves from his pocket for her and began tugging on a pair of his own. Before they were ready, the code flashed on the screen.

"I'll enter the code. You see what's inside," he said.

She nodded and waited.

Hedge punched in the numbers. They both held their breaths as the cabinet made a clicking noise. The top drawer rolled open.

Evan stared at the jewels that glistened in the black velvet-lined tray. The pieces that she wore before were on the right. A bracelet set with rubies rested in the center of the drawer. Two more necklaces and matching earrings filled the remainder of the tray. Across the back of the drawer was a small remote control.

"What does this do?" she asked, holding the small clicker in the palm of her open hand.

Hedge picked it up and looked at it carefully. "Only one way to find out," he said.

"Hey," she protested. Hedge punched the first button. The top drawer slid closed and the second opened.

Evan looked at the control for a second. Reaching over Hedge's fingers, she pushed the bottom button labeled *ALL*. As noted, all of the drawers rolled open at the same time. The pair worked from the top down, recording the contents of each drawer and then pushing each tray closed. When they reached the bottom drawer, they found an emerald necklace arranged flat in a shallow tray. Evan lifted the tray and necklace from the drawer to reveal a false bottom. Under that, they discovered a locked metal box.

Hedge set the box on the cabinet top and retrieved a small knife from his pocket. He flipped it open and inserted the narrow blade into the lock. The latch popped immediately. He poured the contents onto the countertop for examination. A few dozen keys spilled out. Each one had a key ring labeled with the name of a major city in Europe. With a closer look, Hedge saw that the key fobs were actually flash drives.

"This looks like a nice little vacation, don't you think?" he asked.

Evan picked through the cities. "Marseille, Cannes, Nice, Genoa, Barcelona, Ravenna They all sound heavenly right now."

Hedge smiled. "Are you a quick healer?"

"Aww come on," Evan whined. "Don't tease. Healed or not, this job is over. Someone else will get to do the mopping up."

"You're sure about that?"

"Eleanor told me at the beginning of all of this that this mission would last a week to ten days, followed by a month of debriefings and evaluation." Evan stared at the flash drives as she explained.

Hedge moved to the side of the cabinet and hunched down. He crossed his arms at the cabinet's edge and lowered his chin to rest on them. Evan gazed over the keys and into his dark blue eyes. He arched his right brow.

"That's exactly what she told me. I'm just not sure I'm all that excited about a month of meetings and paperwork," Hedge said. He poked his right index finger into the pile and began stirring the keys around.

"Oh, I see," she said with a smirk. "If you don't feel like it, I'm sure Eleanor and her bosses will completely understand. I totally forgot about the 'I don't want to,' exemption."

She leaned over, too, propping her elbows on the cabinet top and dropping her chin into her hands. She couldn't help but smile at Hedge's goofy grin.

"They won't let us track down these leads. We don't even know what these keys go to." She flicked her finger into the mix.

Hedge picked up the one marked *Marseille*. He dangled it in front of her face. "When was the last time you were in Marseille?"

She paused for a moment. "Two years ago, I was there for eleven hours."

Hedge made an injured, puckered face. "Ooh, that hardly counts. What about Barcelona? There is some amazing architecture in Barcelona."

"I've never been to Barcelona." Evan sighed as she shook her head. "We can't, you know. We shouldn't even pretend about it."

"I can be ready to go in six hours," Hedge said.

"I'll be under observation for at least twenty-four," she replied, surrendering to the daydream.

"I'll be discharged by then," Kirk hummed in both of their ears.

Evan's face lit up. "Kirk! Red! You're all right?"

Hedge straightened and moved to put his arm around her shoulders, careful not to bump her scrapes and bruises. "Hey, Kirk! Glad to know you're going to make it."

"I've never been to Barcelona, either," Kirk said.

Evan nudged Hedge's side. "Now you've got Kirk going." She laughed. "Red, I'm afraid we're all headed back to DC to close this file."

Hedge stared at Evan and then at the key in his hand. He held the key to within inches of the dress. "Kirk, would it be safe for the notebook if I plugged in an unauthorized flash drive?"

"Probably," he answered. "But it would be easier and safer to let the dress scan them all at once."

Evan laughed. "Of course. Why didn't I think of that?"

Hedge handed the key and fob to Evan and went back to the notebook. "Let's just try one for starters. What do I do?"

Evan drew a long breath, appearing energized. "What are we looking for, Kirk?" She held the thumb drive over her heart.

"Hedge, bring up the external storage device reader window," Kirk said.

"That one," Evan said, pointing at the screen.

The monitor flashed, and a blue progress bar zipped across the window. A little flashing tab at the top of the page indicated that the contents could be viewed.

"That was fast," she said.

Hedge opened the file with the contents of the fob. A column of pictures ran down the left side of the monitor. Every photo included a description file on the right of the screen. Each file contained names, dates, GPS coordinates and miscellaneous information about the subjects.

"These weren't shot for Christmas cards," Hedge said. He wasn't sure what he expected to see, but it wasn't photos of a middle-aged man in half a dozen compromising positions with Tatiana.

"I should say not," Evan said. "I'm not old enough to see these."

"Neither am I," Hedge said.

"Red, what can you tell us about these keys?" Evan asked.

"I can't see them, remember?" he said, sounding glum. "Tell me about them."

Hedge studied one in his hand. "They're all the same type. They're average-size and have cuts on both sides of the key. They look like they're made of plain steel."

"You said they are marked with city names?" he asked.

"Yes. Well, the attached flash drives are marked, not the keys themselves. Every device is labeled with a different city," Evan said. She picked up another key. "The actual keys are engraved with the manufacturer's name. It's Titan."

"Separate them by countries. Tell me if there are similarities in the cuts by country." Kirk's voice picked up in pace.

"France over here. Spain here. Italy, Greece, and Egypt here." Hedge said as he and Evan pushed the keys into small piles.

They began comparing the keys to each other.

"None of the keys are the same," Evan said. "They're all different cuts, but the same type. There's no indication at all what they fit."

"Maybe there is," Kirk said. "What do all of those cities have in common?"

"They're all on the Mediterranean," Hedge suggested. "All shipping ports. This job isn't over. If we can figure out what these keys open, it might help us find Brawn."

Evan nodded and bit her bottom lip. "What do you think, Red?"

"I think if you want me to back you up on this, you had better let me come with you. And Ramos says him, too." Kirk sighed.

Hedge took her hand and squeezed. "If I can handle Eleanor, will you come with me?"

Evan swallowed hard. "I don't know, Hedge."

"I told you before that there aren't ten women in the world that could wear that dress. I was wrong. There aren't two. You're it, Evan. I need you."

CHAPTER THIRTY-THREE

Eleanor waited for her team at the hospital exit. She opened the doors to the SUV for Evan, Kirk, Ramos, and Hedge. She glared at them like a substitute school teacher with a disrespectful class.

"This isn't a democracy with majority rule," she scolded them as she pulled away from the curb. "Kirk and Tyler should really spend another 48 hours in the hospital."

"You always said that we don't walk away from a job until it's finished," Hedge reminded her. "We need to verify what these keys unlock. We need to know that there aren't other people out there ready to use this information to their advantage. And we need to find Brawn."

Eleanor cast a perturbed glance over her shoulder. "I'm aware of all that. Brawn was my mistake. You aren't responsible for him."

Hedge ignored her last comment. "We need the dress to help us finish this."

"What do you have to say about this, Agent Tyler?" Eleanor asked. She focused on Evan's eyes in her rear-view mirror.

"Ma'am, the dress is incredible. The honor of being chosen for it humbles me. But with all due respect, the dress is a tool. An effective and awe-inspiring tool, but a tool nonetheless. These men are fully capable of completing the job without the dress." Evan said with a tone of regret in her voice.

"Do you think the dress is unnecessary? A waste?" Eleanor asked, not losing her cool gaze on Evan.

"Not a waste at all," Evan explained. "I believe it has more than proven itself in the field."

"May I?" Hedge requested.

Eleanor nodded.

"Evan, you're right. We've been working without the dress for all this time, and we can continue to do so. However, I thought I made myself clear before. I need you on my team. You not only wore the dress successfully, but you were able to kick its butt when needed." Hedge stared at her with a steady eye and a square jaw. "Dress or not, you are coming."

"Yessir," she answered.

Eleanor watched as Evan's expression warmed into a broad smile. "I'm glad to have that settled," Eleanor said. "Ramos, hand out the packets. I'm moving you all to a secure location, but I want you to spend the next twenty-four hours watching the flat and the mansion. Brawn may try to go back to either of these locations. If he does, pick him up."

"And if he doesn't, we're giving him another day to get to wherever in the world he wants to go," Hedge said.

"We flagged him before he had the chance to get to an airport or train. MI-6 has a team on him, too. He's not getting away." Eleanor pulled up at the Hotel Britannique. "For now, get something to eat. I'll send cars for you in two hours."

"Where are you going?" Hedge asked, helping Evan out of the car.

"I'm going in to sweet-talk Fischer into giving me another week. After that, I have some coordinating to do with Interpol." Eleanor sighed. "I'll contact you later. Take a breather and then get back to the job."

CHAPTER THIRTY-FOUR

Hedge watched as she drove away, and then turned back to his team. "At least this place is nicer than the apartment."

They made their way to the third-floor suite, and Ramos used his key to let them in. "Agent McKinnon-Grey moved all our stuff over. There are two bedrooms. Kirk and I are in this one," he said, gesturing to the room on the left.

"Good," Hedge said. His gaze roamed over the walnut-paneled walls hung with extremely well-done copies of Renaissance artwork. Everything in the room was draped in scarlet or covered in gold. He dropped his bag beside the red velvet couch in the salon. He motioned to the black-enameled door on the right side of the room. "Evan, you can have that bedroom to yourself."

She nodded. "Thanks."

Hedge picked up the phone. "What do you all want for lunch? I'll call room service."

"Any kind of sandwich is fine with me," Ramos said. He sat in a plush chair between two pillows and stretched his legs out over the ottoman at his feet.

"Same for me," Kirk said, setting up his laptop at the desk behind the couch.

Hedge waved the phone at Evan. "What about you?"

"I'm not hungry." She disappeared into her bedroom.

"Don't care," he said. He punched in the code for the dining room and ordered lunch. He cradled the receiver and then went out to the narrow balcony for some fresh air.

Why was everything a battle with Evan? She seemed to run hot and then cold. Close and then distant. He looked down to the street and watched the traffic for a few minutes. Deep breath, in and out. He was supposed to be relaxing. That wasn't going to happen as long as there was a job to finish. Hedge shifted the four iron patio chairs around to face each other. He pulled one of the ornate cherry end tables from the parlor to set in the middle of the arrangement.

When the server arrived, Hedge instructed him to take the tray outside. The young man shifted a platter of food and beer from his cart to the small table and then poured out a carafe of water into four glasses. Hedge handed him a generous tip as the man bowed his way out of the suite.

"Let's eat," he called to the others as he latched the door.

Ramos and Kirk found their places on the balcony. Hedge knocked on Evan's door.

"Lunch," he said. "Come out and join us."

Evan opened the door a crack. "I'm really not hungry."

"I didn't ask if you were hungry. Join us at the table. We're having a meeting." He motioned to the door. "We're outside."

Evan nodded and followed him out.

"I want to start by apologizing to you all. I thought this job would be a quick one. I got cocky, thinking the dress would be our ace in the hole." Hedge explained.

"I get it," Evan said with a sigh. "I'm the one who should apologize."

Kirk shook his head. "It wasn't your fault, Evan."

Ramos held up his hands to interrupt, but the apologies began piling up and overlapping. Within seconds the air became a jumble of frustrated gasps and stutters. Ramos shook his head, wedged his right index and pinky fingers into the corners of his mouth, and expelled a shrill whistle that silenced everyone.

"Okay," he said calmly. "I know I'm the new guy here, and I don't know everything there is to know about the dress. But one thing I do know. That dress is not Superman's cape. It's not a magic bullet, and it doesn't hold the secrets of the universe. Am I right?"

Hedge, Kirk, and Evan all nodded.

"Good. We have that out of the way. Did any of us have any idea that Anton was just a pawn for Xandra?" he asked.

The others shook their heads.

"Fantastic. I think we're making progress." Ramos picked up his sandwich and waved it at the others. "Did any of you suspect that Brawn was a lying turncoat or that he was screwing us all?"

Again, they all shook their heads.

"Then I say let's get over all this. We just want to finish the job. So let's just do the job. I love you guys. I'm having fun." Ramos took a bite of his sandwich. "I know I didn't get shot or beat up yet, but my turn's coming. And I can't wait."

The rest of the team just stared at each other. Evan started snickering.

Hedge and Kirk burst into laughter.

"This is what I'm talking about," Ramos said with his mouth full of sandwich.

They all ate their lunch and talked and laughed.

"We should have spent more time talking like this," Evan said. "Maybe then we'd have seen it."

"Stop where you are," Hedge warned. "Like Teo says, 'no more second-guessing.' Right, Teo?"

"That's right," he said, raising his glass of beer and taking a long drink.

"I'm not second-guessing. I'm just thinking out loud, you know?" Evan said. "I mean, we don't know each other. We just trust each other because we have to." She leaned back in her chair and rubbed at her neck. "I know what the job is about. I know or can guess, what we've all done in our lives. I know the things I'm capable of. But when you see and feel first-hand that kind of brutality. The way he strangled my throat, and then how he stabbed poor Charles." Her voice faded.

Hedge stared into her eyes, as the image of a slashed and strangled model flashed in his mind. He knew she had the same realization.

"It's Brawn," he said.

Evan nodded. "Red, can you look up where Brawn was when Sophia Ivanov was murdered?"

Kirk nodded. "I can, but I don't have to. He told me that he's been in Paris for almost two months. If he was telling the truth..."

"Let's be sure," Hedge said. "I don't want to work off of assumptions anymore."

They all went inside and watched Kirk work away on his notebook. "He was here."

"Can you tell us what happened to a couple of other models that Anton had? One named Xenia, the other was Nikki." Hedge hovered over Kirk's shoulder. He looked up at Evan. "I saw their names in Anton's file drawer."

Kirk tapped for a few seconds more. "Got it. Nikki is Colette Reubens. She is twenty-years-old. Reported missing from Roissy by her brother last October; nothing since." He looked up grimly. "Xenia is Gina Marcos. She was found eight months ago floating in the river. She was stabbed and strangled as well." He typed, and his computer beeped in response. "Brawn was within sixty kilometers on both occasions."

"He's Xandra's hit man," Ramos said.

Hedge snarled. "Not just hers. If he killed these women, he killed the men they were seeing at the time, including Ehud Kharu. Kharu's killer has already been linked to six other hits across Europe."

"Wait up. So, if Brawn and Xandra knew that Evan was an agent, how come Anton didn't?" Ramos asked.

Evan shook her head. "Xandra was using Anton and the muses for

193

gathering information. We're all on a need-to-know basis regarding the dress on this assignment. That's why Brawn didn't know all the details of the operation. Xandra may have considered that Anton didn't need to know, either. I mean, she wanted the dress, not me. If she had the dress, then she wouldn't need Anton anymore. If he knew this, he would become a liability to her."

Ramos shook his head and narrowed his gaze. "Brawn was setting us up from the moment he took this assignment." His words were bitter.

Hedge didn't say anything. He didn't have to. They all wanted Brawn taken down. He was first in line for revenge. Hedge nodded and pulled out his phone. He punched Eleanor's number. She didn't say hello.

"Hedge, I was about to call you. We have movement on the bank account for Yakovsky's jewelry shop. Is there any chance that Xandra initiated a deal before we caught her?"

"Brawn is her hit man. There's no telling whether he's taking care of something for her or trying to get at her cash all on his own. Let him access the account and have a trace put on the money," Hedge said.

"What?" she asked.

"You heard me. This is our chance to get a line on him. Follow the transfers and let us know where he's headed. Kirk's going to send you some dots we just connected." Hedge motioned to Kirk. "We'll work from this end, and you can work from yours."

Hedge clicked off. "This is big. He's drawing cash from the jewelry shop account. It has to be him. Elle is going to trace the transaction and let us know where he's going. Ideas? Where do we start here?"

"I'm still not sure about the house. What if we missed something?" Evan asked. "If he's been in Paris for this long, where has he been staying?"

"I'll check his file. It should have a list of addresses," Kirk said. "He won't go back to any of them unless he's stupid."

"He's not stupid," Evan said. "He may keep them in his watch, though. I suppose it depends on if he wants to eliminate us. Brawn might not give us a second thought."

"If he really wanted to get away clean, he would lay low for a while," Ramos said. "He would cut ties and back-pack to the next country. As a company man, he knows what it takes to make convincing forged documents. You can bet he has assets that can set him up with whatever paperwork he wants."

Hedge looked over the report in their assignment files. "He'll want to take us all out if he can. He won't walk away. If he thinks he can get back into the cache of money that Xandra offered, he'll do it. He's proud." He stared at Evan. It was all about her.

"What?" she asked.

"It's you. He'll come after you first."

"Because I'm a woman?"

Hedge nodded. "You're not just any woman. You took him out all by yourself, and not armed with a pistol or a knife or a dress even. You beat him with your bare hands."

Evan smiled.

"He might overlook the rest of us, but in his eyes, you have to pay," Hedge said.

"I have to die, you mean," she said.

"I think that's how he'll see it," he said.

Kirk tapped at his keys. "I have two Paris addresses from previous assignments. I hacked into the traffic camera feeds, and we'll get a hit if he shows up at either place." He looked at Evan. "I agree with Hedge, Evan. I'd feel better if you stayed out of sight until we get him into custody."

Ramos agreed. "I'll stake out his most recent address, and Hedge can watch the mansion. Kirk, you and Evan can stay here and keep us coordinated."

Evan stood up and planted her hands on her hips. Everything about her screamed defiance. "I will not hide out here. I'm the one with the dress. I'm the one who knocked him out. If you think he'll come after me, then I need to get out there and make him show his face."

Hedge grimaced. "That's not why I said that."

"Does that matter?" she asked. "Brawn is a cold-blooded assassin for hire. We know what he's capable of. I didn't sign up for this job so that I could travel the world in pretty clothes."

Hedge laughed. "Unlike me." He hoped a joke might quench her fire.

"Put me out there," she insisted. "If Brawn is still in Paris, we can find him."

Kirk shook his head, appealing to Hedge. "She can't go out alone."

Hedge flipped his file notes closed. "She won't be alone. Ramos and I will be at her side, and you'll be right there in her head."

Ramos shrugged. "Will Eleanor go for it?"

"Leave her to me," Hedge said. "If Evan is up for this, she can't turn us down." He looked at Evan again. "Are you certain?"

"I'll make sure my red cape is back from the cleaners."

CHAPTER THIRTY-FIVE

"He's on his own right now. No Xandra, no Anton, no muses, no mansion. He has two choices. He can stay in Paris, or he can leave town, leave France completely," Hedge stated. "We have his list of known aliases, as well as his face, red-flagged for international travel. All known accounts are frozen, and we're working off of the theory that he's the one trying to get the Yakovsky funds moved."

Evan listened to every word, but her mind wandered back to that night. Anton's dead eyes. The feel of Brawn's rough fingers closing around her throat. The sound of Xandra's collarbone snapping.

She felt like the other three men were staring at her. She looked around the room. They were staring at her.

"I'm sorry, what?" she asked.

"We're just discussing the advantages we have over Brawn. Kirk has him flagged. Ramos' skills give us a tactical advantage at a distance." Hedge motioned to the others and then to her. "You have the dress for defense. We have his history, including his known assets here in France and surrounding countries." He shrugged. "I just wondered if there was some advantage you could think of that maybe we haven't?"

She tumbled a few ideas in her head for a moment.

"You don't have to answer right now," Kirk said. "Just think about it."

Hedge drew a breath to start again, but Evan interrupted him. "He doesn't know that we know," she said.

"We know what?" Hedge asked.

"We know that he was working with Xandra and informing her about our plans. He's aware that we know about that. But he doesn't know that we know that he's the hitman, right?" she asked. "As far as he knows, we just want him for his involvement with Xandra. What if we could get a message to him? Like, if he turns himself in, we will help him out in dealing with MI-6."

Hedge pushed out his bottom lip and stroked his goatee. "I think we could make that work. We'll have to get word to him quickly."

"There are channels," Kirk said. "He'll be listening for information about him one way or another. I'll make sure we include a way for him to get a message back to us."

"Be sure to tell him that I will be there with Hedge when he surrenders himself," Evan said. "Brawn might not risk tangling with Hedge unless he knows he has a shot at me."

"I will," Kirk responded. "Luckily, Eleanor was light on details with her BOLO for Brawn. He'll make contact."

Ramos scratched at his whiskers. "Do you think Brawn will fall for this?"

Evan shook her head. "Only if he thinks he has the upper hand."

Hedge nodded. "We'll make sure he believes he does. He'll play for keeps this time. Every one of us has to stay alert."

Dressed in casual jeans and tee shirts, but armed to the teeth, Evan and Hedge dropped by to visit one of Brawn's known assets, a street artist named Leo. Leo was a short, skinny kid with bad skin and shaggy hair. Evan asked him if he'd seen Brawn recently. As expected, Leo said that he hadn't, but would be happy to get him a message for the right price. They gave him a handful of Euros and a stern warning not to double-cross them. He probably would take the money and skip out, but at least they'd given Brawn a chance to see that they were looking for him.

After leaving Leo on his corner, they made their way to Brawn's former flat, where they saw nothing but an elderly couple tending geraniums on the second-floor balcony. Either he wasn't there anymore, or he had better assets than they imagined for cover.

Evan and Hedge took the scenic route back to Anton's mansion. They parked in the gardens and walked hand-in-hand the few blocks to the estate. Strangers would assume they were lovers, out for pleasant afternoon stroll. Once they were at the mansion, Evan made sure that she was visible from both the house and the street as they walked the perimeter of the grounds. No sign of anyone. No security. No groundskeepers. No one.

"I'm not sure that I like you being out here in the open like this," Hedge said, squeezing her hand.

She laughed and squeezed back. The same thought had just run through her mind. They were vulnerable. The very definition of bait. "If Brawn wants me dead, he'll want to do it up close. He's not going to snipe from a hiding place. Not when he tries to kill me, anyway. With you I'm not so sure," she said. She laughed again, trying not to think about what Brawn really might do.

"I have a message for you, Evan," Kirk whispered in her ear.

"It's Kirk." She took Hedge's arm. "He has something."

Hedge faced her and waited.

"What is it?" she asked.

"Brawn sent a message to me through Twitter using a fake profile. He wants to meet with you both under the Pont de l'Archevêché tomorrow evening. He says that he'll come in without a fight," Kirk said.

Evan relayed the message to Hedge. "He's still here."

"And he wants to meet us under the bridge just beyond Notre Dame." Hedge raked his fingers through his hair. "That's the one where the lovers place their padlocks and throw away the keys. He's bold."

Evan realized she was holding her breath and released it slowly. "We knew he was."

She kept a tight hold of Hedge's hand as they returned to their car. She enjoyed his protection and the warmth of his skin against hers. It was temporary. She knew that. But she was bound to enjoy it while it lasted.

They drove in silence back to the hotel to construct a plan. Evan's stomach tightened as they discussed their options. In less than twenty-four hours they would deliver Brawn to Eleanor, or die trying.

CHAPTER THIRTY-SIX

Hedge watched Evan as she ate her breakfast. He studied her hands for any sign of tremor. He listened to her breathing as she read over her notes. He looked at the scrapes on her arms. They were healing nicely. She was steady and calm. He smiled.

"How are you this morning?" he asked.

"I'm fine, Hedge. The dress is in its bag charging. My shoes are polished. My gear is ready. I stripped and cleaned my pistol last night. I have two extra magazines, ready to be loaded. I'm good." She took another bite of her oatmeal. "Are you nervous?"

"Anxious to get this job done," he said. He inhaled a deep breath and held it for several seconds. When he finally released it, his could feel his whole body pulse with his heartbeat.

"You're going to make yourself sick if you keep doing that."

Hedge looked at her with a furrowed brow, as if he didn't know what she meant.

"That holding your breath thing," she explained, waving her spoon. "Just relax. We'll stroll out casually and get our bearings. It will be fine."

Hedge made it a habit of listening to his instinct. He didn't like what it was telling him this morning. "We should have asked for a different location. We need something we can control better than the bridge."

"That's why we're going out early." Evan put her empty bowl back onto the room service tray. "I don't want you to worry. You'll get wrinkles." She smoothed her thumb over his forehead and grinned.

"I'll be gray before this is over," he said. He stood up when Kirk entered the room from his bedroom. "What do we know?"

"I ran diagnostics on everything this morning, and the modifications I made are good to go. I adjusted things for her injuries. Evan should be fine." Kirk sank into the couch. "I checked my message boards this morning. Brawn is still in Paris. My sources say he hasn't purchased any weapons since he went dark, but that really doesn't mean much. We have no idea what he already had stashed, or where."

The entry door opened, causing all three to jump in their seats. Ramos held up his hands as he entered the room. "Wow, you all need to relax, or we're going to blow this before we leave the hotel."

"News?" Hedge asked him.

"Good news," Ramos assured him. "There's a really good chance that Brawn is staying someplace very near the bridge. Lots of traffic cams all over that area and nothing has flagged him yet. That guy's not going in blind. He's gotta be right there. And there are tons of little shops and businesses all over that area, and most of them have rentals above. Lots of tourists. That's good and bad. Good, because he won't risk making the news by killing a tourist. That would ruin his low profile as an assassin."

"And bad because?" Evan asked.

"Because for the same reasons, I can't blow anything up. Even if I really need to," Ramos said and shrugged.

Kirk smiled. "I feel your pain." Kirk and Ramos fist-bumped each other.

"What can you do?" Hedge asked.

Ramos plopped into the armchair next to the sofa and rested his feet on the ottoman in front of him. "The thing about this particular place on the river is that there is really only one place to perch for cover."

"Good news, bad news?" Evan asked.

"Okay," Ramos said. "The good news is that I don't have to worry about where to hide. My options are limited. The bad news is that Brawn will know exactly where I'll be."

"That is bad," Kirk said.

"But I'm a glass-is-half-full kind of guy," Ramos added. "I can turn that weakness into a strength with a few tiny diversions. I have a couple of little cherry bombs that make a big splash in water without doing real damage. Set in the right place under the bridge, they will make a lot of noise. It will give the appearance of more opposition. It's also a good way to divert foot traffic."

Hedge nodded, calculating the odds. "Good. But only if we need it. I don't want Eleanor having to apologize to the French government for any more than absolutely necessary."

"All right," Ramos said. He sounded almost disappointed.

"How long will it take you to get everything in place?" Hedge asked.

"Done. That's where I've been all morning," Ramos answered.

"Kirk, what do you need?" Hedge asked.

Kirk worked on his program. "I'm ready whenever you are."

Hedge stood in the center of the room, rubbing his palms together. He regarded Evan with a smile and another deep breath. She looked just as beautiful in yoga pants and tee shirt as when she wore the dress. "Are you ready to take a stroll on the river?"

"I'm ready," she said.

Hedge cracked his knuckles while Evan pulled her hair back with a wide headband and tied her sneakers. He pulled his jacket on and zipped it half way. He tossed her track jacket to her, and she tied it around her waist.

"We're going to take bicycles to the bridge and scout out our positions," Hedge said. "Keep your eyes and ears open, and let us know if anything changes."

"Roger that," Kirk and Ramos said together.

Hedge and Evan jogged down to the corner bicycle stand. "This isn't a race, you know," Hedge called to her as she ran ahead.

"I know, but I need to get energized." Evan slowed to jogging in place as Hedge picked out a silver bike for each of them. "I feel like a slug," she added. "I've gotta get my muscles back into shape."

"I'd imagine there are a couple of people who wished you really were out of shape," Hedge said. "Brawn and Xandra got spanked by your flabby figure."

Evan climbed onto her bike. "How far is this little ride?"

From their vantage point at the river's edge, Hedge motioned toward a series of bridges and up to the Notre Dame cathedral in the distance. "We're crossing the Pont d'Arcole, riding over to the Il de la Cite, to the cathedral and then rounding to the other side to the target bridge. It's less than a mile." Hedge took the lead on the bicycle.

Evan caught up. "It's going to be fine, Hedge. It's a good plan."

He led her over the first bridge and past the hospital. They kept to the bicycle lanes to avoid the pedestrians. They rode slowly past the front of the iconic cathedral, turning left at the corner and riding down the narrow road between Notre Dame's flying buttresses and the Seine River.

No matter how often he came to the river, he always saw something new. Sometimes the architecture stood out. Sometimes it was the people. Tourists gathered around street musicians and food carts. Locals hurried by without noticing differences. Noticing differences was his job. He didn't have the luxury of being a tourist or a local. He couldn't afford to become awestruck at something exquisite or immune to the mundane. Even if that was what he longed for most of all.

Hedge thought about how wonderful and dangerous that could be. He'd made that mistake before. He wouldn't make it again. Not with Evan.

After crossing the Pont de l'Archevêché, they found a bicycle station and parked. Hedge led Evan back to the bridge. "All these locks, covering every inch of this bridge," he gestured down the tourist-filled path. "Every lock represents a couple in love."

Evan circled her arm around his waist. "Maybe we should have brought our own lock. You know, to blend in."

Hedge looked into her eyes and smiled. He knew this was just their cover, but he liked the feel of her arms around him. Dangerous. Another risk he knew he couldn't take. He turned his gaze away from her and toward the bridge's end, scanning their surroundings as he did.

They walked another half block to the stone steps that lead to the river's edge. Once they were down the stairs, Evan pulled him aside and out of the foot traffic. She was looking up at the gothic arched windows between the flying buttresses radiating from the back of the cathedral.

"From down here the cathedral looks absolutely majestic," Evan commented. She held her hand over her eyes to shield them from the sun's glare.

Hedge nodded and pulled her into the shade provided by the retaining wall. He put his arm around her this time. This was becoming familiar. He liked it and dreaded it at the same time. He forced himself to focus.

"Notice where the trees are," he said, motioning to the small clump of greenery behind them. "It's the only point of cover at this side of the bridge. If he gets too far under the bridge, or if he shows up on the other side, there will be no place for Ramos at all."

"Probably his intention." Evan looked up with brows raised. "Don't you think?"

They walked to the river's edge and looked down. The murky water swirled into the black shadows cast by the bridge. Hedge imagined the thousands of keys lying just a few meters down, completely hidden by the opaque layer of water.

Evan cringed. "I don't want to take a swim in there," she said.

Hedge laughed. "Let's try to avoid that if we can." He kept his eyes and ears open.

Two men swept the deck of the restaurant boat anchored beside them. They were making comments about all of the tourists now pouring down to the river walkways.

"I guess people are the same all over. Even if you work in the most beautiful city in the world, pushing a broom is still pushing a broom," she said.

"You want something to drink?" Hedge asked. "There's a little vendor just down there."

"Some juice would be great," she said. "Any kind." She looked into his dark blue eyes and smiled. He smiled back. *Oh, that smile.* "I'm gonna talk to the guy at the gangway to this restaurant and see what kind of crowds he's expecting tonight."

"Do you want me to go with you?" Hedge asked. He reached out and took her hand. Her fingers curled around his. It was becoming more natural every time. He squeezed. "I can wait if you want."

Evan shook her head and squeezed back. "No. You go on, and I'll catch up."

Hedge took a deep breath. He knew she could handle herself. He knew he needed to let her do her job without hovering over her. But the knot in his stomach persisted.

"It's okay," she whispered, pushing him toward the sidewalk drink cart.

He walked a dozen steps away and then turned to look at her over his shoulder. She waved playfully as she approached the man at the boat's awning. He turned back to the cart. A bright flash of light caught his attention. He scanned the railing at the street above. The side mirror from a parked car reflected the bright sunlight into his eyes. He realized he was holding his breath again.

"A drink for you?" the vendor asked in stiff English.

"Yes, two bottles of apple," Hedge said. He paid the man and took the drinks. As he turned back toward the bridge, a tour group of school children crowded the sidewalk. He stepped to the far right, against the stone wall, and waited for them to pass.

Their teacher nodded and said, "Pardon," as she herded the preteens down the river. Hedge smiled politely.

He made his way back to the front of the dining boat and waited for a second for Evan to return. The man who had been at the awning before reappeared, but Evan was not with him.

"Excusez-moi, monsieur," he said, catching the host's attention. "Vous avez vu mon ami?" he asked. "La femme avec que j'etais?"

"I saw her a minute ago," he replied. "But when the other man came, she left with him."

Hedge's heart pounded in his ears. "Evan," he said under his breath. He handed the bottles of juice to the man and spun around to find her. He scanned the crowds but saw no one with her red hair. "Evan!" he called out. No answer.

He raced down to the underside of the bridge but found nothing. He studied the face of each person going up or down the steps to the road. "Tyler!"

People stopped in their tracks to stare, but he ignored them. If Brawn had Evan, he wouldn't walk away, he'd be running. Hedge saw nobody running.

His head ached as he strained to see her. She was simply gone. He took a deep breath and tried to listen to the receiver in his ear. "Evan, can you hear me?" he whispered. He hoped.

A glint of light reflected up from the pavement just a few meters away from his feet. He stepped toward it, hoping she had dropped a breadcrumb for him to follow.

He bent down and picked up her earring. It was crushed beyond repair.

Brawn made sure that means of communication was destroyed.

"Kirk? Are you there?" he asked. He hated that he left her alone.

"I'm here, Hedge," Kirk answered.

"Brawn has Evan."

CHAPTER THIRTY-SEVEN

"Why would you do something so stupid as to take me?" Evan asked. She struggled against the nylon flex-ties at her wrists and ankles. "Eleanor was all set to make a deal to bring you in. She won't bargain with you now."

Brawn rocked back in his wooden chair, balancing on two legs. "How long have you worked for the agency? Do you still believe that they follow all the rules?" He played with a butterfly knife as he spoke. "They like people who show creativity and initiative. Not only will Eleanor make a deal with me, but I'll be a free man before you finish filing the paperwork for this assignment."

"Why would you ever think that?" she asked. She looked around the tiny room, trying to figure out where exactly he had brought her. The floor looked like hardened dirt, and the walls were made of cut stone. The wiring to the hanging bulb overhead and to the single electrical outlet was exposed, secured only with wire brads in the ancient mortar.

"This little adventure is just my way of showing our superiors that I know how to take the tactical advantage from anyone." Brawn let the front two legs of his chair hit loudly on the floor.

"You killed an agent of the British government. They won't just let you walk away from that," she insisted.

"Of course they will. We make deals like that every day." He sniffed and blinked with a nervous tick. "If they didn't intend to deal, they would have just sent a sniper out after me. You know that."

Evan nodded hesitantly. She wanted him to think he was convincing her. "How can you consider this a tactical advantage? You went back on your own word."

"Come on, Evan," he said, rising. He walked the three steps to stand directly in front of her chair. "You were just there. You saw very plainly that I chose the one bridge out of all the bridges in Paris that had only one vantage point from which Ramos could offer cover. And when he gets around to looking, Kirk will realize that I asked to meet in the one place where the traffic cams are blinded by the landscaping."

Evan released a long slow breath of defeat. "And you took me before I was dressed for the evening."

"And now your ear receiver is useless. Your cute little earring is smashed to dust."

Evan looked him up and down. She wanted to make him talk, but she hated the sound of his smug voice.

He crossed his arms defiantly and stared down his nose at her.

She blinked and swallowed hard. "And what kind of advantage do you imagine you have over Hedge?"

"I have you," he said, letting his fingers caress her throat. "I have the one thing in Paris he cares about."

Evan tried to lean away from his hands, but he took hold of her jaw with a firm grip and tilted her head back to face him.

"You're mine, and you'll do as I tell you." He pushed her face back roughly. "I know what Hedge wants. He wants you alive. If you obey me, I'll give you back to him in one piece. You're my bargaining chip with him."

She dropped her chin and let herself cry. He slapped her face in response.

"Shut that up," he demanded. "I may need you for Hedge, but I certainly don't need you for dealing with Eleanor or any one of her higher-ups."

She held her breath for a second to clear her mind. She hoped that Brawn didn't lose his confidence, but she didn't want to give away any information he didn't already have. "So you're going through with the meeting tonight?" she asked. She kept her tone timid.

"I will," he said. "You won't be there, of course. I'll give them directions to find you after I'm cleared. Maybe tomorrow. Maybe next week. We'll have to see how they treat me."

"Killing Charles can be spun as an accident. A misunderstanding. Killing me won't be as easy to cover." She glared.

"For whom?" he asked. "You overestimate your value, I think."

Her heart banged angrily in her chest. She again pushed and kicked against the restraints. "I'm going to make sure you pay for this," she threatened.

He slapped her again. "I hate to hear that. I really do plan to let you live." He grabbed her hair and yanked back and down until she could hardly breathe. "But if you give me enough reason to kill you before my meeting tonight," he said, moving his lips close to her ear. "Trust me when I say that I will enjoy every minute of your death." He hovered over her face with a broad, ghoulish sneer. He released her hair from his grasp and watched her fight to recover.

Evan finally regained her breath and turned away from his cold stare.

He walked to the heavy wooden door and peered out through the small warped glass in the top.

"What time is it?" Evan asked.

He ignored her. He flipped the butterfly knife closed and pushed it into his jeans pocket. He kicked his chair into place at the small wooden table. He paced for a second and then knelt beside the cot on the far wall. He pulled out a box from beneath the narrow berth.

Brawn spent the next half hour cleaning and loading his rifle and pistol. With both weapons, he seemed to take pleasure in aiming at her head and pretending to fire. When he had finished with his toys, he put them back into his box and slid them out of sight.

Evan looked up to the arched window that sat high above the table. "Are we below ground?" she asked.

He turned and shot an angry growl in her direction.

"I'm cold," she explained.

"I can warm you up," he said. He walked to Evan's side and wrenched her up from the chair. With one fluid motion, he swung her to the other side of the room and pushed her down on the bed. "You asked for this."

Brawn tossed his knife on the table and started to unbutton his pants as the door flew open. Hedge leveled his Glock at Brawn's chest as he scanned the room for Evan. Brawn took advantage of the hesitation, kicking the pistol from Hedge's hands.

Hedge didn't wait to watch it land. He charged into the dark room, shoulder first, and plowed into Brawn's side. Both men hit the hard dirt floor landing punches from every angle.

Brawn pulled his elbow back and let his knuckles fly into Hedge's jaw. Hedge struck with a swift thrust to Brawn's throat. Brawn raised his knee and pushed Hedge into one of the chairs, sending its pieces across the floor.

Hedge regained his footing and raised his fists in defense. Brawn hooked at him from both directions, but Hedge blocked each advance.

"Give up, Brawn. You can't win now," Hedge coughed. He landed a punch to Brawn's ribs.

"You're old," Jarrett shot back. He spun around quickly and hit Hedge in the kidneys with the heel of his foot.

Hedge dropped to his knees.

"Stop it!" Evan screamed.

Brawn again ignored her and kicked at Hedge's chest. Hedge grabbed Brawn's foot before it landed and twisted, forcing Brawn to turn away. Brawn let his hands hit the floor, and he vaulted his other foot up, catching Hedge's chin and sending him over on his back.

Evan continued to scream. She wrestled with the flex-ties until she had her wrists in front of her.

Brawn dove away from Hedge and scooped up his knife. He stood over Hedge's heaving body and flipped the blade open. "You're stupid to let yourself get into this position. You know what I can do with a knife."

Hedge swept Brawn's feet out from under him. He landed on top of Hedge. The blade sank deep into Hedge's hip, and he roared.

Brawn pulled the knife out and held it high overhead, preparing to plunge it into Hedge's ribcage.

A shot ripped through Brawn's shoulder from back to front. He turned to face Evan, who held his Glock .45 in her still-bound hands.

"I said stop." Her chest heaved with each word.

He howled and lunged at her, and she fired again. This one hit squarely through his heart, and he fell at her feet.

"Romeo, Kilo, Bravo is down. Papa is down. Assist. Please assist, Papa is down," she said, crawling to Hedge's side on the floor.

"Right there," Kirk said. "You okay, Tango?"

"Affirmative, just get here." She pulled her track jacket over her head and shook it down into a wad of fabric at her wrist restraints. She held it firmly to Hedge's hip wound to slow the bleeding. "Teo's coming. You're going to be okay," she said.

Hedge winced in pain. His face was scuffed and swelling. "Are you hurt?" he asked. He started to sit up, but Evan pushed him back down.

"I'm not hurt. But you gotta be still. Wait until help gets here before you start running around on me."

Hedge looked at the heap of man on the floor just beyond his reach. "You got him, Evan."

She nodded. "I was kind of hoping he'd brag about his hits. For a moment I thought he would." She shrugged. "I guess we'll just have to do the regular investigating to wrap it all together."

Evan sat at Hedge's side as he moaned through a wave of pain. Teo entered the room and paused for a moment. He glanced at the holes in Brawn's body and the spatter field on the opposite wall. "Whoa, Hedge. I guess you got him."

Hedge nodded to Evan. "She got him."

Ramos pulled out his medic bag and started stuffing sponge pads into Hedge's wound. Evan wrestled with the jacket for a few seconds before Teo seemed to notice. "Let me give you a hand with that," he offered. He took his knife and cut the restraints apart, so the blood-soaked jacket could come off.

She took the knife from him and finished removing the nylon straps. Three men in uniform entered the dark room.

They helped Hedge and Evan get into the ambulance. Teo gave Evan a thumbs-up before the paramedic closed the door. Teo would stay with the other men to take care of Brawn's body and collect evidence.

Kirk and Eleanor met them at the hospital.

"Are we done now?" Eleanor asked as they wheeled Hedge into a corner behind a sheet. "My UK associate said he could finish up the rest of the project," she said cryptically, to keep bystanders from overhearing important details.

Evan shook her head. "No ma'am."

Eleanor raised her brows as she turned to face the redhead.

Evan took a deep breath and swallowed back any nerves that welled up through her exhaustion. "No ma'am, we're not done. For myself, and I'm sure I can speak for Hedge in this, there is still work to complete. I won't be satisfied if I hand the project off to another team." Her boldness almost surprised herself. "I'm sure you know Mr. Parker feels the same way."

Eleanor shot a glance to Hedge who merely smiled back from his bed.

"We'll discuss this tomorrow morning," Eleanor said. "Go let the doctors attend to you."

Kirk wrapped his arm around her shoulder as she left Hedge's side. "You did great, Evan." He helped her up onto the exam table reserved for her. "Your idea worked."

She slipped her fingers into her neckline and pulled the black underwires from inside her bra. "*Your* idea worked. You should take this before my once-over. I don't want a curious doctor asking me any weird questions about why my bra is making his instruments malfunction."

"You know, we were stumped there for a second. I had your GPS coordinates, but couldn't for the life of me figure where you were. Once you asked about being underground, we knew you were in a room under the street. Hedge just had to figure out how to get to you." Kirk sighed. "Not a minute too soon, either."

"Do you think I was too pushy with Eleanor just now?" she asked him in a whisper.

Kirk laughed. "No, don't second-guess yourself. She likes assertive."

"That's what I've heard."

CHAPTER THIRTY-EIGHT

"I hoped that we might have a moment to chat before the men return," Eleanor said, taking a seat at the end of the red velvet couch and motioning for Evan to join her.

"Certainly," Evan replied. As she sat on the other side of the sofa, she knew her face betrayed her concern.

"Don't worry. I just want a little girl-time. You haven't done anything wrong."

"Yes, Ma'am."

"Call me Eleanor," she insisted. "Girl-time, remember?"

"Okay," Evan said, smoothing the hem of her skirt.

"Over this last week I've seen indications of anxiety from you, and I want to help. What do you need from me?" Eleanor asked.

"From you?" Evan tried to conceal her astonishment. She had been given the assignment that any agent would die for, and her superior was asking what more she could do for her.

"I know we sort of threw the dress at you all at once, but we couldn't read you in until you had it in hand."

"I understand the security measures," Evan said.

Eleanor smiled and drew a slow breath. "Do you feel like you need more training or experience? Or maybe more support?"

Evan shook her head. "I know that I let you down by allowing the dress to be taken, but I really don't think...."

"Of course you didn't let anyone down," Eleanor interrupted. "That was my failure. I got so excited about putting the project into action that I failed to vet Brawn sufficiently." She stared down at the coffee cup in her hand. "Your team paid for my mistake. I apologize."

Evan shook her head again, debating whether to make her confession or remain silent. She swallowed hard and began. "Eleanor, it's not as though I haven't had the very best training or support. I am humbled to be a part of this project. I know that you spent a great deal of time choosing me, but...."

"Let me stop you right there," Eleanor said. "I would do just about anything to wear that dress in the field. I want whoever does wear it to feel the same way. You are the first choice for everyone who worked on the LBD."

Evan swallowed hard. "I love wearing the dress. It's more than I ever dreamed it would be. But I feel that maybe I'm not right for it. Not just for the dress, but the whole job." She paused for a second and then raised her gaze to meet Elle's. "I know this might sound funny to you, but I'm afraid I'm losing myself, my soul, to this job."

Eleanor put her cup on the table at her knees. "I want to tell you something that I think you'll appreciate." She patted Evan's hand. "You and I were both raised in the Bible belt, and I know that you were raised going to Sunday School, too." She paused, and Evan nodded. "My favorite Bible story was about Rahab hiding the Israelite spies in Jericho. She was a prostitute who saved her family from annihilation by harboring the spies and then helping them escape."

"I remember that story. Rahab hung a scarlet cord from her window, right?" Evan asked.

Eleanor smiled and nodded. "And because of her courage, she is remembered and counted in the ancestry of Jesus."

Evan looked at Eleanor with swelling admiration. "Thank you for that reminder."

"Evan, you may not believe this, but you weren't recruited because we thought you had a loose moral compass. Rather, because you were so strong." Eleanor tilted her head and offered a confident nod. "When you were fighting Xandra and Brawn, did you feel you were compromising yourself for the job?"

Evan considered the question. "Honestly, I didn't even think about that. I just had to get the dress back. I just had to do my job."

"But why?"

"People were being hurt, dying. I do my job because I want to make the world a better place." Evan sighed as she listened to her own words.

"Then I'm satisfied that you are still right for this assignment," Eleanor said.

"Thank you." Evan felt her heart pounding hard. Not from fear. Not from nerves. Now it was just beating true. She felt a surge of purpose.

"I've noticed Hedge second-guessing himself these days, too. That's new since our last field-assignment together," Eleanor said.

"What happened? You may not be allowed to say, and I understand," Evan said quietly. "But, like you, I wonder if what happened to you doesn't still affect him."

Eleanor nodded. "I can't offer details, of course. I'm sure you've surmised that Hedge and I were closer than just partners." Eleanor waited for a confirming nod from Evan before continuing. "We got caught in a situation, our subject had both of us, it was bad. They said they were going to let me go if Hedge stayed with them. I was about to leave when I saw a shooter. He was going to take out Hedge, so I ran back."

Eleanor began unbuttoning her chiffon blouse. Evan raised her eyebrows as Eleanor slipped out of the right sleeve and turned away from her. Evan immediately focused on a baseball-sized indention and scar on Eleanor's right shoulder. Eleanor raised the hem of her camisole and indicated a dark blemish just to the right of her spine and below her ribs.

"They shot you in the back?" Evan asked though the healed wounds left no doubt.

"I was lucky." Eleanor redressed and turned back to face Evan. "Our hosts ran. Hedge got us both out quickly. The hospital was close. For all that went wrong, enough went right so that I'm still kicking. Of course, that was a long time ago," Eleanor added.

Evan released the deep breath she'd been holding.

"Now I'm sure that you think of Hedge as an older man, but I can assure you that he knows what he's doing with this whole project," Eleanor said.

"I don't think of him as an old man at all," Evan said, grinning as she considered him.

"Really?" Eleanor raised her brow. "What do you think of him?"

Evan paused to consider how she should proceed. "As a team leader, he is more than competent. He knows exactly how to handle every situation. I never had a moment's doubt of his ability to take control and lead us. I feel completely safe in his hands."

Eleanor blinked. "I see."

Evan decided that she had said too much. A subject change was in order. "I have the dress in the bedroom." Evan gestured to the door over her shoulder. "I'll go get it if you want to try it on."

Eleanor's gaze lingered on the door. "No, I can't. If I put it on, you'd have a terrible time getting it off of me."

"I bet we could sell tickets to that event," Hedge said as he entered the hotel suite. Kirk and Ramos followed him inside.

Eleanor glared.

"What?" Hedge asked. "Brawn isn't here. Somebody had to say it."

Evan frowned before laughing. She patted the center cushion of the sofa. "Come, sit with us."

Hedge shook his head. "Not there." He crossed his arms and leaned against the wall. "I don't want to be caught between Evan and Elle."

Elle shook her head as the others laughed. "And just how long have you been saving that one?"

"Just a little while. Funny, huh?"

"Not if you're the one being called *hell*, it's not." Eleanor rolled her eyes.

Hedge took a step toward the women. "Agent Tyler, make I speak to you in private? It will only take a moment."

"Yessir." Evan stood and followed him through her open bedroom door. He closed it behind them, and she raised an eyebrow. *Was she in trouble? No, he seemed to be in a light mood, making jokes and smiling more than usual. But then again, he had called her Agent Tyler.* "What do you need, Agent Parker?"

She watched him, studied his movements. He started to sit on the edge of the bed but winced in the process. She could see he was still in a great deal of pain from being stabbed in the hip. He stood upright again and faced her with a more serious expression.

"What do I need?" He looked down and then met her gaze again. "I guess I just need to tell you how I'm feeling. I know you're not such a big fan of talking, but I am, so hear me out, please."

"Sure." She didn't know if this was going to be the we'll-get-'em-next-time, or the sorry-if-I-let-you-down, or even the better-off-on-separate-assignments speech. She'd heard them all before. She prepared for the worst.

"Evan, I know technically I'm the team leader, but I see the two of us as partners. You're the one doing all the heavy lifting out there." He reached out and touched her arm. "You're amazing. That word is overused, but it's true. I spent half of the morning thinking about what you've accomplished so far on this job, and the other half trying to find words to say to you now."

Evan laughed. She'd never heard any of those speeches start like this.

Hedge continued. "I have ten sisters, you know, and I think a lot about how men treat them."

Evan nodded. *It was the more-like-a-sister-to-me talk.*

"Evan," he said as he let his hand drop to take her hand. "I have made mistakes. I let my feelings for past partners, for Eleanor, influence the job. I swore I would never do that again." He took a step closer. "I need you. I need you as a partner, but I feel more than that." He took her other hand.

Evan felt the warmth of his body as he moved next to her. This was not what she expected at all. Her heart pounded against her ribcage. This was what she wanted, but also what she feared. She felt a rise in her stomach as though she was on a rollercoaster. She wanted to say something but was afraid to stop his soft words. All she could manage was a trembling nod.

Hedge smiled. "I need you, but I want you to be good with this. To me, you are irresistible in every way. But I won't give in to that if that's not what you want. I don't want you to feel obligated or manipulated. I want this to be on terms you're comfortable with."

Evan shook her head and threw her arms around Hedge's neck. "Would you shut up already and kiss me."

He wrapped his strong arms around her narrow waist and covered her mouth with his full lips. This was real, not a make-it-look-good-for-cover kiss. Evan felt the heat of him all the way to the soles of her feet. Her heart now pounded so loudly, she could hear it.

No, not her heart. The door. Kirk was knocking.

"If you two could hurry it up, please. Elle has a flight to catch."

Evan laughed as Hedge released her from his embrace. "We can continue this later," she said. She wiped a trace of lipstick from Hedge's mouth.

He blinked and nodded. "At your go."

They rejoined the others. Evan took her place on the couch beside Elle. Hedge went back to his arms-crossed stance on the wall.

Kirk parked himself in a chair and propped his feet on the ottoman. "Do we get to finish the job, or are you shipping us all back to the states?"

"You think there is still that much more to do?" Eleanor asked them all.

"I haven't even been shot, yet," Ramos said.

Eleanor laughed. "I can't tell Fischer that you want to stay in the game until you're injured. Why do you believe there is anything more to find than the information on the flash drives?"

Kirk yawned. "Like why the flash drives would be attached to keys from all over the Mediterranean?"

"There could be copies of this information out there, and we can't be sure that someone else doesn't have access to it," Ramos said. "And that someone else could use the information for his own gain."

"True," Eleanor agreed. "But will retrieving the copies, or whatever is out there, require the entire team?"

Evan's brain sparked. "It's not just copies," she said.

Eleanor turned to face her. "Why do you say that?"

"Xandra said something. She wasn't just interested in blackmail for money. She wanted power." Evan nodded. "I think she wants political power. The assassinations weren't simply for influence. I think that she may have been removing obstacles."

Eleanor sat up straight and looked focused. "That's a different situation. Do you have evidence of that?"

"Only what she said about her grandfather and what she believed was rightfully hers. She told me that she intended to have more power than the Romanovs. Actually, she said that she already was more powerful. At the time I thought she was just talking. Considering what we know now, I have to believe there is more to it. And then there's the thing that Brawn said.

I'm not even sure Brawn understood everything that she was doing."

Hedge furrowed his brow. "What do you mean?"

"Something he mentioned the other day," Evan said. "Remember when he said the thing about the left hand not knowing what the right hand was doing?"

"Yeah," Kirk answered. "It's from the Bible in the book of Matthew."

Evan continued. "He said that he didn't like always being the left hand. I thought he was just talking about with us, but what if he meant with Xandra, too?"

Hedge scratched at his goatee thoughtfully. "Agent McKinnon-Grey, I would like to formally request to continue this mission with my team."

Eleanor smiled. Evan watched as she studied each member of the team. Eleanor's gaze fell on Ramos. She smiled and nodded at his enthusiasm. She moved to her old friend, Kirk. She looked at his injured shoulder as if it pained her more than him.

Eleanor's regard shifted to Hedge. She studied him from head to toe. Evan noticed the tiny creases at the corners of Eleanor's eyes tighten and relax with almost imperceptible hints of admiration for the man.

Evan resisted the urge to watch Hedge's eyes reacting to the scrutiny. Seconds later she found herself in Eleanor's sight. Eleanor's eyes narrowed and then softened. Her expression revealed pride. Evan heard her own heart beating in her ears. She wasn't nervous. For the first time, she realized how much she loved her job. She didn't want it to end.

Eleanor nodded. She seemed to see the change in Evan. She reached behind the couch for a box and placed it in Evan's lap. "I'll let Fischer know that you'll be out a while longer. If there is more to this, I don't want to leave the job unfinished. Just keep me posted every day."

"What is that?" Hedge asked. He moved to Evan's side.

"Just a little something I picked up before I left home. Goes with the dress," Eleanor said, nudging at the box.

Evan let a smile curl her pink lips as she lifted the lid from the box. A flutter of tissue fell open to reveal a pair of red leather pumps. Her face lit up like Christmas morning. "These are beautiful."

"Is that what I think?" Kirk asked.

Evan lifted the shoes from the box and examined them carefully. Kirk smiled broadly.

Hedge raised his brow and shot a glance at Eleanor. "The red heels? When did they get approved?" he asked.

"What do they do?" Ramos asked.

Evan pulled off her shoes and slid the red ones on. They fit perfectly. *Of course, they fit perfectly.* She stood and walked to the other side of the room and back. *Heaven.*

She put her old shoes into the tissue-filled box and replaced the lid.

Evan wasn't sure where the next leg of this assignment would take her, but she was going to be dressed for whatever she faced.

Eleanor laughed at Evan's obvious delight. Hedge crossed his arms over his chest proudly, and Kirk leaned back in his chair. A contented grin settled on his face.

"I couldn't let you go running all over Europe with just one pair of shoes," Eleanor said.

"Okay, maybe I just *thought* I asked the question out loud. What do the shoes do?" Ramos repeated.

"Who cares?" Evan said with a sigh. "They're perfectly magical."

THE END

ABOUT THE AUTHOR

Kim Black is an award-winning author and designer. She is a member and has served as President of the Texas High Plains Writers, one of the oldest writing organizations in the country. She has also published historical Christian fiction and children's books under the name Kimberly Black. She lives in the Texas Panhandle with her husband, grown children, two dogs, and two cats.
For more about Kim and her writing, visit her website, www.KimBlackInk.com.

82858487R00123

Made in the USA
Lexington, KY
06 March 2018